There was one more attacker

Annja whirled, expecting her final opponent to be closing the distance between them while her attention was elsewhere.

But that wasn't the case. The other man hadn't moved.

He stood watching her, hands held behind his back, like an instructor evaluating her performance.

"Who are you and what do you want?" Annja asked, and was surprised at the depth of anger she heard in her voice.

Her opponent said nothing.

"I'll give you one last—"

She never finished the sentence.

One second her opponent was standing in front of her with both hands behind his back, and in the next he was leaping forward, a Japanese long sword suddenly appearing in his hands.

Annja just barely managed to deflect the strike as she brought her own sword up.

Where the hell had that sword come from?

It was almost as if he'd conjured the thing out of thin air....

Titles in this series:

ROGUE ANGEL

Alex Archer

THE DRAGON'S MARK

A GOLD EAGLE BOOK FROM

WORLDWIDE®

TORONTO • NEW YORK • LONDON
AMSTERDAM • PARIS • SYDNEY • HAMBURG
STOCKHOLM • ATHENS • TOKYO • MILAN
MADRID • WARSAW • BUDAPEST • AUCKLAND

Recycling programs
for this product may
not exist in your area.

First edition September 2010

ISBN-13: 978-0-373-62145-3

THE DRAGON'S MARK

Special thanks and acknowledgment to
Joe Nassise for his contribution to this work.

Printed in U.S.A.

The
LEGEND

...THE ENGLISH COMMANDER TOOK
JOAN'S SWORD AND RAISED IT HIGH.
The broadsword, plain and unadorned,
gleamed in the firelight. He put the tip against
the ground and his foot at the center of the blade.
The broadsword shattered, fragments falling
into the mud. The crowd surged forward,
peasant and soldier, and snatched the shards
from the trampled mud. The commander tossed
the hilt deep into the crowd.
Smoke almost obscured Joan, but she continued
praying till the end, until finally the flames climbed
her body and she sagged against the restraints.

Joan of Arc died that fateful day in France,
but her legend and sword are reborn....

1

Sengo Muramasa stormed about the room in a fit of rage. The furnishings around him bore silent witness to the strength of his anger; the black lacquer tea table had been smashed repeatedly against the floor until it shattered into pieces. The tatami mats had been ripped to shreds with his bare hands. The paintings on the walls had been torn down and stomped upon until the images they bore were unrecognizable. When one of his servants unwittingly entered the room, Muramasa had beat him to within an inch of his life and left him lying unconscious in one corner of the room.

The old swordsmith barely noticed the injured boy as his thoughts were on the edict that had arrived earlier that morning and the demands it had contained.

He still couldn't believe it. That bastard Tokugawa Ieyasu had actually gone through with it!

He'd heard rumors about the shogun's proposed stance for months, but had never actually believed he would put it into effect.

The words of the edict echoed around and around in his head.

All weapons crafted by the swordsmith Muramasa have been deemed illegal and banned from use by direct order of the shogun. Carrying such a weapon is now considered a crime and is punishable by death. Anyone caught possessing, hoarding, or transporting a weapon fashioned by Muramasa faces the same penalty.

He could not let this happen.

Deny his art? Banish his work? Never!

Already the germ of a plan was beginning to form in the back of his mind and he gave it free reign to grow and expand. He had no doubt the shogun's men would be coming for him, to take his inventory and destroy his forge, to prevent him from creating any new blades. But with winter swiftly approaching, the mountain passes would soon be blocked and it would take months for them to thaw enough to be passable again.

Months he could put to good use.

He had just enough time to produce one final sword—the culmination of his career. He would create a sword to be feared and held in awe in equal measure, a blade to master all other blades, one that would strike terror in the hearts of those against whom it was drawn.

He would call it Juuchi Yosamu—Ten Thousand Cold Nights.

Ignoring the destruction behind him, Muramasa stalked out of the house and across the courtyard to his workshop. His heart was full of feelings of anger and vengeance and Muramasa intended to use them fully.

Entering the forge, he paused a moment to say a prayer at the small Shinto shrine in the corner. The forge was a sacred place and to deny the gods their due would only ensure that his blade would come out weak and brittle. He took the time to ask for blessings and to make the proper offering. When he was finished, he rose and got to work.

Muramasa had been preparing to produce a blade for a customer and so his smelting furnace had already been built. His apprentices had created a thick layer of ash and charcoal as a base and then had surrounded it with carefully made bricks of local clay, until they had a structure that was roughly three feet high with walls nearly one-foot thick. They were ready to begin the smelting process.

The master swordsmith shouted at his apprentices and they came running, eager to begin. Word of the master's fall from favor had already passed through the household and they were as keen as he was to stand in defiance of the shogun's order. After all, their livelihoods were at stake, as well—for who would commission a weapon from their hands when it was revealed that they learned the art at Muramasa's knee? Their futures were at stake, too, and they took to their tasks with all of the energy and attention at their disposal.

For the next three days they stoked the fire, ensuring that it burned at a steady temperature of fifteen hundred degrees. Shovels of iron sand were fed into the mouth of the furnace every thirty minutes—nourishment for the hungry beast—the iron mixing with the carbon and charcoal already in the smelter to create a unique kind of steel. Muramasa watched over the proceedings with an eagle eye, carefully monitoring the molten slag that was vented through the holes at the bottom of the furnace, waiting for just the right consistency and color to appear.

When at last he was satisfied, he ordered his apprentices to tear down the walls of the furnace, revealing a large mass of molten steel in the center, known as the *kera*. Roughly six feet long by one foot wide and weighing nearly two tons, the *kera* was carefully moved by rolling it atop a series of logs to the other side of the workshop where it would be allowed to cool. Once it had, his apprentices would break up the massive block into fist-size fragments that he would personally scrutinize, searching for those that shone with a silvery brightness from the outer edge. The selected pieces would then be hammered flat by his workers, coated with a thin mixture of clay and charcoal to prevent oxidation, and then reheated to thirteen hundred degrees to melt them all together into a single block. After that he would begin the process of forming the blade, hammering the steel and folding it over, again and again and again, making the steel uniform throughout. Eventually he would combine the softer, more flexible core with an outer edge of harder steel, then heat the blade all over again to meld the two layers into one. Later would come the grinding and polishing.

For now, however, it was enough that he had begun.

IT WAS FINISHED.

Muramasa stared at the highly polished blade and could almost feel it watching him, in turn. For three months he had poured his soul into its creation, imbuing it with all the hatred, anger and desire for vengeance he felt toward the shogun, giving it a personality of its own, one that would devour any weapon that dared to stand against it. Like the dragon for which it had been named.

It was the culmination of his life's work.

The door to his workshop burst open and a servant rushed in. Muramasa recognized him as one of those who had been tasked with keeping an eye on the pass in the mountains above. The boy's face was ruddy from the cold and a long gash ran across his brow.

Pausing to catch his breath, the boy finally gasped out the message he'd rushed there to deliver.

"The shogun's troops…"

That was all that was necessary.

The spring thaw had come early and Muramasa had been expecting word of their arrival for days. It wouldn't take them long to negotiate the pass and descend down to the valley floor. He had one hour, two at the most.

But it would be enough.

Juuchi Yosamu was finished. All he needed was to see to its delivery.

After that, let them come.

The old swordsmith sprang into action.

"Quickly," he shouted to the boy. "Find me Yukasawi!"

Still struggling to catch his breath, the boy turned and rushed out the door, intent on doing what his master commanded.

While he waited for his man, Muramasa crossed the room and selected a worn and battered saya from a barrel in the corner of the room. He lifted the blade, intent on securing it safely inside the scabbard.

As he did so the weapon seemed to twist in his hands of its own accord and he felt the sting of its bite as the razor edge sliced cleanly along the underside of his forearm. Blood dripped onto the floor and gleamed wetly against the edge of the blade. But rather than being angry at his carelessness, if that was indeed what caused the injury, Muramasa simply smiled.

The sword hungered for blood, just as it had been created to. Who better than to provide its first taste than the man who had fashioned it?

A noise at his back caused him to turn and he saw Yukasawi enter the workshop. Muramasa took a moment to study him.

The man was a ronin, one of those samurai from the lesser houses who had recently lost his station when his master had gone down in defeat at the hands of the shogun. This is a man who has almost as much reason to hate Tokugawa as I do, the swordsmith thought. It was for this reason that he had been selected. If anyone could get the weapon to safety, Yukasawi could.

It would be the soldier's job to take the sword out of the mountains, past the shogun's troops and into the hands of the samurai in Kyoto Muramasa had selected to receive it.

The man in question, Ishikawa Toshi, was ruthless and wanted nothing more than to ascend to the position of shogun. He was already amassing his army against Tokugawa and his allies, and Muramasa was confident that his gift would be put to good use in the future. All the swordsmith had to do was get it to him.

"Is it time?" Yukasawi asked, his face tight with concern for his benefactor.

Muramasa nodded. "The shogun's troops have been sighted at the top of the pass. They will be here shortly."

"Then there is still time. If we leave now, we can—"

"No." The swordsmith cut him off. "There is no time left for running. Nor will I give that dog Tokugawa the satisfaction. By remaining behind I will delay them long enough to allow you to escape and deliver Juuchi Yosamu as we discussed."

He thrust the now-sheathed weapon into the hands of his vassal. "On your honor and your life, do not fail me."

"Hai!" the ronin shouted. Taking the weapon in hand, he bowed low, then rushed out of the workshop to where his horse was waiting.

The trip down the mountain would be hazardous, but Muramasa was confident his man could handle the task. His other creations might be rounded up and destroyed, but in the depths of his heart he knew that this one would survive.

As his blood continued to drip onto the floor beneath his feet, the swordsmith knew that the world would not soon forget the savage bite of a Muramasa blade.

His legacy would live on.

And Juuchi Yosamu would devour the hearts of his enemies.

A shout sounded from outside and Muramasa knew that that the shogun's troops were near. It was time to meet death.

The old man reached out and picked up a sword. He gave it a few experimental swings, getting the feel for this particular blade, and then turned toward the door with a spring in his step that he hadn't felt for years.

THE BATTLE HAD BEEN SHORT but brutal. His men had fought well and the snow was stained crimson with their blood and the blood of their foes. Of the thirty-eight men who had remained behind to face the shogun's troops, only Muramasa himself still lived. He had intended to die with a sword in his hands, but apparently the shogun had ordered otherwise. His men had surrounded the swordsmith and attempted to overwhelm him, a move that had cost ten of them their lives before the older man had been beaten into unconsciousness.

Now, with his hands bound behind his back, Muramasa stood before his enemies and waited for the end.

The captain of the shogun's troops had been apologetic. This was no way to die for a man of Muramasa's stature, he'd said, but he had his orders and if he did not carry them out as intended, his own life would be forfeit. Muramasa assured him that he understood.

"Do as you must," he'd told the man, and had meant it.

It didn't matter. The resistance, the pronouncement of the verdict against him, the execution to come—none of it mattered, really. It was all stage dressing, anyway— a deliberate attempt to get the shogun's men to focus their attention on what was going on around them rather than searching the countryside for those who might have gotten away. Every hour he delayed them meant another hour that Yukasawi could use to get over the mountains and escape with his precious cargo.

Muramasa had given him as much time as he could.

Two soldiers approached. They each took an arm and led him forward to the clearing in the center of the compound, where what was left of his household staff were assembled as witnesses in front of the massed arrangement of the shogun's troops.

As they drew closer, Muramasa shook off the guards and walked forward on his own. He was not afraid to meet death and he would not go forward to face it looking as if he did not have the courage to do so on his own.

The captain he'd spoken to earlier was waiting for him, naked steel in hand. Muramasa had requested that he be allowed to commit seppuku, but apparently even that last honor was to be denied him.

So be it, he thought. He would still have the last laugh.

Without waiting to be told Muramasa knelt in the snow at the captain's feet.

"Do not worry," the younger man said, whispering so that those assembled around him would not overhear. "I will make certain that the blade strikes deep. There will be no need for a second blow."

Muramasa bowed his head, exposing his neck.

He ignored the long recital of his supposed crimes and the pronouncement of his sentence—death. He'd heard it all before.

As he waited for that final blow, something caught his eye in the distance.

He raised his head slightly, just enough so that he could lift his gaze toward the mountain slopes in the distance. On the side of the mountain, where the trail led to the pass that was used to exit the valley and travel to the world outside, a dark speck moved against the snow. It was barely visible at this distance, and had Muramasa not turned his head at precisely the right moment, he might never have seen it. But he had and deep in his heart he had no doubt at all as to what that speck represented.

Yukasawi had made it. He had managed to work his way past the blockade of the shogun's troops and climb the mountain to the pass high above. From there it would be easy for the ronin to lose himself in the open country on the other side while he made the journey to Kyoto and delivered the blade.

And with that delivery, Muramasa's revenge would begin.

Suddenly filled with satisfaction, Muramasa barely noticed as the captain of the guard brought his sword high above his head.

I curse you with ten thousand cold nights, the sword-smith thought. As the blade descended in a swift, razor-sharp blow designed to separate his head from his shoulders, a smile crossed the old man's face.

2

Paris, France

Annja took the steps two at a time, calling her sword to her hand as she went. The weapon responded, emerging from the otherwhere fully formed and fitting neatly into her grasp as if it had been fashioned for her alone. She remembered the first time she'd seen the sword. It had been in this very house, lying in pieces in the case Roux had fashioned for it. She remembered the heat coming off the fragments of the broken blade and the rainbow-colored light that had exploded from it when she grasped the hilt and lifted it free of its case, somehow reformed. Then, as now, she knew the sword was hers; knew it down to the core of her very soul. Just having it with her made her feel more confident about the confrontation that lay ahead.

She kept her eyes on the landing above, not wanting to be surprised by the sudden appearance of an intruder.

She made it to the top of the staircase without incident. She found herself faced with a long corridor that ran in opposite directions. She knew the area to the right held a series of guest bedrooms, for she had stayed there in the past and was even using one of them now. The left side of the hallway held a bathroom, an office and a small gallery for some of Roux's art. She ignored all of them; the crashing sound had come from the room at the far end of the hall, the one now facing her, and as she moved toward it, she tried to remember just what it was used for.

A spare bedroom? Another office? Maybe a study?

Then it came to her.

A display room.

The room held a portion of the weapons collection Roux had accumulated over the course of his extended lifetime. There were many more rooms just like it scattered throughout his home. But this room was special, Annja recalled. She had spent some time in it during a previous visit, for it contained a certain type of weapon that she had grown rather attached to lately.

Swords.

The collection contained both working blades and a few museum-quality relics, but nothing that was overly valuable and certainly not much that could be moved easily on the open market. The thieves, if that was indeed what they were, were in for a rude surprise if they thought differently.

And they still had to contend with her.

She raced to the door and flattened herself against the wall beside it. She put her head against the wall, listening, but Roux's mansion had been built in the days when they had used quality building materials rather than the cheap substitutes that had become so common today. She couldn't hear anything but her own breathing.

She was going to have to do this the hard way.

Gripping her sword in one hand, Annja grabbed the doorknob with the other, took a deep breath and then pulled it open, slipping inside with barely a sound.

She'd been right; it was one of the display rooms. Swords lined the walls by the hundreds—long swords, short swords, broadswords, cutlasses, épées, scimitars—every make, model and size, it seemed. The carefully polished blades shone in the spotlights that had been artfully arranged to draw attention to the weapons, and here and there the wink of precious gems gleamed back at her from scabbards or hilts.

But Annja barely noticed the swords on the walls, for her attention was captured by those held in the hands of the intruders facing her.

One week earlier

ANNJA WAS CARRYING SEVERAL bags of groceries up the stairs to her Brooklyn loft when her cell phone rang.

"Hang on, hang on…" she said to it as she juggled the bags, managed to get the key in the lock and kicked the door open with her foot.

Her phone continued to ring.

"I'm coming, just hang on!" she told it again, as if the inanimate hunk of metal and plastic could actually hear her. She rushed to the island in the kitchen, dumped the bags on the counter and grabbed for her phone.

Just as she managed to pull it from the front pocket of her jeans it stopped ringing.

"You have got to be kidding!" She scowled at it, ready to fling it across the room in a pique of anger, only to have it ring again.

"Hello?" She practically shouted it into the tiny device.

A deep, rich voice answered her back. "Annja, did I catch you at a bad time?"

There was no mistaking the voice. That teasing tone, that undercurrent of danger—only one man in her life sounded like that.

"What do you want, Garin?"

All that rushing? For him? It said something about her social life, that was for sure, she thought.

"Now is that any way to treat an old friend?"

"Old, yes. Friend, that remains to be seen."

"You wound me, Annja, you really do."

She kicked off her shoes, wandered into the living room and dropped onto the couch.

Garin Braden. Empire builder, artifact hunter, rogue—he had a thousand different faces. The problem was, you never really knew which one you were dealing with, and by the time you did, it was often too late to save yourself. Annja had seen him ruthlessly kill more than one individual and yet had also known him to be charming and tender. She still wasn't sure just what she felt about him; he was larger than life, with his rakish good looks, thick black hair and piercing gaze, but at the same time he had the heart of a devil.

"So be wounded," she said. "Then when you've finished feeling sorry for yourself maybe you could tell me what you want."

Garin swore under his breath and the sound of his frustration made Annja smile. She wasn't the only one with mixed feelings, she realized.

"I am calling," he said, "to invite you to Paris."

Paris? That was a surprise.

"What for?" she asked.

"Can't I just invite you to Paris?"

"You could, but you know I wouldn't come, so what's the real reason?"

Garin was silent for a moment, and then grudgingly said, "It's the old man's birthday."

Annja knew there was only one individual Garin could legitimately refer to that way.

Roux.

Old was right, she thought. More than five hundred years old, if the truth were told. Garin himself wasn't that far behind, for only a few decades separated the two men. The same mystical force that had preserved the sword of Joan of Arc, the sword that Annja now carried as her own, had also given the two of them an extended lifetime. One measured in centuries, rather than decades.

"It's Roux's birthday?"

"I just said that, didn't I?"

Yes, yes, he had. Despite Roux's long life, Annja

knew that he wasn't the type to celebrate birthdays, so that only increased rather than eased her suspicions.

"You're going to throw Roux a birthday party?" She couldn't mask the incredulity in her voice.

Garin had apparently lost his patience with her for he let loose a stream of curses that could have burned the hair off a pirate's chest.

Annja waited him out and then said, "Okay. I'm in. When is it?"

Still grumbling, he named a date only three days away.

"Nothing like giving a girl time to think it over," she said.

"What? Like you've got something else on your social calendar?" Garin shot back and from his tone Annja knew he was rather pleased with himself for that one. Before she could think of a retort, he went on. "I have tickets reserved in your name on the 9:00 p.m. flight out of Kennedy on the twelfth. My driver will pick you at DeGaulle, take you to Roux's for the party and drive you back to your hotel afterward."

And with that, he hung up.

"Garin? Garin!"

Hanging up the phone, she went back to putting away the groceries. While doing so she glanced at her calendar. The bare white spaces stared back at her. Well, what did you expect? she asked herself. Given your lifestyle, it is amazing you have any friends at all.

She had to admit, she'd never been one to stay in one place for long before she'd taken up Joan's sword, never mind afterward. If she wasn't headed off to some remote spot to film a new episode of *Chasing History's Monsters,* the cable television show she cohosted, then she was off volunteering at some dig site in the back end of nowhere just to satisfy her love of history and her need to feel the thrill of discovery. That didn't leave much time for friendships, never mind romantic entanglements longer than a few days in length.

While she occasionally wondered what it would be like to have a normal life, when she really got down to it, she found that she didn't mind all the craziness. After all, boring was the last thing you could call her life.

The party was on the thirteenth. On the sixteenth she was due in studio to shoot some green-screen work for her next episode and to wade through the piles of footage she'd brought back from her last trip. Both would be necessary to cut the raw material into a show worth watching, and while she knew the guys in the editing room could do it without her, she preferred to keep an eye on them to help tone down the inevitable "suggestions" her producer, Doug Morrell, was constantly trying to fill their ears with. Doug was a good guy, but he'd be just as happy to have a show revolving around blood-sucking alien chupacabras as he would some ancient civilization most people had never heard of. He'd once gone so far as to produce and distribute a memorial video of her final moments when she'd lost touch with him during a tsunami in India. That fact that she'd called in shortly thereafter, clearly alive and well, had only added fuel to his marketing efforts and had him envisioning a second volume highlighting her "miraculous" survival. If she'd been closer at the time she might have strangled him herself.

So she'd make the party, but had to be sure to be back in New York by the sixteenth, come hell or high water.

ANNJA WAS FIVE FEET TEN inches tall with chestnut hair and amber-green eyes. She had an athlete's build, with smooth rounded muscles and curves in all the right places. Dressed as she was in a pair of jeans, leather boots and a lightweight tank top, she knew she probably made quite a sight rushing helter-skelter through the airport with her long hair flying out behind her, but it just couldn't be helped. She'd gotten absorbed in research and hadn't left herself enough time. If she didn't make it to the gate on time, Garin would never let her forget it.

As was her usual luck, after convincing her cab driver to set new land-speed records in making it to the airport and then dashing through the terminal after clearing security, she reached the gate only to discover that her flight had been delayed due to a mechanical problem. At least the ticket was for first class, which let her pass the time in the executive lounge while she waited. Once she did board the plane almost an hour later, she popped on her iPod, stretched out and slept through most of the trip, determined to arrive ready to enjoy Roux's party.

Garin had a driver and car waiting, just as he'd said he would, and as she relaxed in the backseat and she watched the Paris streets roll by out her window, she had to admit that the whole thing made her feel a bit special.

Until she remembered just who was waiting for her on the other end.

It's for Roux, she reminded herself, for Roux.

As they drove, she thought about the circumstances that were bringing the three of them—Roux, Annja and Garin—together again. Despite her misgivings, she had to admit to being surprised, pleasantly so, that Garin was going out of his way for Roux; that wasn't something Garin was particularly known for. Ruthlessness, arrogance, a sense of entitlement ten miles wide—yes, he had more than his share of those qualities. But doing something just because it would make another person happy? Not so much.

Still, anyone could turn over a new leaf and in the past several months it was obvious that Garin was trying, in his own way, to smooth over some of the damage from the past, so she supposed she had to give him credit. It wasn't easy for anyone to change, least of all someone so set in their ways as Garin Braden.

The party they were throwing for Roux was, of course, a surprise. Or rather, Garin was throwing the party, with Annja and Henshaw, Roux's butler and majordomo, as the only guests. It pained Annja to think that after such a long life they were the only people Roux could claim as friends, but she didn't consider it too deeply lest she see the glaring similarities with her own life.

That the party was all Garin's idea was equally unusual, given the history between the two men. After all, they'd tried to kill each other on more than one occasion and no doubt would try again at some point in the future. On any given day they could go from friends to enemies in the space of a heartbeat. Still, there was a bond between them that transcended such petty squabbles, and as fate would have it, Annja had become part of their inner circle.

After all, who better to understand just what it meant to carry the sword that had belonged to Joan of Arc than the two men who had once been responsible for protecting Joan herself from the hands of her enemies? The same mystical force that had preserved the sword and ultimately brought it into Annja's possession had also given them their extended life span. It was also part of the discord between them. Neither of them knew what would happen should the sword somehow come to harm. Would they at last be able to live out the rest of their natural lives, free from the influence of the sword, or would time suddenly catch up to them, exacting its toll then and there for all the years they'd escaped its grasp? They didn't know and so, as a result, they had different ideas about how to handle the situation. Roux wanted the sword to remain with Annja, its chosen bearer, while Garin had made it clear he felt the sword should be locked away and protected. If that was even possible.

Annja shifted her attention from the scenery outside the car to the sword itself. It rested there in the otherwhere, just as it always did, glimmering faintly as it waited for her to call it forth with just a thought. For a moment she was tempted, for she loved to feel its weight in her hand, loved the sensation it gave her as she carried it forth into battle, but her good sense reasserted itself before she did so; having a huge broadsword suddenly appear in the back of the limousine probably wouldn't be a good thing for the upholstery, never mind the driver's sense of reality.

It was enough that it was there, waiting for her, and that she could claim it when necessary. She'd had to do so more times than she could count since taking possession of it and she knew that there would be plenty of other such situations in the future. It had become a part of her and she could no more give it up now than she could marry a pig farmer and retire to the country.

The celebration was being held at Roux's estate outside of Paris and it took them about half an hour to reach their destination.

Roux's house was huge, so huge that the word *home* just didn't seem to do it justice. *Palace* might have been better. Ivy clung to the stone walls and helped the structure blend into the trees that surrounded it. It butted up against a hill and the overall effect was as if the house itself were a part of the natural environment around it, and from past experience Annja knew that the design was deliberate. Roux was a man who liked his privacy and went to some lengths to see that it remained protected.

The driver must have called ahead, as Garin was waiting for her on the front steps when they pulled up. Standing with him was Henshaw.

"Welcome back, Ms. Creed," Henshaw said, giving her a small nod of welcome as she stepped from the car.

She grinned. That was Henshaw, positively overwhelming with his emotional displays, she thought.

"Good to see you," she told him. She turned her attention to his companion. "Hello, Garin."

"Annja," he answered just as solemnly, but his eyes twinkled with mischief behind his unruffled exterior.

With her ever-present backpack slung over her shoulder, Annja entered the house with Garin while Henshaw got her overnight bag from the trunk. She could already imagine his scowl as he saw the size of her suitcase. She wasn't the type to travel with more than the few basic items she needed, while he was a firm believer in a woman's right to be prepared for anything and to travel with a wardrobe large enough to let her do so, especially a woman as attractive as Annja. He'd never come right out and said so—the sun would stop revolving around the earth when that happened—but she'd managed to piece together the gist of his viewpoint from the few comments and frowns he'd made to her over the years.

The knowledge that he'd scowl all the more should he discover that she intentionally packed as light as she could just to tease him when coming here made her laugh aloud.

Maybe this was going to be a fun three days, after all.

Annja stepped into the foyer, with its vaulted ceiling and Italian marble floors. No matter how many time she visited, it never ceased to amaze her at the luxury Roux had surrounded himself with over the years. He seemed to be trying to forget the long, hard years he'd served in the field with nothing more than his arms and armor for material possessions and she had to admit he was doing an excellent job of it.

Garin led her through the lower floor to Roux's personal study, one of the largest rooms in the entire house. It was two stories tall and stuffed to the gills with shelves full of books, artifacts and artwork. Stacks of paper streamers rested on a nearby table, along with a pile of balloons. A tank of helium gas stood beside it.

"Roux is out at a high-stakes poker game for the afternoon," Garin told her. "Henshaw will be picking him up around dinnertime, which means we only have a couple of hours to get the place decorated and…"

He trailed off at seeing her expression. "What?" he growled.

Annja laughed; she couldn't help it. Imagining him with those blue and yellow streamers in his huge hands was just too much. It was *so* not Garin. From cold-blooded killer to interior decorator—would wonders never cease?

When at last she could find her voice again, she said, "I'm sorry, Garin, really, I am. I just never expected you to go to so much trouble for Roux and the change is a bit, um, unexpected. Nice, but unexpected."

He accepted her apology with a shrug and the two of them got to work. By the time Henshaw came in an hour later to check on them, they had finished strewing paper streamers throughout the room, even draping them on the massive stone sarcophagus that occupied one corner and wrapping them around the stuffed and mounted corpse of an Old West gunfighter that stood in the other, turning him from a cigar-store Indian-style display to a blue-and-yellow mummy. They were getting started on tying the balloons together into bunches.

Henshaw gave the room a once-over, his only discernible reaction the slight raising of an eyebrow as he took in the steamerwrapped gunfighter in the corner. Turning back to his partners in crime, he said, "I'm off to get Mr. Roux. I shall return in approximately one hour. We shall dine shortly after that."

Garin had several phone calls to make so Annja spent the time wandering through Roux's house, looking at the variety of artifacts that he had on display. While she might not agree with his methods of acquisition, since he had several items that were on current lists of objects either stolen or banned from being removed from their countries of origin, she could appreciate the beauty of the collection itself. She was examining a vase that had apparently been discovered in the remains of Knossos, the king's palace on the island of Crete, when her phone chirped. Pulling it out of her pocket, she saw that she had a text message from Garin.

They're here, was all it said.

She dashed back through the halls, slipping through the main foyer only seconds before Henshaw and Roux entered the house, and joined Garin in the study. There they waited for the guest of honor.

"Surprise!" they shouted when Henshaw led Roux into the room.

The older man started, then scowled first at the two of them and then back over his shoulder at Henshaw.

"Traitor!" he said, "I suppose you're in on this, too, then? What are they doing here?"

Henshaw gave one of his rare smiles. "Celebrating your birthday, of course, sir."

Garin smiled easily, ignoring Roux's brusque manner. "Did you think we'd forget?"

"It's not a question of forgetting. You've never bothered with my birthday before. What's so different this year?"

But he accepted the surprise good-naturedly and even began to enjoy himself as the evening wore on. They ate together in the dining room down the hall—braised duck in a pear chutney, which Annja thought was exquisite— then returned to the study for drinks and conversation.

Garin and Roux had lived so long and seen so much that Annja could listen to them for hours. Roux was entertaining them all with a tale of the time he'd slipped inside a royal palace for a rendezvous with a visiting princess when what sounded like gunfire split the night air outside.

"Did you hear that?" Annja asked.

The other three had for they were already in motion. A lifetime spent in dangerous situations had fine-tuned their senses, including Henshaw's, and they all recognized the sound of guns when they heard them. Annja did, too; she was just surprised to be hearing them at Roux's secluded estate.

Henshaw went straight to the computer sitting on a nearby desk. As he settled into the seat in front of it an alarm began to sound throughout the house. He silenced it with the touch of a button and then pressed another. A section of the wall to the left of where he sat split apart as a result, revealing sixteen security monitors in four rows of four. Each of them showed a different part of the manor grounds and on several of them Annja saw gray shapes racing across the lawn, firing at the hired security force as they came.

The hiss of hydraulics captured Annja's attention and she turned away from the monitors to see both Roux and Garin waiting impatiently for the vault at the back of the room to finish opening. Annja hadn't been inside that room since her first visit to the estate but remembered the treasure trove of multiple currencies and weapons it contained.

Roux could have armed and financed a small private army with what was in room.

It was the weapons stored in the vault that her two companions were going for. Garin armed himself with a pair of heavy pistols while Roux took a rifle for himself and then carried another over to Henshaw.

Garin held up a pistol for Annja. "Here, take this."

She shook her head. "Thanks but I'm already carrying all the weaponry I need."

"Suit yourself," Garin replied, then joined the others at the security station where Roux was trying without much success to reach the head of his security detail on the radio.

When he was unable to get a response, Henshaw gestured to the escape tunnel at the back of the vault. "If we leave now, sir, there will still be time to get you off the estate." Annja knew that it led up to the third floor and from there out onto the slope of the hill against which Roux's mansion had been built. A Jeep waited on the road above, ready to take the master of the house to safety at a moment's notice. Once before, when the estate had come under attack, all four of them had used the tunnel to get to safety. It sounded like a good plan to her now.

Roux was silent for a moment, considering, and then looked over at Garin for his opinion.

The other man hefted the weapon he carried and grinned at Roux. "It's your call, but if I were in your shoes, I'd be a little pissed. After all, it *is* your birthday."

There was no missing the challenge in Garin's answer and Annja bristled to hear it. He was practically daring Roux to make a stand! And of course, given the history between the two men, there was almost no way Roux was going to ignore that and do the right thing, which was to get the hell out of there while they still had a chance.

She was opening her mouth to advise against taking on the intruders themselves when Roux did precisely what she expected him to.

"Garin's right. This is my home and I'll be damned if I'm going to run like a rabbit at the first sign of trouble."

And that was that. Annja knew any further discussion was futile. Roux had made up his mind and, being the good manservant that he was, Henshaw would carry out his instructions to the last. With it being three against one, there wasn't even any sense in arguing.

Annja shot a murderous look in Garin's direction, but he was studying the images on the monitor and didn't see it. Or if he did, he chose to ignore it, which would certainly be in keeping with his usual behavior.

If something happens to Roux…

She would just have to ensure that it did not.

They quickly devised a plan that, when it came down to it, was pretty basic. The four of them would take up position inside the foyer and defend the house against anyone who tried to enter.

Annja just hoped it would work.

They left the study and quickly made their way through the house toward the front entrance. Roux led the way, followed by Henshaw and Garin, with Annja bringing up the rear. They were just passing a wide staircase that led to the second floor when Annja skidded to a halt.

The others ran on, but her attention was caught by the landing on the second floor. Her intuition was calling to her, telling her the problem was above her, on the second floor, rather than out front where the others were headed. Ever since taking possession of the sword she'd been subject to heightened senses and her intuition was just one of them. Right now it was telling her that there was a problem on the second floor, one that would come back to bite them in the ass if they didn't deal with it right away, and she had learned to trust such instincts.

Were they too late? she wondered. Were the intruders already inside the manor house?

Leaving a potential enemy at their backs could prove disastrous, so when she shouted at the others to come back and received no response, she made the decision to check things out on her own.

Turning away from the others, Annja charged up the stairs.

3

There were six of them.

They were dressed in dark, loose-fitting outfits with hoods pulled up right around their heads and ninja masks covering the lower parts of their faces, making it impossible for her to identify them.

Five of them stood in a rough semicircle facing the door, swords in hand. The sixth stood behind the first group, watching, and Annja didn't need to be told that this was their leader. If she was going to get some answers, Annja suspected she was going to have get past the first ranks and confront him herself.

So be it.

They didn't give her time to think, never mind formulate a plan. No sooner had she taken it all in, then they were upon her, the first three rushing forward while the other two closed up ranks in front of their commander.

It was almost as if they had been waiting for her.

The lead swordsman was quicker than the other two, eager for the chance to confront her. As he came forward she sized him up, her mind processing a hundred tiny details in the space of an eye blink, from the position of the sword in his hands to the angle of his hips to the length of his stride.

She moved to meet him.

He struck as soon as he was in range, intending to overpower her with his strength and speed. The tip of his sword came slashing in at her side, then rose at the last second in an attempt to reach her neck.

Annja brought her own sword up in her standard two-handed grip, parried his blow and, using his momentum against him, jammed an elbow into his face as his speed prevented him from stopping in time.

There was an audible crack, blood spurted from the intruder's nose and he dropped to the floor.

Annja kept going, moving in on the other two.

They were a bit more cautious than their comrade, splitting up and moving to either side as she continued forward. Annja knew they intended to force her to confront one of them and allow the other to strike at her exposed back, so she didn't hesitate, choosing instead to rush the one closest to her.

Sword met sword, the blows ringing in the air, as they flew through a flurry of exchanges. From the corner of her eye Annja could see the other intruder getting ready to make a strike, so when her current foe used a horizontal strike to parry her blow, she went with the motion, pivoting on one foot and driving the other directly into her attacker's gut, knocking him to the floor.

Even as he was falling backward, Annja was continuing the turn and bringing her sword around in a sweeping arc, taking the third attacker's blow along its length and letting it slide harmlessly to the side. She let her momentum carry her into a full three-hundred-sixty-degree turn, swiveling sharply around to smack the intruder on the side of the skull with the flat of her blade.

He went down without a sound.

Three down, three to go, she thought.

Gunfire sounded from downstairs, indicating that Roux and the others had encountered the enemy themselves, but Annja couldn't worry about them right now; she had her hands full.

Seeing how well their comrades had done against her, the two attackers now facing her chose a different strategy. With a sudden shout they rushed her as one, blades out and ready to strike from either side.

Annja waited until they were nearly upon her and then jumped upward with one powerful shove of her muscular legs.

The swords passed harmlessly beneath her as she somersaulted over their heads, twisting in midair to land behind them, facing their exposed backs. Her sword was already in motion as she landed on catlike feet and she slashed the backs of their legs without a second thought, taking them out of the fight.

One more…

She whirled, expecting her final opponent to be

closing the distance between them while her attention was elsewhere.

That wasn't the case.

The other man hadn't moved.

He stood watching her, his hands held calmly together behind his back, like an instructor evaluating her performance.

"Who are you and what do you want?" Annja asked and was surprised at the depth of anger she heard in her voice.

Her opponent said nothing.

"I'll give you one last—"

She never finished the sentence.

One second her opponent was standing in front of her with both hands behind his back and in the next he was leaping forward, a Japanese *katana* suddenly appearing in his hands. He lashed out in a vicious strike even before he landed, using his forward momentum to add force to the blow.

Annja just barely managed to deflect the strike as she brought her sword up, backpedaling as she did to give her some much-needed room, her mind grappling all the while at what she thought she'd just seen.

One minute his hands were empty and the next…

Where the hell had that sword come from? It was almost as if he'd conjured the thing out of midair….

The very notion was unthinkable.

She didn't have time to dwell on it as her opponent pushed his attack forward, the ferocity and force of his blows driving her backward across the floor as she sought to defend herself.

She had faced off against talented swordsmen before, but this guy was in another league. It was all she could do to protect herself from harm as she twisted and turned, keeping her weapon between her body and her opponent's deadly blade. Several times he managed to get the tip of his weapon past her defenses, leaving minor wounds in its wake. It didn't take her long to realize that he was toying with her; that, had he chosen to do so, he could have dispatched her more than once during their engagement. In no time at all she found herself backed into a corner, fighting for her life.

She could see several of the fighters she had already dispatched getting back to their feet and she knew it wouldn't be long before she was again horribly outnumbered.

If you're going to do something, Annja, you'd better do it now, she thought.

She gave a shout, putting everything she had into it. It distracted her opponent for the split second she needed to duck his current blow and strike out with her own.

For a moment she thought she'd done it, that she'd punctured his defenses and would score a strike against him, perhaps even a fatal one, but then his weapon came around impossibly fast and caught the hilt of her own. Annja was left watching in dismay as her sword spun out of her hands and away from her, tumbling through the air to clatter against the floor several yards to one side.

As soon as the sword struck the ground that it vanished into the otherwhere.

But even as Annja called it to hand once more, she realized that her assailant's strike was already inside her defenses and time seemed to slow as she caught sight of that shining steel blade arcing toward her.

The gleaming blade grew in her vision, descending in a lightning-quick strike aimed at her exposed neck. But rather than take her head off at the shoulders, as Annja fully expected it to do, the sword was diverted at the last second so that it merely cut free a lock of her hair.

For a moment Annja's gaze met that of her opponent and she could have sworn the other was silently laughing at her. I could have taken you at any time, those eyes said. And for the first time since taking up Joan's sword, Annja felt outclassed.

Then Garin was looming in the doorway, pistols in hand, and gunfire filled the room. He mercilessly cut down those Annja had been unwilling to slay only moments before, their bodies twisting and jerking like marionettes as the bullets thundered into them. He was firing with both hands, so he wasn't as accurate as usual and a few stray shots whined in Annja's direction, forcing her to dive to the floor to avoid being hit.

When she looked up again, her attacker had turned from her and was already halfway across the room, headed for an open casement window that she had failed to notice when she'd first arrived.

So that's how they got inside, she thought. And apparently that's how they intended to get out again. But not if she could help it.

"Garin! The window!" she shouted.

Garin spun in her direction and brought his arms up, the guns roaring in the small confines of the room.

Bullets split the air and slammed into the area all around the window, but Annja's attacker managed to slip through the opening without being hit.

Annja wasn't ready to let him get away that easily.

"Oh, no, you don't," she said through gritted teeth, angry at having been bested so handily. With her sword in hand she ran for the window herself, trusting Garin to stop firing when he saw her move.

Garin shouted something at her, but Annja didn't hear. She was almost to the window itself when a hand appeared from outside and tossed something dark into the room in front of her.

It hit the floor and rolled toward her.

She had a split second to think, *Grenade!* and throw herself to the side before the explosive device went off.

4

It felt as if a giant hand picked her up and threw her against the floor, the concussion hammering her senses until her head reeled. She bounded off the marble floor and slid into the wall with enough force to nearly knock her senseless.

Only the fact that it had been a concussion grenade, rather than an explosive one, saved her life. She was still trying to figure out which way was up when Garin rushed to her side.

"Annja! Are you all right?" he asked, his voice seeming to come from miles away as the roaring in her ears continued.

She nodded, still too caught up in the emotion of the moment to speak. Her heart was beating like crazy and she fought to get her breathing under control as Garin helped her into a sitting position.

At last she found her voice.

"Yes," she said. "Yes, I'm all right."

Using his arm for support she pulled herself all the way to her feet and then stood on still-wobbling legs. Her gaze landed on the lock of hair that the intruder's sword had cut from her head.

Too close.

She glanced over at the intruders. Or rather, what was left of them. Garin hadn't spared any ammunition it seemed; every body was riddled with bullet holes and blood leaked across the marble floor beneath them.

"Did you have to kill them all?" she asked.

"Yes."

Now why didn't that surprise her? "But if you had managed to only wound one or two, we might have been able to question them. Learn who they were and why they were here."

Garin grunted. "Or they might have managed to kill us both. Thank you, but I'll take the safer way out every time, particularly where *my* life is concerned."

Annja did not doubt that in the slightest. When it came to protecting his long life, Garin was exceedingly ruthless.

At any rate, it was too late now to argue about it.

Garin stepped over to the window and cautiously looked out, but the intruder must have been long gone for he turned away, shaking his head. He was on his way back to Annja's side when Roux and Henshaw arrived.

"Is everyone all right?" Roux asked as he stepped into the room, surveying the death and destruction before him.

"We're fine," Annja replied as Garin nodded in assent.

"What happened up here?" Roux asked.

Annja explained how she'd arrived to find the intruders already in the room and what had happened after that. She didn't mention her near defeat at the hands of the final swordsman; that was for her and her alone. No one was too surprised at the realization that Annja had held off six attackers on her own; they had all seen her wield Joan's sword at one time or another in the past and they knew just how deadly she could be with the weapon in hand.

"Did they say anything? Do anything that gave you some idea what they might have been after?"

Annja shook her head.

"I don't get it," Roux said. He glanced around the room, a puzzled expression on his face. "The assault force at the front of the house seems to have been a diversion. They made no attempt to take the manor itself and only put up just enough of a fight to keep the security force occupied."

"Given what we know at this point, I'd say the whole thing was a diversion to allow this group to enter the house from the back," Henshaw suggested.

"A logical assumption, I agree, but why? What was it they were after?" Roux glanced at the weapons decorating the walls and Annja could see him silently cataloging each one, gauging whether there was something valuable enough among them to warrant such an attempt. By the confused look on his face she could guess that the answer to that question was a solid *no*.

As the others looked on, Garin squatted next to one of the bodies. Reaching out, he pulled off the dead man's ninja mask and hood, revealing his face.

The man was Asian. Somewhere in his thirties or so, was Annja's guess. He was dressed in a dark blue coverall, similar to those worn by special forces units all around the world, with dark combat boots on his feet. A quick check showed that any identifying tags or markings had been stripped from the uniform.

"Recognize him?" Annja asked, only half-jokingly.

Garin scowled at her, annoyed by the comment apparently. "No, I don't recognize him," he replied. "Do you?"

Annja snorted. She wasn't the one who dealt in the shadow world of dirty tricks and ruthless competition.

Neither Roux nor Henshaw had ever seen the man. With Henshaw's help, Garin lined the bodies up next to one another and then he began to methodically search them for information while the other three looked on. He stripped them of their masks and pulled back their hoods, gazing at each face as if it might be able to tell him something. He went through their pockets, checked the labels on their clothing and even looked inside the boots they all wore.

Finally he stood, a disgusted look on his face.

"Nothing," he said. "They're as clean as a whistle."

"Professionals, eh?" Henshaw asked, and the expression on his face told Annja how he felt about that revelation. A random break-in was one thing, but the knowledge that this had been planned and executed to within a fair chance of success was something else entirely.

Garin nodded. "Seems to be," he replied. "Though that doesn't tell us what they were after."

"Or whom," Roux added.

Annja had been content to listen in on the exchange but broke in at this point. "What do you mean 'whom'?"

"Seems rather obvious, doesn't it?" Garin answered for him. "They slip a group in the back door while the security team is otherwise occupied dealing with the assault out in front. With all of our attention in that direction, the second group would have had the opportunity to move through the house at will. Probably could have ambushed any one of us before we even knew they were there."

Henshaw glanced over at Annja. "Seems you saved the day, Ms. Creed."

"But that still doesn't tell us what they were after." Roux scowled down at the bodies in front of him. From his expression Annja knew he would have killed them himself had they lived through the assault.

She caught Garin staring at their host and recognized that mischievous expression in his eye.

Uh-oh.

"Pissed anyone off lately, Roux?" he asked, perhaps with a bit more force than he'd intended.

The damage was done, however. Roux noticeably stiffened, then shot back with, "No more than usual. Perhaps they were after someone with a bit less scrupulous business dealings."

Now it was Garin's turn to bristle. "And what's that supposed to mean?"

"Just what I said. You have a far greater capacity for annoying others than I do! Maybe they were here to settle a debt with you."

The younger man threw up his hands in annoyance and took a step toward his former companion. "Oh, I get it. It is *your* home that is attacked, *your* security that is penetrated, but suddenly *I'm* the one to blame."

Rather than back down, Roux moved to meet him. "You're right—it is *my* home that was attacked, *my* security that was penetrated. And I suppose it is just a strange coincidence that it happened on the evening that *you* planned a surprise party for me, now, isn't it?"

Annja watched as Garin's face grew red with anger. "You think I had something to do with this? That I would stoop so low as that? To try and kill you in your own home?" He was shouting now, and Roux was shouting right back, throwing accusations back and forth like some misguided game of catch.

Henshaw stepped between the two men, hands up, holding them back, trying to dissipate the anger before the two went after each other with more than words. The goodwill generated earlier in the evening was gone. If she didn't do something quickly, Annja realized, there would be blood on the floor soon.

"Stop it, both of you!" she said sharply, and much to her surprise, they actually did.

"Given the incredible number of artifacts and pieces of art inside this house, the most reasonable assumption is that this was nothing more than a well-staged robbery. Lucky for us and unlucky for them, they just happened to choose the wrong night."

Both men backed off but it was clear that no one was happy with the situation. After a few minutes of angry silence, Roux pulled Henshaw aside and spoke to him quietly, occasionally casting glances in Garin's direction.

Garin, on the other hand, pretended to ignore him, then announced that he was returning to the study downstairs. Annja went with him. It was a good ten minutes before Roux joined them, which was probably for the best as it gave both men some time to cool down.

Within minutes of his arrival it was clear that the night was over. What had made the evening enjoyable was gone and the chances were slim that they would be able to recapture it. It wasn't so much the armed assault on Roux's home, though that would normally be enough to put anyone off their game, but the suspicions that had been tossed around afterward that made their continued conversations strained and uncomfortable. After a short period of time Garin excused himself, claiming a business engagement early in the morning, and offered to give Annja a ride back to her hotel.

When she refused, he said, "Suit yourself," and left the estate without even a goodbye to their host.

What had started so well had ended badly and Annja couldn't help but wonder how many times over the years the same thing had happened.

No wonder the two of them were reluctant to spend any time together, she thought.

To fill the silence after Garin's departure, Annja asked Roux whether he had called the local authorities or those in Paris. "Detectives from the city would probably be better equipped to handle this kind of thing," she reasoned.

Roux stared at her. "Why on earth would I want to do something so…counterproductive?"

Annja was almost certain that the word on his lips had been *stupid,* not *counterproductive,* but she let it go in order to deal with the issue at hand. "Your estate has been attacked. People have died. How can you not call the police?"

"Quite simply, really. We'll deal with this internally, just as we always do."

"But—"

He cut her off. "I said no police, Annja. I don't need incompetent idiots poking around my house, touching my things, when my staff is perfectly capable of handling this on their own."

At that moment Henshaw stuck his head in the door. "The room's been cleared, sir. The cleaning crew will be in first thing in the morning to scrub the blood off the floor and to patch the bullet holes by the window.

"Very good, Henshaw. Thank you."

Annja was aghast. "You can't just destroy evidence like that!"

Roux laughed and this time it was an ugly sound. "This is my home, Annja. I can do whatever I want in it, including shooting armed intruders foolish enough to enter it. You and your friend Garin would do well to remember that I am not the feeble old man you appear to think I am."

With that he got up and left the room, leaving Annja staring openmouthed in amazement that he had felt the need to threaten her, of all people. Just what had this night come to?

Deciding she'd had her share of five-hundred-year-old egos for the evening, she strode through the house and back to the second floor, intending to collect her backpack from the room she'd stored it in and get the heck out of there before she said something she would regret later.

But once on the second floor, she felt herself drawn back to the room where she'd come close to losing her life, as if called there by the secrets they were trying so hard to figure out.

5

Annja Creed stood inside the doorway and let her gaze just wander about, without focusing on anything in particular. Her thoughts kept returning to those few moments just before the fight, when she'd first entered the room. She could still see them in her mind's eyes, the first five men arranged in two precise rows, their swords out and ready, providing the most protection possible for their leader. They had all been standing still, eyes forward, almost as if they had been…

Waiting.

That was what was bothering her.

They hadn't been moving throughout the room. They hadn't been actively looking through the artifacts on the walls or heading toward the door to join their colleagues at the front of the house.

They'd been standing still.

Waiting.

But for what?

She didn't have a clue.

She looked past the bloodstains on the floor and the pile of extra sheets that had been set there in case more were needed to transport the bodies out of the house, and tried to see the place through fresh eyes.

She was missing something and she knew it. It hovered there, on the edge of her mind, like a presence felt but not seen, a watcher in the darkness. There was something here for her to find, something important, but all she could see was row upon row of swords and the fragments of the window scattered across the floor thanks to the combination of Garin's bullets and the concussion wave of the grenade.

Finally, frustrated and more than a bit annoyed at everyone involved, she turned away, intending to arrange a ride back to her hotel and call it a night.

That was when her eye caught something out of place, a slight anomaly in the otherwise orderly arrangement of the collection.

She turned back and began going over the rows of weapons again, one item at a time, piece by piece, until she could rule each out.

There!

Standing on the hilt of a broadsword that was remarkably similar to the one that had come to her through the centuries was a small figure. When she stepped closer to get a better look, she discovered that it was made from paper. The origami figure was in the shape of a dragon, with swept back wings and a long winding tail.

She stared at it, trying to figure out how it had gotten there.

Annja had been around Henshaw enough times to know that he ruled the cleaning staff with an iron hand. None of them would have dared leave something like the origami dragon behind, no matter how innocuous it seemed. Certainly Henshaw would never do such a thing himself.

The lack of dust on the weapons meant that the display had been cleaned recently, probably in the past day or two. In turn, logic dictated that the paper figurine could only be that old, as well; after all, had the cleaning crew found it they would have thrown it away, if only to save themselves from Henshaw's ire if he found it himself.

While there was certainly nothing innately threatening about a small piece of paper folded into the shape of a mythical creature, something about this one made Annja distinctly uncomfortable.

It was so unexpected and so out of place that it made her skin crawl, the same way hearing a voice in a darkened room when you think you are alone will.

It was almost as if it had been purposely left behind. A small token to remind them that someone other than themselves had been here, in this place, where no outsider should be.

She reached out to pick it up and then thought better of it and swiftly withdrew her hand. If it had been left by the intruders, then she needed to take care to preserve whatever evidence might have been left behind.

She needed to treat it as carefully as she might a

thousand-year-old artifact just recently exposed to the light.

Annja left the display room and walked down the hall to the room, where she'd left her backpack. Retrieving her digital camera, she returned to the display room.

She half expected the origami dragon to be gone when she got back—having it disappear would be about par for the course that evening—but it was still there, right where she left it. She turned on her camera and went to work. She took close-up pictures of the figure from as many angles as possible and then made certain to get some positioning shots, as well, to illustrate just where on the wall the sword on which it stood was hung.

When she was finished, she used a pair of tweezers to lift the paper sculpture off the shelf.

Now it was time to do some serious research.

Roux had already refused to bring the intrusion to the attention of the Paris police, but that didn't mean that Annja was out of options.

Far from it, in fact.

FROM A PUBLIC PAY phone in Paris the call was routed through a number of middlemen and cutouts, designed to hide the origin of the contact should anyone be listening in, until it was at last picked up via cell phone in the back of a limousine.

"Yes?"

"She's an interesting opponent. Perhaps even a worthy one."

"I didn't hire you to evaluate her abilities. Can you carry out the task we discussed or not?"

There was a soft, mocking laugh. "Of course I can. Am I not the Dragon, myth incarnate and legend made flesh?"

"Don't be overconfident. She's survived far too often when the odds were arrayed against her. You'd do well to remember that."

Again the laugh. "Let me worry about the odds. You just be sure the money is in the account as agreed. You have the hotel information?"

"Yes. She's staying at the Four Seasons."

"Oh, fancy. Nothing but the best, I see."

The other ignored the jibe. "Remember, she must give up the sword voluntarily. Anything else will defeat our purposes."

"I know the details. You remember the money and we won't have any issues."

The call ended as quickly and as anonymously as it had begun.

Just the way both parties preferred it.

6

Because Henshaw was still involved in the cleanup at the estate, Roux had one of his other men drive Annja back to her hotel in the city. She was fine with that; if she had seen Henshaw again that night she would have had to tell him just what she thought of his participation in eradicating a crime scene and that wouldn't have gone over well with either of them.

Once back at the hotel, she checked her messages at the front desk and then rode the elevator to the sixth floor. Not satisfied with anything as simple as a basic hotel room, Garin had booked her into a three-room suite, complete with a spa bath, a comfortable sitting room and a separate bedroom.

As soon as she was safely ensconced inside, Annja fired up her laptop and hooked her digital camera to it, downloading the pictures she'd taken of the origami dragon. Once she was finished she chose four of the best images and then attached them to an e-mail to her friend, Bart McGille.

A Brooklyn detective who was also a dear friend, Bart had helped her in the past when she needed information, and he was as good a source as any to start with.

Dear Bart,
Attached are several photos of an origami figure that was left behind by a thief who broke into a friend's apartment in Paris. Due to the owner's reluctance to involve the police, I can't have the authorities here examine the figure but it has certainly sparked my curiosity. Can you do an Interpol search for me and let me know if anything similar has turned up at other crime scenes?
Thanks,
Annja

Her explanation seemed plausible enough to her and she was hopeful Bart would take it at face value and do some digging on her behalf. If he came up with anything, she'd use that to get to the bottom of the attack on Roux's estate. She knew there was more going on there than met the eye, but with Garin and Roux on the outs with each other it was going to take a crowbar to get either of them to talk more about it.

Finished, she suddenly realized how tired and sore she was. Her body ached from a combination of the effort of hand-to-hand combat and the physical hammering she'd taken from the concussion grenade. Never mind the long flight from New York. A hot bath and a decent night's sleep would do her some good, she decided.

The hotel had kindly supplied a selection of bath crystals and she selected one jar at random and threw a handful in while the water was running. Soon the sweet scent of jasmine filled the room.

Annja sighed as she slid naked into the hot water and for the next twenty minutes did nothing but bask in its heated embrace.

Once she had managed to soak some of the soreness from her bones, she got out, dried off and wrapped herself in one of the big, fluffy bathrobes the hotel provided. Not wanting to go to sleep with wet hair, she took the time to comb it out and blow it dry. When she finished, she slipped into a pair of comfortable cotton pajamas and climbed into bed.

Sleep came quickly.

THE LATCH ON THE French doors that led to the balcony in the sitting room snapped open with a soft click about an hour later. The door opened silently from the outside. A shadow detached itself from the others that hugged the exterior wall and slid inside the room without making any more noise than the door had.

The intruder stood to one side once inside the room, waiting for eyes to adapt to the level of light and listening for any sound or sense of movement.

There was none.

The guest slept on in the bedroom next door.

The intruder crossed the sitting room with a few

quick, sure steps, almost as if passing from shadow to shadow. At the bedroom door the intruder paused, listening again.

The door to the bedroom swung open and a shadow slipped inside the room as swiftly and quietly as it had entered the suite itself.

On the bed, the sleeping form of Annja Creed could be seen in the dim light coming in through the window's half-drawn curtains.

The intruder carefully walked around the bed until Annja's face was in sight and stared down at it for several long moments.

Why you?

What makes you so special?

Annja did not reply.

As the intruder looked on, Annja mumbled something in her sleep and flailed about with one arm.

The Dragon watched for a long time, a wraith standing in the darkness beside the bed, eyes alert and ready.

It would be so easy to end it here, the Dragon thought silently. A sudden thrust and it would all be over but the dying. The Dragon could then search the suite in a leisurely manner; no doubt the sword was here somewhere.

But the sensei's instructions had been clear. The sword must be given voluntarily or it was useless to him. Disappointing the sensei was not something the Dragon wanted to do, ever.

It would seem that the easy solution was off the table for now. The Dragon would have to wait to claim its next victim.

The intruder bent close.

"Until next time, Annja Creed."

A SWORD CAME WHISTLING in toward her unprotected throat and Annja knew that this was it. She was about to die…

She awoke, bolting upright in bed, her heart hammering like a thousand kettledrums all at once, a thunderous booming sound. Her eyes were already searching the interior of the room for her opponent, her hand tight on the hilt of her sword as she called it into existence from the otherwhere.

But there was no one there.

The room was empty.

Realization came roaring in.

A dream, just a dream, she told herself.

She pushed back the sheets and got out of bed. With the tip of her sword she checked to see if anyone was hidden behind the curtains, then turned to look out the window, expecting at any moment for a face to press itself up against the glass, horror-movie style, and announce that it was coming for her. But the glass remained empty, the space around her silent.

Satisfied that no one was in the room with her, Annja turned, intending to investigate the rest of the hotel suite, only to come up short when she saw the door leading from the bedroom to the living area was open.

Her mind whirled as she tried to remember—had she left it open or closed it behind her?

She was certain that she had closed it before going to bed.

Or, at least, ninety-five percent certain that she had.

She moved toward it with panther-light steps and carefully eased past, taking in the sitting room just beyond.

It, too, was empty.

The hotel room door was securely shut and locked, as were the French doors leading to the balcony outside.

Despite what her gut was telling her, it appeared that no one had been in the room.

Still, just to be safe, she took another few minutes to search the entire suite, including the closets, the bathroom and even under her bed.

Then and only then, satisfied that she was indeed alone, did she release the sword back into the otherwhere and return to bed.

This time she made certain to shut the bedroom door firmly.

Her last thought, as she drifted off to sleep, was that someone was watching.

7

When she checked her e-mail late the next morning, she discovered a very succinct note from Bart in reply to her.

Call me, was all it said.

A glance at the clock told her that it was early back in the States but she picked up the phone and dialed his number.

A sleepy male voice answered. "McGille."

"Hi, Bart. It's Annja."

"Hey! How's Europe?"

"Not too bad." They chatted for a few moments about what they'd been up to recently and then Bart turned the conversation to the reason she had called.

"So what's this about a robbery?"

Annja gave him the fake story she'd concocted about how her friend's apartment had been vandalized by a thief who'd left behind the origami figure as "payment" for what he'd stolen.

"Sounds like a job for the Paris police. Why send the pictures to me?"

"My friend is subletting the place from the current tenant without the owner's permission. If she goes to the police, the owner finds out and that will be that."

Annja knew that was all she had to say. As a veteran New Yorker, Bart would understand the need to keep the sublet a secret; real-estate prices were so outrageous that subletting rent-controlled apartments had become a thriving black market in the Big Apple and Bart would no doubt believe the same about Paris. For all Annja knew, the situation in Paris might even be the same.

"Say no more," he said good-naturedly.

On the other end of the line Annja breathed a sigh of relief. "So what did you find out?"

"To tell you the truth," Bart replied, "not much. I made a few phone calls, had some folks check some records for me, and what they came up with were all negatives. No similar crimes in your area. No record of origami figures being involved in any crime, regardless of the type, in more than seven years. Basically they found nothing to tie this burglary to any other, in France or elsewhere. Maybe your cat burglar just has a sense of humor."

Annja digested that for a moment, knowing that she was partially hampering Bart's ability to get her information by not telling him the entire story. Still, it couldn't be helped.

Something Bart said jumped out at her. "What do you

mean you didn't find any link to crimes committed in the past seven years? Were there some before that with the same M.O.?" she asked.

Bart laughed. "That's where you nearly gave me a heart attack. Ever hear of the Dragon?"

Annja frowned. "Wasn't there a Bruce Lee movie with that name?"

"No, that was *Enter the Dragon.* Great movie, too. But that's not the Dragon I'm thinking of. This one is an international assassin who likes to leave little folded origami figures at the scenes of his kills."

He said it so matter-of-factly that at first Annja didn't think she'd heard him correctly.

"Did you just say 'assassin'?"

"Yeah, an international hit man, if you can believe that. Responsible for more than eighteen deaths in half a dozen countries, including France. Real son of a you know what."

Annja felt her stomach do a slow roll as she remembered Garin's words from last night. *Probably could have ambushed any one of us before we even knew they were there.*

Bart wasn't finished, though. "And talk about someone who loves their job, this guy managed to get up close and personal to each and every one of his victims. They say he took it as a personal challenge. He'd get in, do the deed and vanish before anyone even knew he'd been there. The police had nothing on him for years, except for those stupid little paper dragons he would leave behind with the bodies in his wake."

Bart laughed. "You sure there wasn't a dead body lying next to that origami, Annja?"

Anger flared. "Jeez, Bart, that's not funny!"

"What? Okay, come on, Annja, lighten up a little. Do you think I'd still be yammering away on this end of the phone if I thought you and your friend were being targeted by some crazed international assassin?"

That was the problem. He thought they were still talking about some harmless burglary.

She couldn't tell him the truth now; he'd be worried sick. "No, I guess you wouldn't," she said instead, laughing it off, while inside she was burning to know more.

Luckily Bart was a talker. "And talk about old-fashioned. Guy manages to pull off eighteen major hits and not once does he use a gun? Come on! What is he, stupid?"

A shiver ran up Annja's spine. Hesitantly she asked, "If he didn't use a gun, what did he use?"

"A big-ass sword apparently. One of those curved Japanese blades, like the one Sean Connery carried in *Highlander.*"

Annja hadn't seen the movie, but there was no mistaking what Bart was talking about. "A *katana?*" she asked, dreading the answer but needing to know, anyway.

"Yep, that's it. A *katana.* Can you imagine getting close enough to a major political figure to try and take him out with a freakin' sword? When everybody else has guns? What a maniac!"

This was getting worse by the minute.

"Did they ever catch him?"

"Of course they did. Why do you think I'm not worried about you, given the kind of trouble you get yourself into?"

She had to admit he was right; ever since taking possession of the sword, she had a knack for getting herself into the biggest messes possible.

Like now.

"So what happened to him?"

Bart snorted. "Got blown up when he tried to take out the British prime minister at a summit in Madrid back in 2003. There wasn't enough left of him to fill a Baggie."

Just when she started to feel better about the situation Bart had go and ruin things again.

"So they never found a body?"

"What did I just say? There wasn't anything left of him to bury, Annja. But trust me, you and your friend can rest easy. Whoever it was that broke into your friend's flat was probably just trying to be funny."

"Some sense of humor," she said, and laughed along with him while inside she was getting more and more nervous by the minute.

She made small talk for a couple of moments more, thanked Bart for what he had dug up and then got off the phone as quickly and as gracefully as she could without raising his suspicions.

As soon as she had, she headed for her laptop.

A quick search online turned up a decent number of feature stories and news reports from the eighties through the nineties that talked about the mysterious

Dragon. All of them told the same basic story Bart had—assassin for hire, no one knew his background or what he looked like, or even if the Dragon was a man or a woman, only that he always killed with his weapon of choice, a *katana,* and would leave a piece of rice paper folded into the shape of a dragon at the scene of every killing. The press had given him the moniker "the Dragon" when word of the origami figures leaked out, and to this day it was the only name they had for him. The Dragon's identity vanished in the same explosion that had claimed his physical body.

She sat back, staring off into space, as she pondered the similarities. An international assassin who killed with a Japanese *katana* and left origami figures in his wake, and an unknown intruder who broke into a rich man's home, carried a *katana* and left an origami figure in his wake. They were too alike to be just a coincidence. Either someone had decided to take up the killer's mantle or the killer himself had never actually died.

After all, there hadn't been a body, she reminded herself.

Maybe the Dragon had spent the past few years in hiding, recovering from injuries sustained from his last assassination attempt, and had only recently chosen to come out of hiding.

But why would a political assassin be after Roux? she wondered.

The most logical answer would be that he wasn't. After all, Roux took considerable effort to stay out of the limelight and something like politics was anathema to a man like him. But what if the Dragon had decided to forgo political assassinations in favor of a mercenary lifestyle? Killing for hire, perhaps? That was a different story entirely.

Garin had been right; Roux had angered enough people over the years that a list of those who held a grudge strong enough to try and kill him would be very long indeed.

More than a few of them had the means to do it, too.

This was not good—not good at all.

8

Given that she was starting to suspect the attack on the estate might actually have been an attempt to assassinate Roux, Annja decided that she was going to take another stab at discussing it with him and see if she could learn anything further that might help her fend off what she was beginning to see as a growing threat to his life.

But when she called the estate, she was informed by Henshaw that Roux was out and wouldn't return until evening. Annja explained that she needed to talk with him, but the majordomo guarded his boss's whereabouts like a mother grizzly guards her cubs and wouldn't tell her where he had gone or exactly when he was expected to return. Rather than spend any time arguing with him, she simply made an appointment to see Roux that evening and that was that.

She spent the next hour pacing back and forth in her hotel room, watching the minute hand creep around the clock and wishing it would go faster. When she couldn't stand it anymore, she decided to get out of the hotel and play tourist for a bit—try to take her mind off her pending meeting with Roux. It had been some time since she'd had the opportunity to wander through the city at her leisure and she vowed that she'd make good use of what little time she had; after all, who knew when she'd be back this way again?

After a quick shower she threw on a pair of khaki shorts, a deep blue T-shirt and her usual pair of low-rise hiking boots, grabbed an apple out of the fruit basket on the table and headed for the concierge's desk in the lobby. Arranging for a rental car to be available upon her return took only a few minutes thanks to the concierge's help, and with that taken care of, she was ready to enjoy the day.

Her first stop, she decided, was going to be Sainte-Chapelle, the palatine chapel in the courtyard of the royal palace on the Île de la Cité. Originally built by Louis IX to store the many holy relics he had purchased from the Byzantine emperor in Constantinople, Baldwin II, including the supposed Crown of Thorns worn by Christ during his crucifixion, the chapel was best known for its fifteen stained-glass windows, each one nearly fifty feet high and picturing Biblical stories from Genesis to Revelation. Annja was as interested in the architecture of the restored chapel—the original having been heavily damaged during the French Revolution—as she was in the artifacts it had once contained. She had always wanted to visit, but had never found the time.

Annja was thankful that the cab ride was reasonably short, for the traffic was terrible and terrifying. When the driver announced that they had arrived, she practically leaped out of the cab and had to suppress a smile at his bewildered expression. She thanked him for the speedy arrival and paid the fare, then turned her attention to the ominous-looking building behind her, with its dark stone towers and conical roofs circa the thirteenth century, known as the Palais de Justice. Now housing several French courts, this wing of the building had once been home to the Conciergerie, the oldest prison in Paris, and had held such infamous prisoners as Robespierre and Marie Antoinette. It was now a museum, but that didn't do much to change the vibe that Annja picked up off the place. Just looking at it made her shiver, as she imagined what it must have been like to be a prisoner there, locked away in a cold, dark, vermin-infested cell.

She walked down the street until she came to the entrance that served the majority of the complex. After buying an admission ticket, she slipped through the gates and made her way in the direction of the chapel.

The royal palace had once stood on the spot the Palais de Justice now occupied and Annja knew it had connected directly to the chapel via a narrow corridor. It was designed that way to allow King Louis IX to pass directly into it without leaving the palace, in much the same way the Holy Roman Emperor in Constantinople had been able to enter the Hagia Sophia from his own residence. The king, who had died of a plague while on crusade, had been canonized by the pope and was now known as Saint Louis. The palace itself had disappeared ages ago, leaving the two-level church on its own, surrounded by the less sophisticated buildings of the Palais de Justice.

There was a fair-size crowd in attendance. Annja worked her way through it, intent on pursuing her own agenda and not wanting to get caught up in any of the guided tours that were taking place. Once inside the lower chapel, she pushed her way past the souvenir stand that seemed to occupy most of the space near the entrance and made her way out into the center of the floor. The high vaulted ceilings rose above her, the beams covered in red and gold, which provided a sharp contrast with the deep royal blue of the ceiling panels. The soft lighting gave the place a gentle and welcoming atmosphere. Annja knew that the lower chapel had served as a parish church for the inhabitants of the palace. It was rather plain, at least in comparison to the grandeur of the upper chapel, but she found a sense of peace and tranquility wrapping about her as she stood, gazing about. There was almost a sense of humility about the place, as if it knew not to overshadow its more famous cousin above, and Annja found that she liked the place despite its lack of sophistication.

Enjoying what she had seen so far, Annja made her way toward the stairs to the upper chapel.

UNNOTICED AMID THE CROWD by the souvenir tables, the Dragon watched Annja as she crossed the chapel floor,

headed for the stairs to the upper level. The decision to
follow her from the hotel had been an impulsive one.
Watching her the night before had generated a certain
amount of curiosity and, after some deeper reflection,
it seemed that a bit of prudent observation might be in
order at this point.

But so far, the target hadn't done anything but play
tourist, something the Dragon found rather annoying.

Why would anyone waste time on such ridiculous-
ness? Time was too precious to be squandered away in
fruitless pursuits; every moment wasted here could have
been spent accomplishing something of value.

Still, there was something intriguing about the woman
and when Annja at last reached the stairwell to the upper
level, the Dragon headed in that direction, as well.

HALFWAY UP THE STEPS Annja felt a chill wash over her.
Bone deep, it seared her with its intensity. It felt as if
Death himself had suddenly taken a particular interest,
his gaze pausing on her for a heartbeat too long, letting
some of the coldness of the grave seep into her flesh as
a result, and instinct told her to run, to get away as fast
as she could.

She shuddered, trying to shake off both the uncomfortable feeling as well as the solution that it had evoked,
and then she casually turned to look back down the
stairs behind her. She let her gaze travel across the floor
of the lower chapel, searching for the source of that
feeling, but as far as she could tell no one was looking
at her and nothing seemed out of place. The interior of

the church was just as it had been moments before, full of tourists taking in the sights and spending their money on souvenirs and cheap baubles.

Her hand twitched and the image of the sword formed in her mind, but she quickly banished it away, disturbed that her first thoughts had been of violence. Equally disturbing, however, was the persistent feeling that she was in danger, and she had learned to trust those feelings. They had saved her life on more than one occasion.

Annja reached the top of the stairwell and moved to the side in order to let those behind her continue forward into the upper chapel. As they did, she watched their faces, but she didn't see anyone who looked even vaguely familiar.

Shrugging it off, she went back to enjoying her visit.

The upper chapel was far more ornate than the lower one; after all, this had practically been the king's private worship area. Supported by slender piers, the ceiling seemed to float high above the collection of magnificent stained-glass windows, giving the whole place a feeling of fragile beauty. The brochure she had been given along with her entrance ticket told Annja that there was more than six and a half thousand feet of stained glass around her, and within the deep reds and blues of the glass were some eleven hundred illustrated figures from the Bible.

Annja spun in a circle, drinking it all in. It was truly beautiful, there was no doubt about that, and her only regret was that she hadn't come to see it in the late afternoon when the setting sun would have been blazing through the colored glass, setting the room alight with its glow.

The huge rose-shaped window at the back of the church drew her attention and she was headed in that direction when that cold, uncomfortable feeling from several minutes before swept over her again, making her skin tingle.

Determined to get to the bottom of it, Annja stopped where she was and spun in another slow circle, ostensibly drinking in the view but actually checking out the area on all sides.

Across the chapel, in the shadow of one of the pillars that lined the walls, someone stood watching her.

Whoever it was—and from this distance she couldn't even tell if it was a man or a woman—wore a gray sweatshirt and a pair of jeans. The hood on the sweatshirt was pulled up, hiding the person's face, but even through the shadows Annja could feel the other's eyes upon her.

As if sensing her attention, the watcher suddenly stepped back and disappeared behind the column.

Almost before she'd thought about it, Annja found herself in motion, headed across the church at an angle, trying to intercept whoever it was that she had seen. There was only one exit from the upper level, the stairs by which she'd entered, and so she knew if she could reach them first she'd have a chance.

The gray sweatshirt flashed into view again. Her watcher was hugging the rear wall, headed for the stairs just as she'd suspected, and she quickened her own pace, trying not to lose sight of her quarry in the process.

She was almost upon him when a group of tourists spilled out of the stairwell onto the main floor, obscuring her view and making it difficult to move forward as quickly as she had been. She pushed her way through, ignoring the looks she was getting in return. No way was she letting him get away at this point!

But when she reached the stairs she was alone.

Her quarry was nowhere to be seen.

She turned slowly about, searching through the crowd, ignoring the stares and the resentful looks as she tried to figure out just where he could have gone.

She saw a flash of gray slipping between two tourists and rushed to catch up.

"Hey!" she shouted, startling those around her. "Hold it right there!"

Annja pushed her way through the crowd, determined not to let him get away a second time. She was going to get to the bottom of this right now!

She could see him, just a few people in front of her. He had not once looked back, which in itself was suspicious to her. Didn't he hear her calling? If he was innocent, wouldn't he look back and see what she was shouting about, just like so many of the others around them were now doing?

They were only a few steps away from the staircase when Annja put on a little extra burst of speed, pushed past a family of four who suddenly froze directly in her path like a bunch of deer caught in the headlights of an oncoming car and reached out.

"Hey!" she said, grabbing his arm and spinning him around. "I said, hold it!"

She had been expecting resistance and so was surprised when the other person turned suddenly toward her, nearly throwing them both off balance. A kid of about eighteen stared out at her in bewilderment from under the hood of the sweatshirt he wore. He shrugged her off and let out a stream of rapid-fire French. Although fluent in French Annja didn't need to know the language to understand what he was saying. "What the hell is wrong with you?" sounded pretty much the same in any dialect, given the tone and the look that went along with it.

Annja stepped back, holding her hands up as if to show they were empty and that she wasn't a threat. Clearly she had made a mistake. This wasn't the guy.

"Uh, sorry," she said, and then repeated it in French. "*Pardon, pardon.* I thought you were someone else."

A male voice spoke up immediately behind her. "Mademoiselle? Is there something wrong?"

Annja jumped at the sound, not having seen anyone approach, and turned to find a gendarme standing nearby, his gaze on both of them. The officer's hand was uncomfortably close to his pistol and it didn't seem to be the kid who had him upset.

She smiled and tried to look embarrassed, which wasn't hard to do, considering. "I'm sorry," she said. "There's no problem. None at all. I thought I saw an old friend and was trying to get his attention. I didn't mean to make anyone upset."

The kid spouted off an angry stream of French, determined to tell his side of the story. As the gendarme listened to the kid's explanation of what had happened, which included more than one reference to the "crazy American lady," Annja stared over their heads at the crowd, searching for the person she had seen.

But aside from a number of bewildered tourists, there wasn't anyone there.

DUMPING THE SWEATSHIRT INTO a nearby trash bin was all it took to transform the Dragon into someone else. Disguises work best if they are simple and this was as simple as it got. Looking like a completely different individual now, the Dragon was even able to walk directly past the Creed woman without her being the slightest bit the wiser.

With that kind of anonymity, the Dragon could have stepped right up and slipped a knife into her back without her even suspecting that anything was wrong until the cold blade pierced her flesh. It gave the Dragon a certain sense of heady power and it was only the orders that precluded the woman's death that prevented it from happening.

Another time, the Dragon thought, and reveled in the superior feeling all the way down the stairs, across the complex and out into the street.

Exiting the tourist attraction, the Dragon hailed a cab and went directly back to the Creed woman's hotel, intending to take a good look around the room while she was still dealing with the gendarme.

The Dragon had long ago learned that looking as though you belonged allowed you to get away with being somewhere you didn't almost ninety percent of the time. It was all about acting the part and having the right attitude. The employees at the hotel where the Creed woman was staying were no different than those anywhere else in the world; the Dragon marched straight through the lobby and into the elevator as if it were the most natural thing in the world and no one said a word.

Once inside the hotel, it was a simple matter to "accidentally" bump into a maid and pick the passkey right out of the pocket of her uniform. A quick trip up the stairs, a knock on the door to be certain no one was in the room and not ten minutes after entering the hotel the Dragon was standing inside the Creed woman's suite, just as easily as the night before.

This time, however, the Dragon didn't waste any time pondering the situation but set to work immediately to try to find the sword. The weapon had been described as a plain, unadorned broadsword and something like that could only be hidden in a few areas. The safe was out of the question; it was far too short and shallow. The shelf above the safe, on the other hand, was long enough and that was where the Dragon began.

From there the search progressed through the room. Under the bed. Under the mattress. Behind the curtains in the corner of the room. Under the cushions of the sofa. Inside the entertainment center. Behind the bathroom door.

The Dragon looked everywhere that made sense, even taking the time to stand on a chair and look inside the heating vent, but it was no use.

The sword was nowhere to be found.

A glance at the clock said it was time to get out of

there; almost half an hour had already passed and the Creed woman might return at any moment.

But still the question nagged.

What had she done with the sword?

ANNJA SAT IN THE BACK of a cab, trying to decide what to do next. The misunderstanding in the chapel had put her on edge, that was for sure, but Annja was determined not to let it ruin the rest of her day. She'd have enough tension once she had the opportunity to speak with Roux, she knew; for now, she needed to stop being so paranoid and enjoy herself. It wasn't as if the Dragon was after her, anyway; it was Roux who should be worried.

Having satisfied her need for architecture, she decided to take in some of the city's art. She directed the cabbie to take her to the Musée d'Orsay, overlooking the Louvre along the left bank of the River Seine. The building itself had once been a railway station serving Paris-Orléans, so she hadn't fully escaped the tug of form and design, but it now housed one of the more formidable displays of art in all of Paris, short of the Louvre itself. Once there she spent hours wandering up and down the long rows of displays, drinking in the creative talents of Renoir, Degas, Monet and van Gogh, just to name a few.

Her visit was marred, however, by the memory of the figure she'd seen in the chapel and the now-constant feeling that she was under observation. More than once she tried to catch someone in the act, but each time she looked, she was unable to see anything or anyone out of the ordinary. No one turned away too quickly. No one let their gaze linger too long. The museum was full of patrons and they had their eyes on the paintings, not on her. Yet the feeling persisted and made her uncomfortable enough that she eventually decided to call it a day.

She returned to the hotel around sunset, took some time to freshen up and to calm her nerves and then, after picking up her rental car, she headed out of the city for her rendezvous with Roux.

The drive south passed without incident and it wasn't too long before she was pulling up in front of the massive gates that guarded the entrance into the estate.

As usual, once inside the house, Henshaw led her to the study, where she found Roux seated in the leather chair behind his desk, reading the day's copy of *Le Monde*.

Seeing her, he rose and smiled. "Annja, to what do I owe the pleasure?"

She had already decided to play it straight. "I wanted to talk to you about last night."

"Of course." Roux ushered her over to a pair of leather armchairs and offered one to her while settling into the other one himself. "Before you say anything else, let me apologize for my boorish behavior at the end of the evening. My remarks were totally uncalled for and I hope you let them pass as the angry grumblings of a man whose home had just been invaded by thieves."

He smiled pleasantly and Annja realized that he was being sincere; he really did feel bad for the things he had said to her. She gracefully accepted his apology and moved quickly past it to the reason she'd made the drive all the way out here.

Reaching into her backpack she withdrew a cardboard box in which she had safely tucked away the paper dragon, then withdrew the latter from inside the box. She stood the little paper dragon on the table between herself and her host.

"What's this?" Roux asked, picking up the dragon and turning it over in his hands. "What a marvelous specimen. I didn't know that you did origami."

"I don't," Annja replied. "I discovered it in the display room last night while helping to clean up in the wake of the attack."

Roux stopped looking at the figure and turned his head in her direction instead. She wasn't surprised by his carefully blank expression—after all, he was a world-class poker player—but the very fact that it was there told her what she needed to know.

Roux understood the significance of what he was holding.

He wasn't going to make it easy, though. "I'm sorry?" he said, as if he hadn't heard her correctly.

She relayed the tale as quickly as possible—how she'd gone back to the display room looking for something, she didn't know what; how she'd found the paper dragon and what she'd done afterward to try and understand just what the simple figure might mean. She told him of her suspicion that it had been left there intentionally, as a type of calling card, to let them know that this wasn't yet over and that they were up against a foe who made your typical hired gunman look like a schoolboy compared to the skills the other could bring to bear.

"I think your life is in great danger," she told him finally, and then sat back to await his reaction.

Roux had been silent throughout, had let her get her facts on the table and had patiently waited through her explanation as she pointed out the things she'd done and the thought process she'd used to arrive at her conclusion.

When she was finished, he sat quietly for a moment before speaking.

"You can't be serious," he said at last.

It was not the reaction Annja was hoping for.

"Of course I'm serious! Did you think I would drive all the way out here to talk to you just for the heck of it?"

"But, Annja, seriously. Do you really think an international assassin, this mysterious Dragon, a hired gun who specialized in political killings, is really trying to kill me? Whatever for? What possible reason could he have? And let's not forget the fact that this Dragon is supposed to be dead."

"I don't know what reason he might have. That's what I was hoping you could tell me," she answered.

Roux scowled and waved his hand in dismissal. "Now you sound like Garin, for heaven's sake. 'Pissed anyone off lately, Roux?'" he mimicked, in a passable imitation of the other man's voice. "I'm the least likely man ever to be involved in politics, Annja."

"I know that, Roux. But what if it's something more? What if the Dragon is no longer interested in political killing but has decided to branch out, handle contract work, for instance?"

Rather than convince him of her sincerity, her plea only made him laugh. "Now you sound like something out of a spy novel, Annja. Political killing? Contract work? It was a simple robbery, nothing more."

"If that's the case, then what were they after?" she asked hotly.

For just a second she thought she saw a triumphant gleam in Roux's eye. It was there and gone again in less than a second, so she couldn't be sure, but something deep down inside said she'd just played into his trap.

"While you were gone we were doing our homework, too, Annja. And we think we've found the answer to that very question."

The older man rose and walked over to his desk. From behind its massive bulk, he lifted a sword box and carried it back to Annja. Handing it to her, he said, "Go on, open it."

Annja did so, revealing the long curved blade of a U.S. cavalry saber, circa the late eighteen hundreds, with a leather-wrapped hilt and brass guard. It was pitted in a few places, but she could still make out the initials *GAC* etched into the blade just above the guard.

"What is it?" she asked.

"The saber worn by General George Armstrong Custer the day he fell in battle at the Little Bighorn," Roux answered proudly.

Annja winced. "I wouldn't be so quick to defend that claim."

"Nonsense," Roux said, taking the box back from her and closing it up tight. "I can assure you that the provenance of this blade is without blemish. Custer carried this sword the day he died and it has hung on my wall in that display room ever since I acquired it at a very private auction. It was the only item of any serious value in that room last night."

Roux's idea of "serious value" was enough to bankroll a small country, but that didn't mean he was right. Annja would have bet her left arm that no one had come looking for that sword, namely because it wasn't worth the steel from which it was made. She knew Custer hadn't worn a saber at the Battle of the Little Bighorn and neither had any of the other officers in the Seventh Cavalry. Popular art showed him holding his cutlass aloft as the Indians surrounded him, but eyewitness accounts from that terrible day told a different story.

She tried to point this out to Roux, but he wanted nothing to do with it. Nor did he accept her arguments that a single experienced thief would have had an easier time breaking into the display room to steal the sword than a group the size of the one she'd encountered there. He had convinced himself that there wasn't any real danger and it seemed that nothing she said would sway him from that conclusion.

When she finally left, hours later, she had gotten exactly nowhere. Her instincts were telling her that Roux was in danger, but he refused to see it.

As she climbed into her rental car, she was already

trying to figure out what to do next. One thing was for sure, she wouldn't leave one of her friends in danger.

ROUX WATCHED THROUGH THE window as Annja descended the front steps, climbed into her rental car and drove off toward the gates. He heard someone enter the room behind him and without turning, he said, "You heard?"

"Yes, sir," Henshaw said. He never would have dreamed of listening in on his own accord, but Roux had ordered him to do just that.

"And?"

"I'm not sure, sir. I don't think we have enough information."

"Even with the rumors we've been hearing about the Dragon's interest in a certain sword?"

"Even so, sir. After all, as you say, they are just rumors. The Dragon, if that indeed was who it was, could have been here for an entirely different reason."

Roux thought about that for a moment and then shook his head. "I don't see how. If the Dragon had been hired to kill me he wouldn't have gone about it the way he had. The assault was staged and I think we both know why."

"If you say so, sir."

After a moment, Roux made up his mind and said, "I want her kept under surveillance twenty-four hours a day, seven days a week. Here and in the States, until I say otherwise. And she isn't to know that you are there unless there is trouble."

Henshaw nodded. "Understood—24/7, no interference unless her life is threatened."

As Annja's car finally disappeared from sight around a bend in the road, Roux turned to face his employee. "I want you to find me everything you can on the Dragon's movements in the past two months. Use whatever resources are necessary. If he's after Annja, I want to know how and why. In the meantime your people have authorization to do whatever needs to be done to keep her safe."

"And you, sir?" Henshaw asked.

"Me?" Roux replied. "I'll be perfectly fine, Henshaw. I'm not the target."

Henshaw hoped those words wouldn't come back to haunt either of them.

9

Kyoto, Japan
1993

Those who knew better disappeared like rats from a burning ship the moment the two men appeared at the mouth of the alley. Seen with the naked eye, there wasn't anything noticeably strange about them, but those who had been on the street long enough developed senses different than the usual and something about the pair screamed danger like an air-raid siren.

It was a feeling that spread quickly, like a virus passed from one street hustler or teen runaway to another, and those who encountered it made themselves scarce if they knew what was good for them. Those who were too sick or stoned or weak to move on their own were grabbed, swiftly examined and then either tossed aside like garbage or trussed up like turkeys headed for slaughter and left where they lay for collection once the men were finished.

Most of them ran, but the girl near the end of the alley in the large cardboard box did not.

She'd only left home a few days before and already she was bone weary from all the hiding and running and scavenging. Life just shouldn't be this hard, she'd told herself time and time again, and at last she had begun to believe it. Life that was this hard just wasn't worth living, it seemed. When the owner of the box, a thick-faced Chinese boy named Wu, suddenly deserted his home, she wasted no time rushing in to get out of the rain. Flopping down among the discarded cushions and bags of trash that did double duty as Wu's bed, Shizu sat there, waiting for the newcomers to get to her, too tired and worn out to care anymore.

It didn't take them long.

Much to her surprise, when they reached into the box, seized her about the ankle and began to drag her back out into the rain, she discovered that she wasn't so tired, after all.

Suddenly she wanted to live.

She kicked and screamed, fought them tooth and nail, threw everything she had into getting away, and none of it did the least amount of good.

When she got to be too much to handle, one of the men simply reared back and smashed her in the face with his huge, meaty fist, sending her plunging into the swirling darkness of unconsciousness.

SHIZU HAD BEEN IN THE cage for just shy of a week when the big man arrived to claim her. She didn't know that yet, of course, being kept in a room all alone, without light, and inside a six-by-six-foot steel cage, but she would meet him soon enough as it turned out.

The guards came for her sometime after breakfast but before lunch, if you could call the cold gruel they fed them anything even close to the definitions of those words. Still, despite its horrible taste, she ate it when she could; every ounce of energy was important in a place like this. They dragged her out of the cell and stripped her clothes from her, an act which required several of them to hold her arms and legs down while they cut the material off her bucking form. If she had been a little older, if she had learned of such things at home the way most young girls do, she might have been afraid for her virtue, but these men were acting under orders and the thin, featureless body of a twelve-year-old girl did not excite them in any way.

When they were finished removing her clothes they dragged her into another room, still kicking and screaming, and left her on the floor in a heap.

They were gone only long enough to get the fire hose.

The water shot out of the nozzle, slashing across her body, pushing her about the floor like a discarded toy until she smashed into a nearby wall. She'd been through this once before, on the night she'd been brought here, and she understood what was happening enough to force herself to her feet and brace herself against the wall with her back to the water to keep from drowning. Her captors apparently took this as a good sign, for the force of the water eased off a little and she was scrubbed clean by the pounding water without too much difficulty.

When they were finished they gave her a light smock to wear over her naked form and led her down a series of hallways to another room. Inside were ten or twelve others girls who were dressed just like her in pale-colored smocks and bare feet. None of them said anything to her, their eyes cast dutifully downward as weeks of captivity had taught them was correct, and so Shizu didn't bother speaking to them, either. Instead, she took the time to examine her surroundings and to wonder just why they were all gathered here.

She didn't have long to wait to find out.

The guards came back a few minutes later and ordered the girls to line up shoulder to shoulder, facing one wall. From the door before them came an over-weight man in his mid-fifties, surrounded by body-guards. Shizu figured, rightly so, that this was the man in charge of kidnapping them in the first place.

With him was a tall gaijin, or foreigner, dressed like a *sariman* in a gray suit the color of river rock. His hair was long and he wore it loose about his face, his eyes alight with curiosity and fire.

Shizu couldn't stop looking at him.

She hadn't seen many gaijin before and so for that reason alone he was a curiosity in her eyes, but it was the sense of power that emitted from him that truly caught her attention. This was a man used to being in control, used to having his every word obeyed without question; even Shizu's young mind could figure that out quickly enough. This man was a predator, her instincts screamed, and all that was left to determine was the identity of the prey.

He sensed her interest, though he didn't acknowledge it in any way. Instead, he walked with the fat man to the end of the line and slowly began to move along it, looking at each of the girls, in turn. Sometimes he would ask them to do simple things—stand on one foot, touch their fingers to their noses—and other times he would examine them the way a doctor might, turning them this way and that, looking into their eyes, asking them to open their mouths and feeling their teeth.

When he got to her, he stopped and looked her over, just as he had the others. But rather than ask her to do any of the things she'd seen so far, he spoke to her in passable Japanese instead.

"What is your name?" he asked.

Afraid, she did not speak.

"Come, come, girl. I'm not here to hurt you. What is your name?"

This time she told him. "Shizu."

"Would you like to leave this place, Shizu?"

Daring to meet his gaze, she said, "Very much."

"Would you like to go away with me, Shizu?" he asked, softly this time.

She felt tears welling up at his kindness, something she hadn't experienced in a long time, and she could only nod.

When she had dried her eyes and dared look again, she found him still standing in front of her, waiting patiently. He smiled and extended his hand.

"Come, Shizu. It's time to go."

She let him lead her out of that place and off to a different life.

10

Now

Concerned that Roux wasn't taking things seriously enough, Annja woke the next day determined to get some answers. She knew there was more going on than met the eye. If Roux didn't want to talk, there was still one other person who might be able to tell her what she needed to know.

Garin Braden.

She had his cell number—or one of them, at least—and used it to call him that morning.

"I need to see you," she told him when he answered the phone.

He laughed, a low, throaty chuckle. "Just how much of me would you like to see?"

He sounded like the cat who'd just eaten the canary, positively delighted that she'd chosen to call him and propose such an unusual request. She, however, didn't have time for his antics.

"Cut the crap, Garin. Roux is in trouble and I need to talk to you about it immediately."

As she snarled at him she did her best to ignore the mental image his response had called to mind. Seeing more of Garin wouldn't be such a bad thing, at least in an aesthetic sense….

But Garin apparently didn't hear her reprimand or he simply chose to ignore it. He was still laughing when he said, "I'm free for lunch, if that will suffice."

It was good enough. They agreed on a place and time, with Garin suggesting he send a car and Annja firmly stating she'd get there on her own.

She had the concierge arrange a cab and she settled into the back, prepared to enjoy the ride. Paris had always been one of her favorite cities and it was particularly lovely on a spring day like this one. The streets and open-air cafes were full of Parisians enjoying the day, and the ride, short though it was, cheered her in a way that she hadn't expected.

As it turned out, the restaurant Garin had chosen was only a few blocks from her hotel. It was also one of the most popular luncheon spots in all of Paris, judging by the line that waited at the door to get inside. She began scanning the crowd for a sign of her host even as she exited the cab.

"Ms. Creed?"

She turned to find a good-looking, curly haired man dressed in a sharply pressed gray suit standing nearby.

"I am Michel, the maître de'" he said. "If you would be so kind…" He indicated the entrance with the sweep of his hand.

Ignoring the daggerlike looks she received from those waiting in line, particularly the women, Annja walked to the front doors, stepped inside and then allowed Michel to take the lead.

"This way, please," he said, and then headed across the dining room floor. He led her to a small, private dining room in the far corner of the building, opened the door and ushered her inside.

Garin was waiting for her at the room's only table. He stood, a smile on his face, as she entered and took her seat, then he sat across from her.

"It's good to see you again, Annja," he said, after Michel left the room.

"The dining room would have been perfectly fine," she replied, uncomfortable with the situation. This wasn't a date, for heaven's sake.

"Nonsense," Garin replied. "You wanted to talk about Roux and this way we are free to do so without fear of being overheard." He poured her a glass of wine from the bottle on the table, the red liquid a sharp contrast against the perfectly pressed white linen tablecloth.

"Now what's on your mind?" he asked.

Annja looked at him over the top of her glass and spoke without preamble. "I'm worried about him."

"Oh?" he said, leaning back and enjoying a sip from his own glass.

She told him everything she had told Roux the night

before, from the discovery of the origami figure to her belief that the intruder at Roux's estate had been none other than the Dragon himself. She brought it back to Roux, saying, "He's acting like the attack on his estate was an afternoon lark, rather than a possible attempt on his life. He refuses to involve the authorities and ignores me when I try to discuss it with him."

Garin laughed. "I'm surprised at you, Annja. The man's home has been invaded, and with it his pride, and you act as if he should be happy to chat about it. With a woman, no less! That is not the Roux we know and love."

He had a point; she knew that. But given the possibility that the intruder actually was the Dragon, Roux should've been able to set aside such things in favor of protecting himself and, by extension, those around him.

She said as much to Garin. "For an old soldier, he's not acting with much tactical sense. If the intruder *was* the Dragon, Roux could be putting himself, and those around him, in serious danger," she concluded.

Garin waved one hand in dismissal. "One does not need tactics to deal with a pack of common thieves," he said, but Annja saw it for what it was—a poor attempt to distract her from the truth.

She'd seen him stiffen when she'd mentioned the Dragon, just as Roux had. They knew something, something she did not. This time she wouldn't be distracted so easily.

"What aren't you telling me?" she asked.

He tried to brush it off with a laugh. "I don't have any idea what you are talking about, Annja."

She wasn't buying it. She had a sudden suspicion that Garin knew far more about what was going on than he wanted to admit. "That's a load of bull and you know it. Spit it out, Garin, or so help me, I'll…"

"You'll what?" he teased, still smiling. "Skewer me in a public restaurant?"

Without a second thought she called forth her sword and poked him with it beneath the table. "Damn right, I will. Now talk!"

He glanced down to where the tip of the blade rested against his thigh and shook his head at what she assumed was her audacity. She didn't care, as long as he told her what she needed to know.

"All right, all right. Calm down and put away the pig-sticker. No need to get unfriendly."

With a quick thought the sword was back in the otherwhere, where it would be ready when she needed it again. "What do you know about the Dragon?" she asked again.

Garin leaned back, staring at the wineglass in his hand, as if the answers they sought might be found in the depths of that ruby liquid.

"What do I know?" he repeated. "Nothing. I *know* nothing. But I do have certain suspicions that I am willing to share."

The waiter came in at that moment and their talk was put on hold as Garin ordered for both of them. Normally this would have annoyed Annja to no end—she could order her own lunch, thank you very much—but she cared more about what Garin had to say than eating at this point and so she let it go.

When the waiter left the room, Garin continued. "A man in my position, a man with business interests as diverse as my own, is always conscious of security to one degree or another. Political leaders are not the only ones who get assassinated, you know."

Annja rolled her eyes.

"Given that, I employ people to keep me abreast of developments in certain areas. And it was through them that I first learned of the Dragon.

"No one seems to know who he was or where he came from. He just announced his availability for hire by assassinating the French Deputy Minister of Defense one evening in Paris, killing the man so quietly that his sleeping wife never even stirred in her sleep. The Dragon departed as silently as he had arrived, leaving the wife to wake up next to her dead husband several hours too late to save him.

"From that point, he seemed to be everywhere at once. The next decade was like the rest of us had stumbled onto his personal playing field. Diplomats. Ambassadors. Bankers and lawyers. Powerful people create powerful enemies and there is always someone willing to pay an exorbitant sum to keep others down. The Dragon didn't care about their political affiliations or issues. He killed them all—every race, color, creed and political party—provided those hiring him could pay his price."

Annja frowned. "You seem to know a lot about him," she said.

He shrugged, unconcerned with her suspicions. "No

more than anyone else in my position. For all I knew I could have been next on his list, as my unflinching approach to business has earned me more than a few enemies along the way."

Unflinching, Annja thought, try bloodthirsty. And the idea that you've generated a "few" enemies has to be the understatement of the century.

"What made the Dragon so unusual was that he always killed his targets by hand, usually with a Japanese *katana,* and if the sword wasn't strange enough he would also leave behind a token of his presence at every murder scene."

"Let me guess," Annja said. "An origami dragon."

"Always said you were as intelligent as you are beautiful, Annja."

She ignored his comment and took a moment to think over what he'd just told her. Something didn't make sense. Why would an assassin renowned for killing with a sword suddenly decide to use explosives? "So what happened in 2003?"

Garin grinned. "I see I'm not the only one who knows a little something about the Dragon."

Ignoring her scowl, he went on. "I've heard a hundred different theories over the years as to what happened that day and I don't agree with any of them. Killing is an art form, particularly for a man like we're talking about. For him to resort to a suitcase full of plastic explosives when every single one of his victims before that date were killed by his own hand is simply ludicrous.

"What happened in 2003 is that the Dragon, the real

Dragon, had nothing to do with the attempted assassination of the British prime minister. It was someone else."

The waiter came in with their meals at that point, giving Annja some time to digest what Garin had said. She barely noticed what she was eating as the implications of what he had just told her poured through her mind.

"You think the Dragon is still alive," she said after a few minutes.

Again the shrug. "For the past year or so there have been rumors that the Dragon has returned. Nothing more solid than that, understand, just rumors. Given what you found at Roux's, however, I'd say the possibility just grew a little more distinct."

"Why would the Dragon be after Roux?"

"Who said he was?" Garin shot back, and that brought Annja up short.

"You think the Dragon is after you?" she asked.

"No."

If not Roux, or Garin, then who?

"No," she said flatly when she realized what he was suggesting.

He looked at her with a strange gleam in his eye. "Not Roux. Not me, though I must admit to being a bit concerned over that last one for a little while. No, I don't think the Dragon is after either of us. I think he is after you." He leaned forward, holding her gaze in his own. "And after what I've heard recently about the sword the Dragon always carries, I think I know why."

Her frown deepened, her lunch all but forgotten. "You *are* going to tell me, right?"

He paused, gathering his thoughts, and Annja had the distinct impression that he was trying to figure out just what to tell her and what to keep close to the chest.

After a moment, he continued. "Everything has an opposite, a dark twin on the cosmic scale of balance, if you will. The world itself is built on duality. How could we recognize white without black? Laughter without sorrow? Goodness without evil?"

He looked at her, as if to gauge whether she was following the argument, and she nodded to show that she was.

"The sword that you now carry is a symbol of truth, of justice, of all that is good in the world. It emulates the moral and emotional qualities of the one who bore it into battle all those years ago. And because you represent those things, as well, the chain continues, like an heirloom passed down through the generations.

"You, me, Roux—we are all bound to that sword in one way or another. For Roux and me, our association with it, and with its original bearer, has resulted in a lifespan measured in centuries rather than decades. In your case, the sword has given you increased agility, speed, strength—even your senses are better than they once were."

There was little there for her to argue with. It was true; the sword had certainly changed her in ways that she hadn't thought possible. Knowing that Garin was aware of the changes as well, made her a little uneasy, but she buried the thought as he went on with his explanation.

"You know better than anyone else that the sword comes with a certain set of responsibilities. Defend the weak. Protect the innocent. Stand as a barrier against the evil in the world around you, just as its original bearer strove to do so many years ago."

He was right again. Her life had become far more complicated since taking possession of the sword. Where she might have turned away from a difficult situation in the past, maybe even told herself that it wasn't any of her business, now she practically leaped into the fray whenever the opportunity presented itself.

Garin continued. "So it stands to reason that if all things have an opposite, a yin to the yang, then there must be another weapon out there somewhere that represents the side of darkness as much as your weapon stands for the cause of light."

Biting back her unease, she forced herself to follow his line of thought.

"You're saying the Dragon has such a sword."

Her companion shook his head. "No. I'm saying that there are rumors that the Dragon, if he is still alive, has such a weapon. I don't know for sure."

Annja thought back to the swordsman she had faced in the display room and the way his sword had suddenly seemed to appear in his hands, a sword she would have sworn he hadn't had moments before.

Of how it mirrored the way she handled her own so perfectly.

"But you believe it, don't you?" she pressed.

Garin thought about it for a moment, and then nodded at her. "Yes," he said, "I do."

His admission sent Annja's pulse skyrocketing.

"Why?"

"For the past year or two I have been hearing rumors about a sword, one that is supposed to have considerable power, being carried by a man available for hire. Not just any man, but one with an impressive résumé, full of what has euphemistically been called 'wetwork.' At first I thought that the rumors were about you and the weapon you carry, that those who passed it along simply couldn't imagine that it was a woman in such a role, but it only took a little bit of investigation to learn that the sword in question was not a broadsword, like your own, but a Japanese *katana*.

"After that, it wasn't hard to put two and two together. I think the Dragon is back. I think somewhere, somehow, he learned about you and the sword that you carry. And I think he is curious to discover whether you are like-minded individuals or incompatible opposites."

He took a long sip of his drink. "If the former, I suspect he just wants to talk with you. If the latter," he said rather bluntly, "then I'm quite sure he won't hesitate to kill you."

ABOUT THE SAME TIME that Annja and Garin were sharing lunch, Henshaw was walking into a meeting in a pub along the docks by the Seine. It was a far cry from the restaurant that Garin had selected, but then again, the people that Henshaw was meeting were more concerned about anonymity than they were about how many varieties of wine were available to go with their meal.

Marco was already in the booth at the back when he arrived.

"It's been a while," Henshaw said when he reached the table.

"That it has, mate, that it has." The two men eyed each other warily for a moment and then Henshaw abruptly laughed and wrapped the other man in a bear hug. Had Roux seen such a display of emotion from him, Henshaw was certain his employer would have assumed he'd suddenly lost his mind, but he and Marco went back quite a ways and had literally saved each other's lives more than once over the years.

Of course, Henshaw didn't talk about those days.

Marco hadn't changed much since then; his hair was long, but his grip was still as strong as steel and his gaze never stayed in one place too long as he was constantly assessing the situation around him, alert for whatever was to come.

The two sat down at the booth opposite each other and waited a moment while the waitress brought them a couple of pints. Then they got down to business.

"So what's this gig that you've got for us?" Marco asked.

Henshaw had thought long and hard about how to convince his old friend to take the job and had finally settled on playing it as straight as possible. "Executive protection," he told him, slipping a photograph out of his coat pocket and passing it across the table.

The picture showed Annja striding across the street, her hair flowing back behind her in the slight breeze.

The jeans and T-shirt she wore hugged her body in all the right places, which was one of the reasons Henshaw had specifically chosen this one. As he'd hoped, Marco's eyes lit up at the sight of her.

"Good God, isn't she gorgeous," he said, pulling the photo up for a closer look. "Who is she? And what's she do? Recording artist? Film star?"

"Her name is Annja Creed. And she is an archaeologist, actually."

Henshaw met his gaze squarely when the other man glanced up to see if he was pulling his leg.

"You're kidding me, right?"

"Not at all."

The photo was tossed back down on the table. "Okay, this I gotta hear. You wanna hire around-the-clock surveillance and executive protection for an archaeologist? What'd she do, piss off the Vatican by discovering the tomb of Jesus or something?"

Nothing like that, Henshaw thought. She's just the current bearer of a mystical sword that once belonged to Joan of Arc and is now being pursued by one of the world's most dangerous assassins.

But he couldn't say that.

Instead, he explained that Annja's work had made certain terrorist groups aware of her as a potential target of opportunity and that his employer was interested in protecting the investment he had made in her work without her knowing the extent of the danger she was in. As stories went, it was a decent one, and certainly good enough to pull Marco and his team into the mix.

Henshaw felt bad about deceiving his old friend, but what else could he do? It wasn't as though he could just come out and tell the man the truth.

They spent a few minutes discussing terms and pay rates and concluded the deal over a handshake. Both men knew the other was good for it.

When they were finished with their beers, Marco said, "Come on, I'll introduce you to the rest of the team."

The left the pub, climbed into Marco's old sedan and drove a few blocks deeper into the warehouse district, stopping at a small nondescript building to the west of the pub. Marco pulled out a set of keys, unlocked the door and ushered Henshaw inside.

This was where the rest of the team waited for them.

There were three women and four men. Marco introduced them to Henshaw one at a time—Dave, a cheery, good-natured sort who couldn't have been more than twenty-five; Olivia, a dark-haired beauty with a background in demolitions; Jessi, a former SAS commando; Arthur, a quiet, unassuming man who was the group's electronics expert; Clive, a former U.S. Marine who had turned his skills to the private sector; Glen, the team's covert infiltration expert; and last, but not least, Sara, a short, pudgy woman who could shoot the cap off of a soda bottle at four hundred yards.

They looked like a good, solid unit. Henshaw was pleased. After Marco introduced him, Henshaw laid out the requirements and expectations of the job in a clear, concise manner. There were a few questions, but none that he couldn't answer and certainly none that might have brought his explanation into question. Not surprisingly, none of the team members recognized Annja. *Chasing History's Monsters* just wasn't their cup of tea.

From inside his briefcase Henshaw produced a thick dossier of information on Annja, including her usual habits and preferences, the hotel she was currently staying in, address and layout of her loft in Brooklyn. Essentially anything he could think of that might help them do their job. After all, Annja's life was possibly at stake and he wasn't going to cut any corners. He informed them of her prowess in martial arts and commented that she often practiced with various types of weaponry, just in case they witnessed her with sword in hand.

When he was finished, he left them to their perusal of the documents and joined Marco off to the side, where he passed him an envelope.

"My employer will spare no expense," Henshaw told him. "Inside the envelope you'll find the access information for a bank account you can use for expenditures. Do whatever you need to in order to keep her alive."

Marco looked at him for a long moment. "This isn't a hypothetical, is it? You really think someone is going to make a go at her."

Henshaw nodded. "I do. And I'm counting on you to stop them from succeeding."

Marco smiled. "That's what they pay me the big bucks for, mate. Don't you worry. We've got it handled."

11

After her lunch with Garin, Annja decided to walk back to her hotel rather than catch another cab. It would give her some time to digest what she had just learned and she could do with some fresh air and a bit of thought.

She suspected that the individual she'd fought the other night was, indeed, the Dragon. When you combined the stealth with which they had infiltrated Roux's estate, the skill the swordsman had displayed when wielding his weapon and the presence of the origami dragon left behind at the scene of the attack, there weren't too many other conclusions that made sense. She'd been so focused on figuring out why an international assassin was after her mentor and friend that she never stopped to consider the other possible targets in the picture, namely herself and Garin.

If what Garin was telling her was true, then she had reason enough to be concerned.

She'd been hunted before. That was nothing new. Since taking up the sword it seemed that everywhere she went she ran into some psycho with an ego the size of California who saw her as an obstacle to their plans for world domination or whatever this week's fiendish plot might be. She fought back against them, each and every time, and had always managed to come out on top.

This time, though, she wasn't so sure.

She'd never faced off against an international assassin for hire before.

And to make matters worse, he'd already beaten her once.

Her thoughts turned to the rest of what Garin had said. Rumors about a mystical sword were all well and good, but she was probably one of the few people on earth who had the personal experience to actually take them seriously. The very idea that there might be another sword with powers similar to her own was extremely unsettling to her. Where had it come from? What was its purpose? How had the Dragon gained possession of it?

Garin had once told her that her discovery of the last piece of the sword that had been missing for so long was nothing short of a miracle. At first she had believed it to be the fortune of fate, the result of a chance earthquake that occurred while she was in the vicinity. Later, after hearing the stories related to her by Garin and Roux about the long search for the pieces of the sword, she began to question the validity of her early theory.

Maybe the sword had recognized something in her

and had done what it needed to do to bring them together. Could the same thing have happened to the Dragon?

Not knowing was going to drive her crazy; she knew herself well enough to see that coming from a mile away.

Since she didn't have enough information yet to come up with a decent answer for the questions that were bothering her about the sword, she decided to try to focus on the Dragon himself. What did he want with her? And how did he know about her in the first place?

She had to admit that she'd had a few close calls; she'd been forced to use her sword now and then when other people were nearby. But she'd always thought she'd done a good job of keeping it out of sight. People had seen her with it—there was no doubt about that—but she'd been confident that no one had ever seen her draw the sword out of the otherwhere. Or, at least, no one had seen her draw it and lived to tell the tale.

So how had the Dragon known to come looking for her? Did his sword act like her own, providing the occasional flash of intuition or gentle nudge in the right direction? Had the Dragon come to Roux's estate for some other reason, only to turn his attention to her after he recognized a kindred spirit?

She had too many questions without answers.

Annja had only walked a few blocks when the feeling of being watched fell over her. She recognized it right away, that creeping sensation at the base of her spine that let her know she was under someone else's scrutiny.

She casually stopped and looked around, making note of those in her immediate vicinity, but she didn't see anyone who looked familiar. Still, she spent a few minutes checking out those she did see, trying to remember their faces and what they were wearing so that if she did see them again she would know it.

After a few minutes she continued on her way.

She was just starting to think the whole thing had been a figment of her imagination, just a result of the conversation she'd had with Garin, when the feeling returned. At the same moment she caught a mental glimpse of her sword, hanging there in the middle of the otherwhere, gently glowing, and that seemed enough of a warning for her not to brush aside her intuition.

There was a bank ahead—she'd seen it on the way to the restaurant—and its windows were made from reflective glass. She waited until she drew abreast of them and then stopped, pretending to be searching through her pockets for something while actually using the glass to watch those who were coming up behind her. She was looking for someone who stopped suddenly, or who turned away abruptly, anything that might give them away as the watcher she knew was back there somewhere.

But aside from an elderly woman on an electric cart, no one seemed to be paying her the least bit of attention.

If they were out there, they were good—she had to give them that.

She set off at a brisk pace, nearly twice what she'd been doing before. She cut down a side street, using the opportunity to look back in the direction she'd come for anyone cutting through the sidewalk crowd quickly enough to catch up to her, but again, no one seemed to be giving her any undue attention. She headed north at the next intersection, then cut back east at the next side street, bringing her back to her original route. Each time she changed direction she used the opportunity it presented to take a quick look at those behind her, watching for familiar faces, but there were none.

She hadn't seen them at first the other day, either, though. Just because she couldn't see them didn't mean they weren't out there.

She decided to try one more trick. She was approaching an intersection and as she got close she kept a near watch on the lights, waiting for her chance.

Just as the lights turned green, Annja shot out into the street, across the flow of automobiles and one very large city bus, rushing to get to the other side before any of them could move. More than one driver blew their horns, but she didn't care; she was too busy reaching the opposite sidewalk and then looking back the way she had come to see if she'd left anyone flat-footed on the other side, trapped behind a wave of vehicles.

There was no one paying the least bit of attention to her.

Maybe I imagined it all, she thought.

While it might have been a possibility, Annja didn't think it was a very likely one.

She stood on the corner for a long pause, watching those behind her, wondering.

Where are you?

HIGH ABOVE, ON THE ROOFTOP of the building adjacent to the corner where Annja stood, the very individual she was searching for at ground level watched her through a pair of military-grade binoculars.

From Annja's erratic movements over the past few minutes, the Dragon knew that Annja suspected she was being watched again, but without any hard evidence to confirm the suspicion she would have no choice but to brush it off. Not once in the past few hours had the target looked up, so the Dragon was confident Annja would not be able to locate where the surveillance was coming from. The decision to use the rooftops, rather than put a team on the ground, was apparently paying off.

Maybe you're not as good as you think you are, Annja Creed.

12

That night Annja spent hours on the computer, trying to learn everything she could about the Dragon. Unfortunately, as Bart and Garin had both explained, there really wasn't much available out there that could tell her anything of value. Rumors abounded—about the Dragon's background, personal tastes, business partners, weapons of choice, even what kind of women he preferred. But it was all nothing more than will-o'-the-wisps in the night, suppositions, maybe an occasional educated guess, but certainly nothing that could be labeled as cold, hard fact. She hadn't seen anything so far that even assured her the Dragon was a man, though the general consensus seemed to be that he was.

She also wasted a fair amount of time trying to track down any rumors about a mystical sword on the various conspiracy Web sites and newsgroups that she knew about, but aside from half a dozen spontaneous sightings of Excalibur, the legendary sword of King Arthur, that was a dead end, too.

Finally conceding defeat, she decided to call it a night and get some sleep.

AN INSISTENT BEEPING woke her.

She reached out with one hand, fumbling for the switch, trying to remember just what on earth she had set the alarm for, where she was supposed to be this morning, when she discovered the alarm clock wasn't where it was supposed to be.

Rather than resting on the bedside table where it had been when she'd gone to sleep the night before, it now stood across the room on the window sill.

That's weird.

She had no memory of moving the alarm clock, but she'd been pretty tired when she'd finally tried to get some sleep, so maybe she'd done it so that she'd be forced to get out of bed and therefore had no chance of sleeping through the alarm.

But why had she set it in the first place?

Her eyes caught site of something on the pillow next to her and she turned her head to get a better look at what it was.

The origami figure of a dragon stood atop the pillow, its wings unfurled, staring at her with its featureless face.

Annja recoiled, throwing herself back off the bed in order to get as far away from the little paper figurine as possible. At the same time she called her sword to her, holding it out in front like a symbol of protection as she scrambled frantically to get her back to a wall and ensure that she couldn't be attacked from at least one direction.

Then, and only then, did she look around.

Sunlight streamed in through the thin gossamer curtains over the windows, lighting up the room and showing her immediately that no one else was standing in the room with her.

She could hear the cars in the street below going about their early-morning business, but the noisy growl of their engines and the squeal of their brakes sounded as if they were from another country. She could see the curtains blowing in the morning breeze coming in the open window, could feel the shafts of sunlight reaching out across the room, intent on blanketing her in their warmth. But all she could feel was the icy touch of dread crawling about inside her mouth like a pair of disembodied fingers.

One thought kept repeating itself over and over again in her head, blotting out everything else.

The Dragon had been in her hotel room last night.

Had been standing there, right beside her bed.

Watching her sleep!

Being watched in public at the Chapelle was one thing. Being followed on the streets of the city was another. But having a killer there in her bedroom while she was fast asleep?

It was almost too much to take.

Only the thought that she might not be alone, that the intruder could still very well be there, inside her hotel room, perhaps in the bathroom or the sitting room, just waiting for his chance to strike, released her from her frozen state and got her moving again.

Just as she had the night before, she searched through the entire hotel suite, looking for an intruder. No one was there, not now, but the big smiley face with the *X* drawn through it in red lipstick on her bathroom mirror was enough to show that the Dragon had been in there, as well.

She stared at it, momentarily numb, and then, making up her mind, swung into action.

13

Annja packed as quickly as possible, throwing what little clothing she had with her into her bag and jamming her computer into her backpack. She made sure to keep a low profile and not stand in front of any of the windows or the French doors while moving about the room. Just because the Dragon had never used a high-powered rifle before didn't mean he couldn't suddenly change his mind. She had no interest in being taken out before the fight had actually begun.

Rather than grab a cab at the taxi stand outside her hotel, she slipped out a side door and hustled down the street, cutting down the occasional alley, until she reached the main thoroughfare one block over. Then and only then did she flag down a passing cab and ask him to take her to the airport. The front door of the hotel was sure to be watched, but maybe she had avoided giving herself away by taking the alternate route.

She went straight to Terminal One at Charles de Gaulle International Airport and traded in her first-class seat to New York on the next day's flight for the first available seat that morning. She ended up riding coach, and paying a hundred-dollar change fee, but it was all Garin's money, anyway, and there was no way she was staying in Paris given the Dragon's interest in her. She hoped the sudden flight back home would throw him off her track, at least for a little while. That should give her time to figure out just what she intended to do about the whole mess. If she could discover more information about the sword he carried, maybe she could divine his intent or at least find a way to neutralize his abilities.

She grabbed her cell phone and called her producer, Doug Morrell, while she waited for her flight to be called. She wasn't worried about him being busy or asleep. It was a Tuesday, the show was his life and, without her finishing off the edits for the episode slated to run later that week, he was sure to be at home panicking.

Right, she was.

"Annja!" he said when he recognized her number on his caller ID. "Tell me you're finished and the show's ready to go."

"Not yet, Doug, but it's close." The truth was she hadn't even thought about it, but what was a little hedging between friends? "But I'm stuck and need some help."

"Are you having trouble with the editing boys again? Need me to come down there and knock some sense into them?"

For his young age, Doug took his authority pretty seriously—or at least, challenges to his authority—and he didn't like folks in other departments giving his hosts a hassle. Not that he'd ever actually leave his office to deal with the troublemakers, but it was the thought that counted, Annja told herself with a sigh.

"No, Doug," she said. "I'm just fine and the editing team is great."

"Aren't they, though? You should have seen how they handled that Jamaican zombie stuff last week. Totally class act, I tell ya." A bright thought suddenly hit him. "Hey, any chance of zombies in this one? We could do a two-part special, you know? Zombies from…"

"No, Doug, no zombies." She cut him off before he could go any further. Doug was her friend, but still, sometimes it took a bit more patience than she had to listen to him when he got on a roll.

"But I need your help in getting me in to see a hypnotist ASAP."

"A hypnotist? Whatever for?"

Annja winced; she hadn't thought of a decent excuse. She went for the mystery line. "I can't tell you that yet."

"Can't tell me? Why not?"

"Because I'm not sure if I can use it or not. I have to talk to the hypnotist first."

Doug was silent for a minute. "All right. I think I can line somebody up. There was this guy we used for the office party last year who might work. Lenny the Magnificent or something."

If she'd been in the same room she would have reached out and swatted him across the back of the head. It served her right for trying to pull a fast one, she thought, but she was in too deep to back out now.

"No, Doug. I need a real hypnotist. Preferably a doctor or at least a licensed therapist."

"Lenny won't work?"

"Definitely not. No Lenny."

She could hear him flipping through some paper, maybe an address book or even the yellow pages. She didn't care as long as he came through.

"All right, all right. Let me think. This might take me a little bit. How about I call you back when I have something?"

"I'm just about to catch a flight so can you leave me a message on the voice mail?"

"Catch a flight? Annja, where are you?"

Oops.

"They're calling me, gotta run! Thanks, Doug!" she said, and hung up before he could ask her anything further. Just to be safe, she also turned off her cell phone.

She had more than an hour to kill before they boarded her flight and she spent the entire time holed up in a corner of the waiting area with her back to the wall, watching everyone who came even remotely close or showed the slightest interest in her. Was that man in the janitor outfit watching her too intently? How about that woman with the stroller? Was that even a real baby? Maybe it was just a doll, designed to throw her off the scent? Or how about that businessman two rows over who kept looking in her direction and smiling? Was that smile a little too forced? His gaze a little too intent?

Every loud noise made her jump, every person she saw was a potential enemy, and it kept ratcheting her anxiety level higher and higher until she realized that the flight crew and gate attendant were constantly looking her way.

If you want to get on this flight, you'd better relax, she told herself. Closing her eyes, she tried to do just that.

When at last she got on the plane, Annja settled into her seat and then carefully scrutinized each and every passenger who had gotten on behind her. She had no idea what she was checking for; she just expected to know it when she saw it. She was still looking when the flight attendants gave the all clear and shutting the main door, prepared for takeoff.

Finally she managed to calm down.

BACK AT THE GATE IN Paris, the watcher approached the attendant, looking anxious and concerned.

"Excuse me? That wasn't the plane to Chicago, was it?"

The attendant smiled. "No worry, love. That was New York, not Chicago."

The watcher pretended to be relieved. "Oh, thank goodness, for a moment there I thought I'd missed it."

Turning away, the watcher wandered back down the concourse and over to the ticket counters.

New York, it is, then. Now when is the next flight?

ANNJA SPENT MOST OF THE flight either dozing fitfully or watching the people around her, trying to find one who was watching her, in turn, but she had no luck.

By the time she got off the flight in New York, she was nearly numb with fatigue.

She was too exhausted to take the train, so she splurged for a cab, asking the driver to take her to her address in Brooklyn. A long fare was a good thing and the cabbie, a tall, thin, bald fellow with a Ukrainian accent, was more than happy to oblige.

Annja lived in a run-down neighborhood in the heart of Brooklyn. She liked to think of it as lived-in, but that kind of rationalization was also what made die-hard Manhattanites call an apartment the size of a postage stamp a one-bedroom studio. Still, it was home and when the cabbie pulled up in front of her four-story building, one of the oldest on the block, she breathed a sigh of relief.

In practically no time at all she stood in front of her door, the wood scarred and chipped but still strong. The 4A was written in small white figures and affixed to the varnished surface of the door.

She dragged her keys from her pocket, disengaged the five locks that prevented access, then stepped inside and locked them all over again, just to be safe.

One thing was sure, if the Dragon had followed her here, he was going to have a bit harder time getting inside than he had in Paris. For one, there weren't any balconies. For another, this was her home and she would brook no one inside its walls that didn't belong.

The big room had a fourteen-foot ceiling. Shelves lined the walls and many of them sagged under the weight of the books or rocks and artifacts that filled them nearly to overflowing. A desk sat in one corner, all but buried by the sketch pads, books and file folders scattered across its surface.

Stacked haphazardly around, and in one case under, her desk was a veritable sea of electronics, from the hollowed out shell of an Xbox video console to a brand new LCD projector the size of a cigarette pack she'd gotten on loan from a company that was looking to have her test it in the field.

All the nervous energy she'd been expending since she'd left her hotel room in Paris finally caught up with her. She dropped her bag and backpack by the bed, toppled into it and was asleep in less than a minute.

14

True to his word, Doug had called back and left a message on her voice mail, which she found when she finally returned to the land of the living early the next morning.

"Hi Annja, it's me, Doug. I managed to call in a few favors and get you an appointment to see Dr. Julie Laurent. She's in the Village, on Houston, and can fit you in for a nine-thirty tomorrow morning. You might want to call her ahead of time and give her a little bit more information about how she can help you, as she had a lot of questions that I just couldn't answer, but otherwise you're all set. You owe me one. How about dinner on Friday at Domenico's? Talk to ya later." He rambled off the address and then hung up.

Just as he'd suggested, Annja called the doctor ahead of time and gave her the story she'd come up with to explain why she wanted to be hypnotized. Dr. Laurent took it all pretty well, only asking a question here and there that focused on her family history and the state of her insurance, then said she'd see her soon.

Annja took the subway to Manhattan, changed trains at Thirty-second Street and then rode another train the rest of the way to the Village.

Once on the street, it didn't take her long to find the building, sandwiched as it was between a deli and an office park.

The doctor's office had its own entrance with a buzzer, but the gate was unlocked and the door to the foyer open, so she didn't bother ringing and instead climbed the steps just inside the door to the narrow landing at the top. A small brass plaque was tacked to the wall next to the only door in sight. Dr. Julie Laurent, Hypnotherapy.

"Well, here goes nothing," Annja said to the silence around her. Reaching out, she knocked on the door.

"Coming, coming" came a voice from within, and a moment later the door opened to reveal a gray-haired woman in her mid-sixties, dressed in cream-colored pants and a pale blue sweater. A pair of wire-framed glasses hung on a silver chain about her neck. Her dark eyes sparkled with intelligence.

"Are you Annja?"

"That's me," Annja replied, and extended her hand. They shook and the doctor led her inside the office and over to an arrangement of leather couches and chairs that occupied one side of the room.

"Thank you for seeing me on such short notice,"

Annja said as she sat down, taking in the room around her as she did so.

It was a bright and airy place, despite its small size, and Annja was immediately charmed by it. French doors made up the external wall and beyond their gossamer curtains she could see a tiny balcony, with just enough room for a wicker chair and a table. In the far corner of the room, cloaked in shadow, was a masculine-looking desk that appeared to serve more as a storage depot than a work area.

"Not quite what you were expecting?" Dr. Laurent asked, startling Annja out of her examination.

Annja laughed. "No, not quite. I was expecting something a bit more doom and gloom, I guess."

Laurent nodded knowingly. "My clients bring enough of that with them on their own," she said. "So I try to give them something a bit less intimidating. Can I get you anything? Coffee? Tea?"

Annja shook her head. "No, I'm fine, thanks."

"All right, then. Tell me what I can do for the star of *Chasing History's Monsters,*" the doctor said as she leaned back in her chair.

Annja relayed the same story that she'd given over the phone—how she had been plagued for months with this recurring dream of a swordsman, the blade he wielded with such skill and fervor, and the hand-to-hand combat they ultimately engaged in. She knew the dream was trying to tell her something, she said, for she'd never had one with such intensity or frequency before. Except every time she woke up, all she could remember was the fact that she dreamed of a man wielding a sword, and nothing about who he might be or what he might want. Annja hoped the dream story would cover any slipups she might make under hypnosis.

"Our dreams are often a way for our subconscious mind to try to tell us something—you are certainly correct about that. And given your line of work, I'm not surprised that your subconscious is using metaphors like the ones you describe to try to reach you. After all, if it had manifested in your dreams as an overweight clown with bright red hair, you might have simply brushed it off, no?"

If it were only that easy, Annja thought.

"It's possible that something about the man's face, the clothes he is wearing or even the weapon he carries is a symbol for something else in your life, something that is bothering you. No worries, we'll get to the bottom of it for you.

Dr. Laurent took a sip from her glass of water, then asked, "Have you ever been hypnotized before?"

Annja shook her head. "I almost did so at a comedy club once, but chickened out at the last minute."

The doctor smiled, trying to put her at ease. "That's fine. The process is pretty simple, actually. First, I'll take you through a series of muscle relaxation techniques that are designed to put you in the right frame of mind for phase two, which is the trance itself.

"While in the trance, you'll relive the dream, but you will have complete control over it this time. You can speed it up or slow it down, even bring it to a complete stop if you like, just like using the pause button on your DVD player."

"Will I remember what I see in the dream when I wake up?" Annja asked.

Dr. Laurent shook her head, saying, "You're not actually asleep, but I know what you mean and the answer is no. You won't remember any of the session consciously. However, I will be recording your responses the entire time and you'll be able to sketch anything you see during the trance, so between the two we should be able to capture the essence of what your subconscious mind is trying to tell you, all right?"

It sounded as if that was the best she was going to get so Annja agreed. There had to be some detail she could uncover that would help her find the Dragon.

"Shall we begin, then?"

As Annja settled back on the couch, something strange happened.

Once several years earlier, she'd come face-to-face with a king cobra while working a dig in southern India. She hadn't even known the snake was there until it reared up beside her as she knelt by the supply chest. Hood spread, it had stared at her with alien eyes and she'd felt the cold hand of dread squeeze her spine in its iron grip.

Lying back, as the gentle grip of the couch shifted beneath her frame, Annja felt the very same sense of fear creep over her as she had that day at the dig. Something deep in her soul was telling her to get out of there, to make her apologies and slink out the door with her metaphorical tail between her legs.

Her heart began to hammer in her chest and her

breath came in quick, short gasps. She felt her right hand flex in just the same way it always did as she settled her grip around the hilt of her sword. Miraculously she managed to stay in control and didn't call it to her; it would have been a little difficult explaining to the doctor just where she'd been hiding a massive broadsword, never mind what she intended to do with it.

What's wrong with you? she asked herself. Get a grip, for heaven's sake.

Annja willed herself to calm down and take a few deep breaths. As she did so, her anxiety began to recede. Fortunately, Dr. Laurent had stepped over to her desk to start the tape recorder and hadn't noticed her difficulty. By the time the doctor returned, sketch pad and pencil in hand, Annja had managed to get herself under control.

"Here," Dr. Laurent said, handing her the pad and pencil. "Hold these loosely in your lap. When we encounter something important, I'll tell you to draw it on the pad."

Thanks to her work as an archaeologist, Annja had been sketching things—ancient artifacts, dig sites, even fellow workers—for years and felt confident that she could capture whatever images she needed to in this fashion.

Just as she'd said, Dr. Laurent took Annja through a series of relaxation exercises. She was instructed to take a deep breath, hold it and squeeze the muscles in her toes for the count of five before releasing them, breathing out while she did so. Then her toes and the soles of her feet. Then her toes, the soles of her feet and the muscles in her calves, squeezing, holding and then letting them relax. Muscle by muscle, body part by body part, they worked up her entire body—up her legs, across her torso, down her arms and finally to her jaw and face. All the while Dr. Laurent spoke to her in a soft, soothing voice, helping her to relax mentally as well as physically.

By the time they were finished, Annja rested in a gentle trance, aware of her surroundings, able to listen to and respond to the doctor's questions.

"Can you hear me, Annja?"

"Yes." Annja's voice sounded distant, muted, as if it were coming through a thick blanket or maybe from a room down the hall. It was the sign Dr. Laurent was waiting for and it let her know that Annja was deep in the trance state.

"Very good, Annja, very good. Remember—nothing can harm you here. You are the one in control. Whatever you see or hear or feel during our session are just memories. They do not have the power to hurt you in any way. Do you understand?"

"Yes."

"Excellent. Okay, now I want you to think back to last night, before you went to bed. Let's say about dinnertime. Can you tell me what you were doing?"

Bit by bit, Dr. Laurent led Annja through the early evening and then into the beginning stages of the dream. When she felt Annja was ready, she said, "Now I want you to focus on the swordsman. Do you see him?"

"Yes."

"Very good. Can you tell me what he is wearing?"

"It's a black jumpsuit. The kind that Air Force aviators wear."

"Okay, Annja, that's good. Very good, in fact. Now I want you to look at his face for me, Annja. Can you tell me what he looks like?"

"No."

Dr. Laurent frowned. "Why not, Annja?"

"I can't see it."

"What do you mean you can't see it?"

"His face is covered up. I can't see it."

"Covered up? As in bandaged?"

Annja shook her head. "No. Just covered. He's wearing a black face mask and a dark hood. All I can see is a thin stretch of skin around his eyes."

"What color are his eyes, Annja?"

"Black. A deep brown that looks like black."

Dr. Laurent made a note on her pad. "Okay, you are doing very well, Annja. Let's forget his face for now—we'll come back to it later. Can you see any insignia on the jumpsuit? A patch or a name tag, maybe?"

Annja was quiet for a moment, as if she were examining the individual standing before her in the landscape of her memories.

"No."

"Okay, that's not a problem. Not a problem at all. What's happening now? What is the swordsman doing?"

Even as the doctor watched, Annja physically shrank back from what she was seeing in her memory.

"Rushing toward me with his sword already drawn. I have to be ready with my own!"

Recognizing the rising concern in her patient's voice, the doctor stepped in quickly. "It's all right, Annja. Remember, you are in control. Nothing can happen that you don't want to happen. I want you to pretend you have a great big pause button right there beside your hand and I want you to press it. Right now, press the pause button, Annja."

Annja stabbed at a spot on the couch with her left hand.

Seeing this, Dr, Laurent said, "Now the swordsman is standing completely still, isn't that right, Annja?"

Annja nodded, then answered aloud. "Yes."

"And he will only move when you are ready to let him do so, right?"

"Right."

"Okay." The doctor thought about the situation for a moment, wanting to be certain to avoid accidentally tripping over Annja's obvious anxiety again. "Here's what I want you to do, Annja. I want you to make the swordsman come toward you, just as he does in your dreams, but I want you to have him do it one step at a time. Imagine you are watching a movie and the swordsman is the star. He doesn't have the remote control, you do. The movie can only play when you want it to—you are in control. And right now you are advancing the movie frame by frame, so the swordsman appears to be moving toward you in slow motion."

After a moment, the doctor asked, "Where is he now, Annja?"

"Just a few feet away."

Step by step the doctor walked her through the scene—the swordsman's approach, the battle between them.

Then came the final, crucial moments.

"I see the sword, sweeping toward me," Annja said. "I'm trying to get out of the way but I'm not fast enough. The blade is getting closer and closer—"

"Stop," the doctor said.

Annja's hand stabbed at the couch again. "It's stopped."

"Can you see the sword clearly?"

"Yes."

"Describe it to me, please."

"It is a *katana*. Fifteenth, maybe sixteenth-century. The blade must have been recently polished for it reflects the light in the room, except where the etching is located."

Dr. Laurent sat up straighter in her chair. "What does the etching say, Annja?"

"I'm not sure. They're kanji characters, I think."

"Is that all?"

"No. A dragon is there, as well, above the kanji."

"Can you draw them for me?"

Annja's hands found the pad and pencil she'd been given and she began to sketch, the tip of her pencil moving swiftly over the blank page without hesitation. The first sketch only took her a few minutes and when she was finished she flipped the page and went right to work on the next.

And the next.

And the next.

By the time Annja started in on the fifth drawing, Dr. Laurent couldn't contain her curiosity any longer. Getting up out of her seat, she stepped behind the couch and looked over Annja's shoulder at the sketch pad.

"Oh, my!" she said when she saw what Annja was drawing.

ANNJA CAME BACK TO HERSELF to find Dr. Laurent sitting in her chair nearby, watching her closely, a tight expression on her face.

"How are you doing, Annja?" she asked when she saw that her patient had emerged from the trance.

I feel good, was Annja's first thought, and she truly did. She felt rested in a way she hadn't for a long time, as if she'd laid down for a quick nap and had awoken a dozen hours later instead. Her physical and emotional batteries felt recharged and ready for whatever was to come next.

"Is it over?" she asked, glancing around for a clock. Just how long was I out, anyway? she wondered.

"Yes, it's over," Dr. Laurent said. Realizing what Annja was looking for, she answered her unspoken question. "You've been in a trance for just about an hour, give or take a few minutes."

"And did it work?"

"I believe so." The doctor picked up the sketch pad off her lap and handed it Annja. "Does this look familiar?"

While the drawing wouldn't win any awards for its artistic merits, it was immediately clear what it was she had drawn—the face of the swordsman she'd encountered at Roux's. The figure in the picture stared out at her from behind the concealment of a hood and face mask, but she would recognize the look of superiority in those eyes anywhere. She felt the hair on the back of her neck stand up as she stared at the image and had the eerie sense that the image was looking back at her at the same time.

"Yes, that's the man from my dreams," she said in reply to Dr. Laurent's question, and gave herself a quick shake to dispel the lingering sense of disquiet the image was giving her.

"That's what I thought. How about what's on the next page?"

Annja flipped the page and found the image of a *katana.* But it was the two images she'd sketched onto the blade itself, just above the *tsabo,* or hilt guard, that really caught her attention. The first was a set of Japanese characters that she couldn't read so she had no idea what they said. The second was easily recognizable, however; it was an elegantly drawn image of a dragon straight out of Japanese mythology. The beast had been rendered standing on its hind legs, its wings outstretched to their full extent and its long whiskers drooping past an open mouth full of teeth.

Annja was surprised, as the drawing was not only well done but extremely detailed. It was considerably better than the first one, as if she had tapped into some long-forgotten well of artistic talent deep in her soul. "I did this?" she asked.

"You did that," the doctor replied. "Perhaps you have a second career as an artist."

"Yeah, maybe so." As she stared at it, Annja

realized the etching had been on the sword that the Dragon had wielded, the one that had almost taken her head off. Her unconscious mind had seen and made note of the details even in the midst of the fight that her conscious mind and body was trying frantically not to lose.

Annja also knew that just as artisans today signed their creations, so, too, did the ancient swordsmiths, etching small sets of kanji characters into their blades to show evidence of their craftsmanship. You could tell the provenance of a blade from those tiny images, and once you knew what type of blade it was, you had a shot at tracking it down as the ownership and heritage was often carefully cataloged.

For the first time since her search started, she'd found a solid lead.

Dr. Laurent asked her something, but Annja missed it.

"I'm sorry. What was that?" she said, looking up from the drawing.

The doctor's eyes were filled with sorrow.

"I asked if you were ever injured in a fire."

No sooner had the words left the doctor's mouth than the sense of fear and danger that had reared its head at the start of the session came sweeping back in like a tsunami. Cold fingers scurried up her spine and her breath caught in her throat. It was as if her entire system had been shocked into immobility; she couldn't have responded to Dr. Laurent even if her life had depended on it.

Then, as quickly as it had come, the feeling passed and she could breathe again.

"No," she managed to whisper back in answer to the question.

"Lose a loved one to a fire, then? Maybe when you were younger?"

"No," she said, more firmly this time. "I was raised at an orphanage in New Orleans. I never knew any of my family." The doctor hadn't asked if she'd ever had nightmares about dying in a fire, so Annja had no intention of mentioning them. Besides, she'd outgrown that long ago.

Dr. Laurent leaned forward in her chair and said, very gently, "Turn the page, Annja."

As she did as she was asked, Annja said, "I don't know what this—"

The rest of the sentence died. She stared at the page in complete shock.

She'd drawn an executioner's fire straight from the history books—a central pole surrounded by a heaping pile of bound hay and wood that burned out of control, the flames reaching for the edges of the page as if hungry for more. A great cloud of smoke and ash filled the space around the image and Annja had the sense of figures standing there, watching the spectacle as if enjoying an afternoon at the movies.

But what made her heart pound and her thoughts freeze like ice was the suggestion of a figure at the center of the image, the thin slender shape of a woman, just the whisper of a ghost at the heart of the inferno.

"Oh, my God," she breathed.

Frantic, she flipped the page, only to find the exact same image on the next sheet in the pad.

Dr. Laurent was speaking to her, but Annja's head was filled with a great roaring noise, a curtain of sound that blotted out everything else, and she didn't hear anything that was said. All she could do was stare at the pages in front of her, astounded at what had come bubbling up from her subconscious like some ancient beast waiting to devour the unwary.

Page after page, the sketches were the same, until she came to the very last page of the drawing pad. Maybe her subconscious mind had recognized that this was it, there were no more pages to draw upon, for a small detail had been added to this image that was not present in any of the others.

In the right-hand corner of the page, almost lost in the swirling cloud of ash and smoke that covered the area, the image of a dove had been added to the scene, wings spread as it soared toward the heavens.

It was too much for Annja. With the pad clutched to her chest, she mumbled her apologies and got out of there as fast as she could.

15

Thailand 1996

"No!" old man Toshiro barked. "Feel the pattern, do not think it."

Shizu nodded at her instructor and returned to the starting position, ready to run through the kata again from the beginning, all two hundred specific moves, despite her exhaustion and pain. She'd been at it for two straight days and the lack of food and drink was starting to take its toll on her concentration and on her fifteen-year-old body. And Toshiro would brook no error; if she made a mistake, she would start again from the beginning, just as she was now. A single complaint or groan of pain would only prolong the session; Toshiro had once kept her going for five straight days, when she'd voiced an argument over why she shouldn't have to practice the basics with such fervor and repetition, until she'd finally passed out from exhaustion.

It had been three years since she had first arrived here at Toshiro's. She remembered that morning as though it was yesterday. The old man had been waiting outside when she and Sensei had arrived. She had clung to Sensei in the limousine, scared of the wizened little man waiting outside the car.

Sensei had spoken to her gently, but firmly. "You are going to stay here with Toshiro for the next few years, Shizu, and he is going to teach you many things. When you are finished, when you have learned all you need to know, then I will return for you. Your destiny awaits you, but destiny is a harsh mistress and you must be strong if you are going to bend her to your will. Can you do that, Shizu?"

She remembered staring into his eyes, seeing the challenge there, and knowing deep down in her heart that if she did not get out of the car and do as she was asked, then the second chance at life that she had been granted when this man walked into the warehouse in Kyoto would be finished. He would abandon her as quickly as he had taken her in.

With a trembling hand, she had opened the car door and presented herself to Toshiro.

"Again! Begin!"

Focusing her concentration, Shizu started the sequence of movements that began the kata, letting her thoughts drift as she felt the proper movements more than thought about them. Katas had been developed to allow a martial artist to practice against an imaginary opponent—or, in this case, opponents—and as Shizu moved through the sequence she concentrated so strongly that she could picture them before her. She could see their strikes, feel the passage of their limbs, as they punched and kicked and spun, trying to defeat her. Shizu was a good pupil, probably one of the best Toshiro had ever trained, though he'd never tell her that, and she moved from defense to attack and back again with almost effortless ease.

Toshiro had been a harsh taskmaster over the years, but a fair one as well. He had taught her so much—art and language, history and culture, math and science. She took to it with an aptitude and a hunger that had surprised both of them, and in a very short time she had surpassed even his brightest students.

It was in the second year of her residence that the physical training began. Strength conditioning to prepare her body. Meditation to train her mind. Martial arts to prepare her for what was to come in the years ahead. Karate. Tae kwon do. Brazilian jujitsu. Thai boxing. Wing Chun kung fu. Ninjitsu. A mishmash of styles and disciplines, all designed for one end—to prepare her for the destiny that Sensei said awaited her.

She had learned much, it was true, but even she knew there was more to come. Toshiro was not done with her yet. This was just another of his seemingly endless tests, but Shizu welcomed it as she had all the others.

Besides, this day was different.

Sensei was there.

She did not know how she knew; she just did. She had not seen him, had not heard Toshiro speak of his presence, but she could feel him, out there, somewhere, watching.

And so she strove to perform the kata without error.

Seeing the near perfection of her movements, Toshiro decided to show his unseen guest just how good his pupil actually was. With a nod at the doorway in the back of the room, the martial-arts master summoned those he had handpicked for the occasion.

Five darkly clad warriors rushed into the room, armed with a variety of weapons, from a bo staff to a *katana*. Without hesitation they rushed across the room and attacked Shizu, who was still moving through the sequence of her kata.

The young prodigy felt them coming, could sense them in her mind's eye, and she waited for them to reach her.

Then, once they had, she fell on them like a lightning storm.

It didn't matter that they were armed and she was not. It didn't matter that they were warriors who had been studying for decades, well versed in their particular disciplines, while she had been studying for only three years. It didn't matter that she had been enduring a grueling training session for forty-eight hours without a break while they were well rested, well fed and eager to show Toshiro what they could do.

None of that mattered.

What mattered was the heart of the warrior, and Shizu had that in spades.

She made it look easy.

One by one, her opponents were disarmed, beaten, battered and tossed aside like leaves before a gale-force wind. Even as they lay there groaning, trying to figure out what had just hit them with such ferocity, Shizu continued with her previous exercise, flowing into the next step in the kata as smoothly as if she had never been interrupted.

Behind her, out of sight, the old teacher smiled in grim satisfaction.

When she had finished all two hundred steps of the form with perfect execution and flawless precision, she turned to her teacher and bowed low, just as she'd been taught on the very first day.

But then Shizu did a surprising thing.

As Toshiro watched, his pupil turned to face the wall behind which their guest stood, observing the session. With just as much respect as she had shown her teacher, Shizu bowed to their unseen guest.

The move brought a bark of laughter from Toshiro, something his students heard so seldom that it caused Shizu to spin around and stare at him in surprise.

TOSHIRO SAT AT THE FEET of his guest and served him tea prepared the old way, the only way that mattered. As any true warrior would, the man accepted the proffered cup and then offered it back again to Toshiro, indicating that the elder should be the one to drink first. Back and forth it went until honor had been satisfied and his guest took a long drink from the tiny cup.

With the ceremony out of the way, the two men could get down to business.

"You saw?" Toshiro asked.

The other man nodded. He'd been watching from behind a hidden slot in one of the studio's shoji screens, the same one Shizu had so impertinently bowed toward, and was privately thrilled with how far his protégé had come. "She has learned well, yes?"

"She is a good student. Still thinks too much, but we'll drive that out of her yet."

Toshiro's guest frowned. "You think she needs to remain here longer?"

The shorter man beamed. "Oh, yes. Another year, maybe two. She is not yet ready."

"But I thought you just said she was a good student. That she *was* ready."

The grizzled old warrior shook his head. "Not ready. Still has not learned the path of the lotus flower, the way of the crane, the—"

His guest held up his hands. "Okay. Enough. I will not argue. You are the master here, not I." Still seated, he bowed low to show his respect and to apologize for his doubt.

The older man slapped him on the knee, an affectionate move that one might not have expected for a man of his reputation, but the two of them had known each other for a long time, a long time indeed.

"You shouldn't worry. I will forge for you a weapon with such precision that not even Death will know she is coming."

The other man smiled. "I know you will, Toshiro, I know you will."

16

Now

Feeling very flustered by what she had experienced in the hypnotherapist's office, Annja wandered the streets for a bit, keeping her mind purposely blank. She didn't want to think about the drawings on the pad in her hands, didn't want to think about the possible implications, how it all might be interpreted. Not yet, at least. She just wanted to calm her racing heart and get her pulse back under control.

She found herself standing before a quaint little café on the corner of Bleaker and Main. The place was only half-full, with several of the tables outside under the canopy empty. She sat at one and glanced over the menu until a waiter came to see what she wanted.

"What can I get for you today?" he asked.

She ordered lunch—a glass of water and a chef's

salad—even though she wasn't all that hungry. It was more about giving her something to focus on, something for her hands to do, rather than needing to fill her stomach.

Once she had relaxed she pulled out the sketch pad she had taken with her from Dr. Laurent's office and flipped it open to one of the pages where she had drawn the execution scene. With the detached eye of a scientist she studied it.

Had she seen the image before? she wondered. When she had first acquired the sword she'd done a tremendous amount of research into the woman who had once carried it—could she have seen it then? In a museum or an art book? Maybe a research site on the Internet?

There was really no way to know.

The other solution—that it wasn't something she had seen, but a memory from another time and another place—freaked her out more than she expected. She had always known that there was a reason the sword had chosen her, but having it do so because she was…what? A descendant? A distant blood relative? Or even crazier yet, the reincarnation of Joan herself?

Heaven only knew and right now it didn't seem to want to tell her.

Tired of chasing down streets that seemed to have no end, Annja gave up on those images and turned to the other set that she had drawn, marveling again at the detail she'd been able to capture.

She was examining the image of the sword itself when someone said, "Excuse me?"

Annja looked up to find an Asian woman standing

beside her table. She wore ripped jeans, a black concert T-shirt, and a jean jacket that had been drawn on with Magic Marker so many times that the words had long since blended into an incoherent stream of letters. Her long black hair hung freely down her back.

"Excuse me, but are you Annja Creed, from *Chasing History's Monsters?*" the young woman asked.

Not now, Annja thought, but it was too late. Might as well get it over with.

"Yes," she said, a bit abruptly.

The woman couldn't help but notice the tone. She dropped her eyes to the ground and began backing away. "I'm sorry to have bothered you. Sorry."

Way to go, you coldhearted idiot! Annja berated herself. Probably took all her courage just to come over and say hello.

As she turned to go, Annja said, "No, I'm the one who should be sorry. Please, don't go."

The woman hesitated, clearly uncertain what to do.

"Come on, join me for a minute," Annja said, forcing a smile to show that she meant it. Her audience was small enough; she didn't need to go chasing off any of her viewers, no matter how badly her day had been going.

The fan sat down and, smiling shyly at her, held out her hand.

"I'm Shizu," she said.

"Annja, though you already know that."

"Right. And, like, don't worry about it, by the way."

Annja was confused. "Don't worry about what?"

"That you were going to dis me like that. I mean,

you're a celebrity, right? You must get people interrupting you all the time—like, what a bummer. I completely understand."

Annja stared at her as if she was from another planet.

Someone up there must hate me, she thought, but she smiled graciously and said, "Thanks. For letting me apologize, that is."

"Like, no problem."

Once she got beyond Shizu's annoying speech habits, Annja actually began to enjoy herself. She discovered that Shizu was going to New York University, was majoring in philosophy and had lived most of her life in the San Francisco Bay Area before moving to the Big Apple. The girl was actually quite well-read and Annja began to suspect that the vapid airhead exterior was really just a front she'd developed through the years to allow her to fit in with others her age.

Annja, in turn, answered her questions about what it was like to work on a cable television show, how she'd gotten involved in archaeology, and whether or not she thought her cohost, Kristie Chatham, was any good at her job.

Lunch passed quickly and for a short while Annja actually forgot about the disturbing events in Dr. Laurent's office.

Eventually Annja excused herself to go to the restroom and when she returned she saw that the waiter had left the check on the table in one of those black plastic sleeves. She was in the process of reaching for it when Shizu jumped to her feet and grabbed her hand.

"Oh, my God, like, I totally didn't realize what time it was!" Shizu exclaimed. "I was supposed to meet my boyfriend twenty minutes ago! Thanks for talking with me for so long. My friends are never going to believe this!"

They shook hands and Annja watched her disappear into the crowd moving past at the corner. Still laughing over the uniqueness of the whole encounter, she picked up the small plastic folder with her bill inside and opened it up, intending to pay, only to recoil in surprise.

The bill had been folded into the shape of a dragon.

Alarm bells blared in her mind.

She shoved back from the table and managed to restrain herself from calling on her sword right then and there. Only the thought that drawing it in public might be just what the Dragon wanted her to do kept her from actually doing it; she didn't need to be on the five-o'clock news wielding a sword in a public restaurant. She was already notorious enough as it was.

Heads turned in her direction as she surged to her feet and she glared at them all, mentally wrapping each face in a ninja hood and mask, searching for a pair of eyes that looked familiar to her, but none of them were.

She knew she had only seconds to pinpoint just where the origami had come from and every second wasted was another that the Dragon could use to either prepare for an attack or fade into the background, only to disappear once more.

She wasn't going to let that happen this time.

Having eliminated those around her, Annja realized that the Dragon must be inside the café. After all, that was where the bill had come from and no one but her and her waiter had touched it.

She focused on the waiter.

She hadn't even looked at him when he'd taken her order, not really. She'd been too wrapped up in her turmoil over the sketches. So for all she knew he could be the Dragon himself, though it was more likely that he had simply given the other man access to her check case. Either way, the waiter would have some answers.

Like an enraged lioness, Annja stormed inside the café itself and then, not seeing the waiter anywhere in the room, she pushed her way through the small crowd of customers near the bar and slipped into the kitchen.

A man in a dishwasher's apron intercepted her just inside the doors. "I'm sorry, miss, but you can't be in here."

"Where is he?" she snarled, and watched in satisfaction as the help quickly backed away from her. She followed, deeper into the kitchen, until she could see the guy who had served her. He was in one corner, talking to the chef.

Hands reached out for her, trying to stop her, but she pushed past and cornered the waiter against the wall.

With one fist wrapped in his white shirt and the other holding the folded-up bill in front of his face, she shouted, "Who did this? Did you do this?"

The guy shrank back from her. "Lady, I don't know what you are talking about! Who did what?"

"Folded my bill up like this! Did you do it?" She shook him a little, being none too gentle about it.

His eyes grew even wider, if that was at all possible. "Easy, lady! Take it easy! I can't even fold a napkin right, never mind do something like that!"

There were murmurs of assent from the group that was gathering around her. Looking into his eyes, she could see he was being honest. He had no idea what she was talking about.

She released him and turned away, her thoughts racing. If the waiter hadn't done it himself, nor allowed it to happen in the back before it reached her table, then it had to be someone else on the staff.

But who?

She replayed the final minutes of the meal in her mind: she was sitting talking to Shizu, the waiter had come by and placed the check on the tabletop, she'd gotten up to use the restroom. When she had returned, Shizu had thanked her and raced off to meet her boyfriend.

Annja stopped the mental replay and backed it up again, watched as the waiter placed the check folder on the edge of the table between Shizu and her, watched as she excused herself to go to the restroom.

Thinking it through, an uncomfortable suspicion was starting to form in her mind. The only time the bill folder had been within anyone else's sight was during those few moments that it had rested on the tabletop. And the only person within reach of it at the time, aside from herself, was…

Shizu.

Annja was already in motion by the time her conscious mind caught up with her intuition. She threw some cash at the waiter, ran out of the café, vaulted the small iron fence that surrounded the outdoor terrace and rushed into the nearby intersection, her eyes already scanning the crowd for any sign of the girl who had shared a drink with her over lunch.

The girl worked for the Dragon.

Annja hunted up and down those streets for more than an hour, hoping she might show herself, might give Annja the chance she needed to grab her and ask a few, all-important questions, but it was no use.

The young woman, whoever she had really been, was gone.

17

As Annja was confronting the waitstaff at the café and trying to determine just who had left the folded paper dragon in her bill folio, the Dragon was headed for the offices of Dr. Julie Laurent, hypnotherapist.

Something had happened to Annja there. Her agitated state had been proof of that and the Dragon wanted to find out what had riled her so badly.

Finding the office was easy. The Dragon climbed the steps and knocked on the doctor's front door.

"Coming!" said a faint voice from behind the door.

The Dragon put a finger over the peephole, preventing the doctor from looking out and seeing anything.

A moment passed. The Dragon heard the locks being turned on the other side, and then the door was opened to the extent the security chain allowed it. The Dragon reared back and slammed a foot into the door right next to the handle.

The door flew open, knocking the older woman behind it backward into the office and down onto the floor. The Dragon followed swiftly. A knife was put to the doctor's throat.

"Scream and not only will I kill you, but I'll carve you up before I do," the Dragon said.

Wisely, the doctor clamped a hand over her mouth to keep from crying out.

The Dragon kicked the door shut, relocked it and turned back to face the woman still cowering silently on the floor.

"You and I are going to have a little chat, all right?"

Dr. Laurent nodded.

"If you answer my questions, you'll be fine. If you do not answer them, I'm going to have to hurt you. Do you understand?"

With tears streaming down her face, the doctor nodded.

"Good."

The Dragon instructed her to get up off the floor and to take a seat in one of the nearby chairs. Dr. Laurent immediately did so. That was a good sign; a submissive attitude was much better than the defiance that had been expected.

Taking out a photograph of Annja, the Dragon handed it to Dr. Laurent.

"The woman in the photo was in here earlier this morning. What did you talk about?"

A little bit of the doctor's uncertainty came back at the idea of breaching her client's privacy. "I can't possibly give you that information. It is covered by doctor-client confidentiality and—"

Still smiling, the Dragon reached out, grabbed the doctor's left pinkie and brutally snapped it.

Dr. Laurent let out a short, sharp yelp of pain that was quickly cut off as the Dragon slapped a hand over her mouth.

Leaning close to her ear, the Dragon said, "Next time I'll break all of the fingers on that hand. And then I'll go to work with my knife. Now answer the question!"

The doctor's bluster seemed to have fled in the wake of the violence and she answered the best she could around her sobs of pain.

"Ms. Creed came in for a consultation. She's been having the same dream for several nights and she…she wanted to understand just what it was trying to tell her."

"See? That wasn't so hard, now, was it?" the Dragon asked. "What kind of dream?"

"A man…attacking her with a sword."

"Did she describe this person?"

"Not really."

"Why not?"

"Because all she could see was the swordsman's eyes. The rest was covered up with some kind of mask." Dr. Laurent cradled her injured hand in her other one and glared at the Dragon.

In response, the Dragon smiled and then nearly laughed aloud as Dr. Laurent recoiled in fear, pulling her hands against her body as if that would protect them from harm.

Little good that will do when the time comes, the Dragon thought.

"What else can you tell me?"

Dr. Laurent explained how her patient had been focused on identifying the swordsman and had even drawn images of the sword that he carried in the dream. When asked if she had these drawings in her possession, the doctor admitted that she did; there were copies in the file with her written notes.

"And the file is here, in the office?" the Dragon asked.

Dr. Laurent sighed at this further violation of a client's privacy but had learned her lesson the first time and didn't object. Instead, she showed the Dragon where she kept the file.

The images were well done, surprisingly so since they had been created while the artist was in the midst of a hypnotic trance. The Dragon stared at the face in the picture; it was an excellent likeness.

The image of the sword, however, was more disturbing.

There wasn't enough detail in the portrait for the Dragon to be worried about being identified through it. But the image of the sword was another story. It was close enough to the real etching and signature that Annja Creed might be able to trace it back to the Dragon's master and that would never do.

"Is this the only copy of the drawing?" the Dragon asked.

Dr. Laurent nodded.

Something passed between them, a feeling, a premonition, maybe. Whatever it was, the doctor suddenly realized the purpose of the question, her eyes going wide with the recognition of what was to come. She gave a frightened little squeal and tried to run, bolting from her chair and heading for the door.

The Dragon let her get close to the door, let her hope rise as she realized freedom was only a few steps away, and then bounded across the room, seizing the doctor by her hair and spinning her around to face the interior of the room. With a flick of the wrist a blade appeared in the Dragon's hand, a blade that was used seconds later to slash the doctor's throat.

It happened so fast that the doctor never had time to scream.

Blood fountained up from the wound and the Dragon shoved the body away to avoid being splashed.

Dr. Laurent tumbled forward, collapsing across the sofa, her hands going to her throat as she tried to staunch the flow of blood.

It took less than a minute for her to die.

Messy, but unavoidable, the Dragon thought.

Being careful to avoid the splatters of blood across the floor, the Dragon walked to the desk and picked up the photocopies of the drawings the Creed woman had made, as well as the file containing the doctor's impressions about the patient and her condition. The doctor's final few patients would automatically come under suspicion if the police followed their normal procedures, and the last thing the Dragon wanted was to have the police trailing the target. By taking the materials the Dragon hoped to eliminate any connection between the doctor and the target, which, in turn, would throw the police off the track.

Just to be certain that all traces of the Creed woman's appointment had been dealt with accordingly, the Dragon stole the doctor's appointment book and erased the tape on the answering machine.

Stepping over to the window to be certain of better reception, the Dragon took out a cell phone and dialed a number. When it was answered, the Dragon said, "I need some men. A combination of muscle and general surveillance experience would be best. I'll meet them in the location we discussed previously."

With that, the Dragon hung up, took one last glance around and then left the office behind, carefully locking the door with the doctor's own set of keys.

THE MEN ASSEMBLED AT THE warehouse two hours later.

The Dragon looked all six of them over. They were average looking, nondescript. Several had short haircuts that suggested prior military service. A few had prison tattoos. None of them would stand out in a crowd and even the tallest among them wasn't so tall as to be memorable.

It was a good group.

"This is your target," the Dragon said, handing them each a photograph of Annja, taken as she came out of her apartment building. It was a good shot, with a clear view of her features, and they would have no trouble identifying her from it.

The Dragon gave them a minute to look it over, and then said, "There are two addresses on the back. One for her home, the other for her place of employment. I want her watched. I need to know where she goes, who she sees and what she does."

The men nodded. One of them had the audacity to make suggestive comments regarding what he'd like to do to her. That wouldn't do. The Dragon walked over and without warning slammed the blunt side of one hand into the man's throat.

His eyes bulged; his hands went to his neck as he realized his windpipe had been crushed and his air supply cut off. He reached out in his panic, but the Dragon stepped back and let him fall to the floor, calmly watching as he suffocated to death.

It took several minutes.

The rest of the men looked on in silence.

When it was over, the Dragon turned to the group and asked, "Anyone else like to offer their opinion of the target?"

No one said anything.

The Dragon knew that men like this were influenced by two things—fear and money. With the first established, it was time to move onto the second.

Stepping over the dead man's body, the Dragon walked back up the row, examining each man in turn. "If the opportunity presents itself, or if you are made and she knows you are following her, I want you to stage a confrontation. She is in possession of a certain sword, one that is worth a hefty sum of money. If any of you get the location of that weapon, or the sword itself, I will provide you with a reward above and beyond the fee for the job itself."

There were murmurs of appreciation.

The Dragon looked them over. "Do you understand?"

There was a chorus of agreements.

The Dragon handed them all a slip of paper.

"Here is a cell number. Memorize it. When you have completed the assignment, call me."

After a moment, the Dragon collected the slips of paper and then dismissed the men.

The plan had been set in motion. It was time to wait to see if it bore any fruit.

18

Between the events in Dr. Laurent's office and the encounter at the café, Annja had had enough excitement for one day. She caught a cab and headed home, but not until she'd had the driver make a few sudden turns and run a red light or two. At this point, it made sense to be cautious.

Just because you can't see them, Annja thought, doesn't mean they aren't out there.

She had the cabbie drop her off a block from her loft and ducked into a local Chinese restaurant for some takeout. Once back at home, she sat down and looked at the drawings, trying to make some sense of them.

She stared again at the face of the swordsman, searching her memory for a familiar face, trying to determine if she had ever seen him before. With only the eyes and the upper half of the nose to work from, it was like trying to find a needle in a field of haystacks. It could be anybody, really.

She turned her attention to the images of Joan of Arc's execution. Recalling her thought that she might have been reproducing a painting or an image she'd seen somewhere before, she turned to her laptop. A search turned up nearly ninety thousand images.

It would take days to go through them all.

Still, she glanced through the first few pages of images, looking for something that resembled her drawing. But, aside from the fact that they all showed a young woman being burned at the stake, none of them were a match.

The mystery remained and Annja decided to leave it that way.

Later that night, while she was trying to get organized for the work she needed to do in the studio the next day, her phone rang.

Answering it, Annja said, "Hello?"

Only silence greeted her.

"Hello? Is anyone there?" she asked.

Still nothing.

Assuming it was a wrong number, she hung up.

A few minutes later the phone rang again.

A feeling of unease swept over her as she stared at the receiver. It rang twice, and then a third time. On the fourth ring she overcame her reluctance and snatched it up.

"Hello?"

Silence greeted her a second time, but this time it was different. This time there was a depth to it, a sense that someone was there, even if they weren't answering her.

That silence angered her.

"I know you can hear me. I don't know who you are or what you want, but I'm not the type of person you want to mess around with. I suggest you leave me alone."

When she still didn't get an answer, Annja hung up the phone.

No sooner had she done so, then it rang again.

Grabbing the phone for the third time, she snarled, "Now you are asking for trouble."

A man's laugh echoed down the line. "And here I thought you just didn't understand me, Annja."

"Garin?" Finding him unexpectedly on the line startled her.

"I'm headed out of town for a week and thought I'd check in before I left. You returned to the U.S. rather abruptly, after all."

It took Annja a moment to focus on what he was saying; the prior calls had unnerved her more than she had expected. Finally she said, "After your little altercation with Roux I saw no sense in staying, not when I had work that needed to be done here."

"And does that work pertain to the information we discussed before you left?"

Annja was about to say yes, but bit her tongue at the last minute to keep from doing so. If there really was an international assassin after either her or Roux, she suddenly didn't want Garin to know about it.

"No, nothing like that. Just some editing for the show that needed to be done." She tried to change the subject. "So where did you say you were going?" she asked.

Garin answered with a laugh. "I didn't say, actually,

but if you must know I'm visiting some of my electronic plants in Japan for the next few days. No luck tracking down the Dragon, then?"

So much for her change of subject.

"I spent a day or two looking into it, but I haven't found anything solid. Why? Have you learned something new?"

Garin shouted something unintelligible to someone on his end, then said to Annja, "No, nothing new. Just thought you might have. You're so good at that kind of thing, after all."

Another shout, though this time he covered the mouthpiece of his receiver so that it came out muffled.

"Sorry, Annja, gotta run. They're holding the plane for me. Best of luck and let me know if you find anything."

Before she had a chance to say anything back, he hung up.

She stared at the receiver in her hand for a minute, muttered, "Idiot," and hung up.

Garin's call made her uneasy for a reason she couldn't quite put her finger on, and she lay in bed wondering about it long into the night.

THE NEXT MORNING SHE ROSE early and prepared for her day at the studio. Doug Morrell was counting on her and the editing team to cut nineteen hours of video down to a thirty-minute segment, a task that was never easy for Annja. She wanted her viewers to get as much information as possible and there was only so much she could jam into a lousy half hour.

Still, it had to be done and she didn't trust anyone else to work on her shows if she was available to do so. The few times she'd let Doug handle the chore, he'd stuffed so much garbage into the show that it had looked like one of Kristie's episodes. And if there was one person in the world Annja couldn't stand, it was her cohost, Kristie.

While she would just normally take the subway over to Manhattan, today she decided to splurge on a cab. Along the way she tried to shake any tail she might have picked up by having the cabbie make half a dozen turns at the last minute and double back a time or two down the same streets. When she was at last satisfied that no one was following them, she let him take her the rest of the way to her destination by a more direct route.

The editing team was already assembled in the cutting room when she arrived and for the rest of the day Annja threw herself into the work in front of her. She didn't think about the Dragon. She didn't think about a mystical sword, hers or anyone else's. All she did was focus on making her next episode of *Chasing History's Monsters* the best it could be. They had less than an hour of work to go when quitting time arrived, and Annja convinced the others to stay around and finish up so they wouldn't have to come back in the next morning. To make the decision easier for them, she offered to have pizza and beer brought in for dinner.

That did the trick.

By seven o'clock they were finished. The video had

been cut, the still shots selected and Annja had even recorded the necessary voice-overs that were needed to pull the whole thing together as a cohesive unit.

When Doug came into work the next morning, he'd find the entire package on his desk, ready to go down to production for the final assembly.

Not bad for a day's work, Annja thought.

Perhaps more importantly, it left her next day free so she could look into a few of the details she'd uncovered earlier that morning, which had been the entire point of the exercise in the first place.

She said goodbye to the three technicians, grabbed her backpack and the precious drawings it contained and headed down the street toward the subway station where she intended to catch a train back to Brooklyn.

She had only walked a few blocks before she felt a stranger's eyes upon her again, just as she had the other day. In the middle of the block she abruptly stopped and bent down to tie her shoe, glancing backward as she did so. Maybe it was because it was getting dark and they didn't think they'd be seen or maybe they just didn't expect her to be as aware of her surroundings as she was, Annja didn't know, but whatever the reason, her little stunt worked.

About a block and a half back, two men abruptly stopped and turned away from her. One pretended to be examining a magazine stand and the other pulled a cell phone out of his pocket and acted as if he was answering a call.

Annja knew the truth, though. She'd seen how intent

they were on watching her in those first few seconds before they'd turned away.

She was being followed. There was no doubt about it.

The man in front was short and thick, with shoulders that looked as if they belonged on an NFL linebacker. His shaved head gleamed in the streetlights. His partner was taller and thinner, with a thick head of wavy hair and a goatee. Both were dressed in dark pants, shirts and jackets.

Annja stood and continued walking, but this time she glanced back over her shoulder a few times, watching the men behind her.

They clearly weren't from New York, as they hadn't yet developed a New Yorker's odd talent for moving through a crowded sidewalk without disturbing the slower pedestrian traffic moving around them. Where Annja slipped through the crowd, moving easily with the changing patterns of those around her, her pursuers plowed their own path and it was this disturbance in the natural flow that had caught her eye and let her know that they were still back there.

Even as she watched, the two men quickened their pace, obviously trying to close the distance between themselves and Annja.

She wasn't about to let that happen.

Let's see if I can flush the foxes out of the henhouse, she thought, and then broke into a run. Her sudden move caught them off guard and her long legs allowed her to widen the distance between them in those first few seconds, giving her some precious lead time.

She raced across the traffic against the light. Horns

blared, people shouted, but she didn't stop, counting on a little bit of luck and a lot of divine provenance to get her through. She barged through the crowd standing on the opposite corner and shot down the street perpendicular to the direction she'd been traveling in, headed for the subway station on Broadway a block and a half away.

By the time she reached it, she had widened her lead to almost two whole blocks. Unfortunately, her pursuers had doubled in number, as well, for as she stopped for a moment at the top of the steps leading down to the subway station, she could see four men shoving their way through the crowd toward her.

Time to go, she told herself, and raced down the steps two at a time.

At the bottom she caught sight of a couple of transit cops standing around chatting and she momentarily considered getting them involved, but decided against it at the last minute. If it was the Dragon's men behind her—and really, who else could it be?—then she didn't want to drag them into her mess.

Instead, she charged forward, vaulted the turnstile and dashed down the steps in front of her, headed for the center platform. The station serviced four different sets of tracks, two northbound and two southbound. The center platform would give her access to one of each, which seemed her best bet at the moment. When she had managed to lose her pursuers, she could always get off at another stop, cross over to the opposite platform and head back the other way, if necessary.

Once on the platform she slowed her pace and began

to mix in with the crowd around her. The little magazine-and-snack stand was selling Mets caps for fifteen bucks, so she hurriedly bought one and, stuffing her hair up underneath it, jammed it on her head. She thought about grabbing a pair of sunglasses while she was at it, but decided against it. She didn't want anything to hinder her vision of the people around her.

There was a commotion on the stairs and Annja turned away, not wanting to be caught gawking and give herself away. She moved down the platform and then looked back the way she had come.

Her original pursuers were coming down the stairs, shoving people out of the way when they didn't move fast enough. As she watched, a young college student angrily tried to push back and ended up being tossed down the stairs for his trouble.

That got people's attention and they cleared a path, allowing her pursuers to descend that much faster.

A glance to her right to the northbound platform showed that her other two pursuers were already amid the crowd over there, searching for her.

Where the heck was the train?

She looked down the tracks, hoping to see the telltale glow of the oncoming light, but only the darkness stared back at her.

For a second she thought about jumping off the platform and disappearing into the tunnels, but she wasn't desperate enough yet to take a chance of getting caught on the tracks with an inbound train.

When she turned back toward the crowd, she saw that

her pursuers had reached the bottom of the steps and were on the platform itself. They stopped for a moment, talking it over, and then one headed her way while one went the other.

If she was going to reach the stairs, she was going to have to confront at least one of them.

Annja knew she couldn't count on the crowd to keep her hidden forever. Sooner or later one of them was going to catch a glimpse of her and then she'd have to deal with all four of them together. Going on the offensive, while they were still separated from each other, seemed like a smart move and it didn't take her long to decide to do just that.

She began to work her way through the crowd back in the direction that she'd come from, keeping her face averted as much as possible. As she drew closer to where the bald man stood searching for her, she gradually drifted in his direction. When she was only a few feet away she stopped and waited for him to close the distance.

He was trying to see over the heads of the people around them when Annja stepped up beside him.

"Looking for me?" she asked.

As he spun to face her, Annja delivered a massive punch to his right temple, stunning him. She followed it with a left cross that started somewhere around her waist and ended up catching him right beneath the chin, slamming his head back.

He dropped to the ground like a felled tree.

The crowd around them suddenly backed away, the typical New York response to trouble—stay out of it.

Annja was ready to deliver another blow but realized she didn't need to; he was out cold, at least for the time being.

Her frontal assault had an unintended consequence, however. From the platform across the way she could see a number of commuters gesticulating in her direction. Aware of the movement of the crowd, her pursuers glanced in the direction the commuters were pointing.

They saw Annja at the same time she saw them.

Time to go, she thought to herself.

She turned, ready to make a dash for the stairs and the freedom they represented, only to find herself looking down the barrel of a very ugly handgun.

"I don't think so, Ms. Creed," the man with the goatee said, shoving the gun closer to her. "You're coming with me."

No way, she thought. The minute she gave in to them she was signing her own death warrant. Better to go down fighting than to be led like a lamb to the slaughter.

Besides, the gunman had already made a fatal mistake.

He'd underestimated her.

Annja was already in motion by the time the "No!" came rolling off her lips. She used her shout to distract him; all she needed was a few seconds. Her left hand came up in an arc, the outer edge crashing into the gunman's arm just above the wrist, sending the gun away from her face. In the same motion her hand locked on to his wrist, pulling him forward and down.

The gun went off, the sound deafening so close to her ear, but she was already out of the line of fire thanks to her deflection strike. The bullet bounced off the concrete beneath her feet, disappearing somewhere into the crowd. Annja was still in motion, pivoting on the balls of her feet and using the swing of her hips to bring her right arm around vicious arc that ended against the side of his head.

No sooner had she connected with that blow than she delivered another, a hammer strike to the face with her left hand as she completed the circle she'd started with the first blow.

Her assailant staggered, but did not go down.

The crowd around her was screaming, a result of the gunfire and the violence that had suddenly broken out in their midst, but even that was drowned out as a northbound train roared into the station on the tracks next to her.

About time! she thought.

If she could get on that train before they did, she had a chance of getting away.

The gunman was shaking his head, trying to clear it, as he brought his arm back up, searching for a target.

Annja didn't give him any time to find one.

Her right foot came up in a scissor kick, delivering a thunderous blow to the exact same place she'd already struck him twice.

Apparently the third time was the charm, for he dropped to the ground, the gun spinning out of his hand across the platform.

Annja turned, intent on going after it, but was prevented from doing so when several bullets cracked off the floor near her feet.

As she dove to the side, desperately trying to get out

of the line of fire, she saw the other two gunmen standing at the top of the stairs, firing down at her.

She hit the ground and rolled for cover behind a nearby column. Several other people were already huddled there and Annja knew that if she didn't get out soon it wouldn't be long before some innocent bystander was caught in the cross fire and seriously injured or killed. For all she knew, it could have happened already. Those bullets had to end up somewhere and she could just imagine them finding a home in some commuters' unprotected flesh.

The train across the platform had discharged its passengers out the opposite side and now the doors on her side swished open. She could hear the conductor's voice indicating what the next stop would be and giving the all-clear announcement, but a fresh barrage of gunfire designed to keep everyone in place and under cover, trembling with fear, prevented anyone from heading for the open doors.

Annja knew she didn't have the same choice. She had to get on that train, had to take the battle out of the station to keep any more innocents from getting hurt.

Another volley of gunfire echoed around the station. Expecting a hail of bullets, Annja was shocked when none came her way.

She chanced a look around the pillar she was using as cover and was astounded to see a second group of men shooting at the first set from the cover of the magazine stand at the other end of the platform.

Who the heck are they? she wondered.

It didn't matter. While they kept the first group distracted, Annja saw her chance.

She surged to her feet and raced for the doors of the subway car even as the bell sounded and they began to close.

A fresh volley of gunfire, from both grounds, filled the air with lead but Annja was committed. There was no turning back.

She was halfway across the platform when she realized it was going to be tight. The doors were closing and even if she got her hand in the door it wouldn't do her any good; they wouldn't just pop back open like an elevator's doors did. It would take some time and she'd be stuck there with one arm in the door and the rest of her standing exposed against the unyielding surface of the train car outside, for too long.

It would be like shooting ducks in a barrel for anyone with an ounce of experience with a firearm. And from what she had seen so far, they probably had a better than even chance of hitting a nonmoving target.

All this went through Annja's mind in a split second, and in that time she realized she really only had one course of action left available to her if she wanted to get out of this alive.

With a final burst of speed and a huge downward thrust of her long athletic legs, Annja launched herself like a missile at the closing doors of the subway car.

19

Annja shot through the opening just as the doors closed behind her. She tucked herself into a ball to cushion the impact she knew she was about to experience.

She careered into a metal pole, bounced off that and then slammed to a stop against the closed doors on the other side of the train.

She felt the car lurch into motion beneath her as she climbed cautiously to her feet. Several passengers were staring at her openmouthed and she was sure she looked quite the spectacle after a stunt like that, but Annja didn't care. She'd survived; that was all that mattered.

No sooner had she risen to her feet, however, than she was throwing herself back down to the floor as the windows in the subway doors shattered under a hail of gunfire. Safety glass went flying, and through the opening Annja could see her two pursuers racing toward her, guns extended. Behind them she could also see her first assailant, the bald man, back on his feet and closing the distance as well.

What do they think they're going to do, jump on the moving train? she wondered.

No sooner had she thought it than the lead gunman threw himself against the door and hung on, letting the train carry him with it. With the glass in the windows gone, he was able to stick his arm inside the train and point his gun at her.

You have got to be kidding me! Annja thought, even as she hurled herself down the center aisle and away from the door.

Gunfire followed her and several passengers went down in a shower of blood.

With so many passengers watching, Annja didn't dare draw her sword, so she scrambled forward on hands and knees, trying to reach the door to the next car, while around her the other passengers huddled in terror.

The gunplay stopped, as her pursuer turned his attention to getting inside the subway car before the motion of the train or some hanging piece of equipment swept him off the outside. She could hear him swearing and hollering at the person closest to him to help him haul open the doors, but Annja didn't stick around to see the results of his efforts. Instead, she rose to her feet, hauled back the lever to open the door and stepped onto the narrow platform connecting her car to the next.

While in that no-man's-land between cars, Annja summoned her sword from the otherwhere. Its presence made her feel almost instantly better; she always felt as if she could take on any challenge with the sword by her side and this time was no different.

She stepped across to the next car, hauled open that door and disappeared inside.

As one, the passengers in the next car turned to see what all the commotion was about and more than a handful started screaming the moment she stepped into the car, sword in hand.

"Stay down!" she shouted at them and they did, cowering in their seats. Annja had been concerned that a stray bullet might injure them, but then she realized they weren't afraid of being shot at all. They were afraid of her!

Come on, now, she thought, it's just a broadsword. I'd be far more afraid of the dudes with guns.

She kept moving forward, rushing for the other end of the car as fast as she could and counting on the passengers to get out of her way.

To a one, they all did.

Must be the sword, Annja thought with a smile.

She guessed she was seven, maybe eight, cars from the end of the train. She made it through six of those cars before her pursuers caught up to her, which was pretty damn good, all things considered.

It just wasn't good enough.

"Hold it right there!" a man's voice shouted, and Annja didn't need to look to know who it was. The sound of the slide on the gun was extraloud in the current silence of the subway car.

Slowly, so as to not be mistaken for making any heroic moves, Annja turned to face her assailant.

Three of them stood there—the bald man, the guy with the goatee and one of the newcomers. The fourth man wasn't there, but Annja didn't bother to ask where he was.

"Put down the sword and kick it over here," the bald man said.

Knowing she'd reached the end of the line, Annja did as she was told. She bent down and put the sword on the floor. Then, before she could change her mind, she kicked it along the length of the car toward him. She wasn't sure what would happen next.

When she looked up again, over their shoulders, Annja saw an astounding sight. The second group of gunmen she'd seen at the subway station was cautiously making their way toward the group ahead of them. Annja had no idea who they were or what they wanted; all she knew was that their guns were pointed at the other shooters, rather than at her, and that was good enough for now.

The gunmen hadn't noticed them yet.

Pointing behind them, Annja said to them, "I see you invited a few more guests to the party."

Maybe it was the way she said it. Maybe it was the half smile of satisfaction on her face. Whatever it was, it seemed to do the trick. The gunmen turned as one to look behind them.

With the speed of thought, Annja made her sword vanish back into the otherwhere. Then she turned to escape.

The sound of gunfire filled the car, the crack of the shots and the buzz of the bullets echoing in the narrow confines of the car. Annja instinctively ducked into a crouch to present a smaller target, but she needn't have worried. The two groups were blazing away at each other and weren't paying attention to her.

She ran for the last car.

On the other side of the door a few scattered passengers were watching the gunplay behind them as if it were a spectator sport and Annja grimaced.

Only in New York.

Crossing the car, she came to the final door on the train. Looking through its window, she could see a small platform on the other side and, just beyond it, the tunnel itself.

If she could get off the train…

The door, of course, was locked, to prevent people from doing the very thing she was about to do. Not that that was going to be a hindrance to her.

While everyone's attention was on the gun battle going on in the car behind her, Annja called her sword into being and shoved it right through the lock.

There was a tearing, grinding sound and then the door popped open.

Rather than trying to haul her sword back out of the splintered steel of the door, Annja simply let it go, willing it back into the otherwhere as she did so. The sword vanished, leaving a gaping hole in the lock.

Annja stepped out onto the tiny platform at the end of the train. A small metal railing that came up to her midthigh was all that kept her from falling off the back of the train. The wind whipped all around her and the tunnel was filled with the roar of the moving train and the squeal of its brakes as the conductor tried to slow it down and bring it to a stop as a result of all the shooting. There was a ladder bolted to the subway car on her left, but since it led to the roof of the train she ignored it. With the ceiling of the tunnel so low, climbing up there was practically suicide, which meant she didn't have many options available to her. She could either go back the way she had come or she could get off the train.

A quick glance back into the car showed her pursuers passing through the door at the other end. They would figure out where she had gone in just a few seconds, and if they caught her on the platform it was all over.

Knowing that if she gave it any real thought she'd chicken out, Annja backed up a few steps until she was against the door, then took a running start and launched herself over the rail and off the train.

She hit the ground hard and rolled, her arms and legs tucked in tight to avoid hitting the rails nearby. She sprang to her feet and headed down the tunnel as fast as she could run. In the back of her mind she marveled at the fact that she had just jumped off a moving train and survived, but the other half of her chalked it up to the sword's influence on her physical abilities and left it at that. The important thing was that she had gotten away.

A bullet bounced off the wall next to her in the split second before the report of the shot reached her ears, echoing in the narrow confines of the tunnel.

The tunnel curved to the right a few feet ahead and

she ran for all she was worth, praying she could get around the bend before a bullet found her flesh.

Two more bullets bounced around her, ricocheting in the dim light and then she sped past the curve and was out of range, at least for a few minutes.

Between now and the time the gunmen reach you, you have to come up with a plan. And it had better be a good one, she told herself.

The tunnel smelled of dirt and exhaust and a thousand other things she couldn't identify. It was dimly lit by a series of bare bulbs hanging on the left-hand wall every ten feet. There was just enough light for her to see so she hurried along as fast as she could, staying to the middle of the tracks and trying to be careful where she put her feet.

From behind her came the sound of running footsteps.

At least one of her pursuers, maybe more, as still back there.

Annja pushed herself, trying to put as much distance between them and herself as she could. The tunnel branched several times and she let intuition be her guide, making a left here, a right there, until she realized that she was no longer certain she was even on the same track. At that point she slowed down to a walk to try to figure things out.

She hadn't yet come upon another subway station, so she had no way of knowing where she was. Common sense told her to keep moving in one direction; eventually she had to hit another station and from there she could gain access to the street. So far she hadn't seen any trains, either—maybe traffic control had shut them down temporarily.

She kept walking.

After a few more minutes the earth around her began to vibrate with a steady rhythm and she knew that the trains were up and running again. That made her more nervous than she wanted to admit; if something happened, there wasn't anyplace she could go. She had to find a subway station and soon.

Annja was just starting to wish she'd headed in the other direction at one of the previous forks she'd encountered when a pursuer caught up to her.

He charged her out of the darkness, ramming his shoulder into her midriff and lifting her with his forward momentum. They careered across the width of the tunnel until he slammed her bodily against a nearby column supporting the roof above.

She took the impact badly, not having had time to prepare herself and thought she heard a rib crack as she was crushed between his massive shoulders and the concrete behind her. He kept the pressure on, trying to suffocate her while using his arms to pummel her sides with his massive fists.

As she hadn't had time to grab a lungful of air, she was already fading quickly, and Annja knew that if she didn't do something drastic she was going to be in serious trouble.

She brought her right knee up sharply, hammering it into his stomach, but it was like hitting a concrete block with a rubber mallet. She did it again and again, but had no greater luck with her subsequent blows than she'd had with the first. They just bounced off him; the man was a human tank, it seemed. All the while he kept up the punishment with his fists.

Air started to become a scarce commodity and she knew she had to make a move or she was going to pass out. Once that happened it was all over; she'd be completely at her attacker's mercy.

Her arms were free so she considered boxing him about the ears, but with his head pressed against her side she would have only be able to get to one. She needed something a bit more powerful than that.

Her vision began to dim around the edges, a gray haze floating at the periphery of her sight and slowly moving toward the center. He must have sensed her distress, for he suddenly shifted his feet and shoved forward, driving his shoulder another inch into her solar plexus, sending a wave of dizziness washing through her.

Now or never, Annja, she told herself.

Her hands moved spiderlike over his face, searching. He twisted his head, trying to get away, but she managed to find an eye socket with one hand and rammed her thumb into it.

He let out a howl of pain that filled the air around them like the death knell of some strange beast.

The pressure on her gut relaxed as the man stumbled backward, his hands going to his face. Annja sucked in a great lungful of breath and stumbled away, fighting to clear her head, knowing that he would be on her again in seconds.

Annja straightened up, blinking back the darkness that had threatened to overwhelm her. The bald man stood a few feet away, shaking his head like a dog, trying to clear the fluids running down his face.

"I'm going to kill you for that," he said, and charged forward.

Annja dropped into a crouch, ready for him, and as he rushed forward, she grabbed the front of his shirt with both hands and went over backward, using her hands and feet to toss him up and over her head as she rolled.

He slammed to the ground, dazed, and Annja didn't waste any time. She was already there, sword in hand, the point at his throat.

"Who sent you?" she asked, still trying to suck in enough air to calm her screaming lungs. "What do you want?"

She never heard his answer, however, for it was drowned out by the shriek of a train whistle.

She spun around, looking down the tunnel. A light flared there in the depths. As she watched, it drew closer.

A train was coming down the tracks.

Right toward them.

Annja didn't hesitate, didn't wait to see what her opponent was doing or how quickly the train might be coming. She knew she had only moments to get out of the danger zone or none of that was going to matter at all.

Annja ran like the devil himself was on her heels.

While moving through the tunnels she'd noticed a shallow niche in the wall every hundred yards or so. She knew these were emergency nooks designed for the transit workers to use in the event that they were accidentally caught in the tunnel with a moving train. The niches weren't much more than hollowed out spaces in the walls, roughly half a foot deep, if that, but she figured they were enough if you kept your head about you and stayed put until the train passed.

Of course, she had to find one first.

The train whistle wailed again, warning her to get off the tracks, and this time the sound was much closer. She chanced a look back, noting that her opponent was up and on his feet, chasing after her as fast as he could go and that the train had closed half the distance between them already, with no sign of slowing down.

They had two minutes, maybe less, before the train would be upon them.

She faced forward and kept going, her gaze frantically scanning the walls on either side.

There had to one here somewhere! There had to be!

The train closed in.

Annja had only seconds left.

Come on! Where the hell is it?

Then she saw it, barely visible amid the darkness of the tunnel, a shadowy outline that suggested depth.

She flung herself into the emergency niche against the far wall, squeezing her body in as deep as she could get it, worried that the effect of the passing train might be enough to pull her out again into the danger zone.

The man pursuing her was still ten feet away and his body was suddenly silhouetted in the harsh light of the train roaring toward them.

"Run!" Annja screamed, but she couldn't even hear herself over the roar of the train's whistle. She had a moment to see his face plainly in the light of the train, could see the terror that distorted his features, could see his outstretched arm as it reached for her…

Annja turned her face away at the last instant, pressing her cheek against the cold concrete behind her and trying to shrink back into the wall itself.

The train flashed by just inches from her face. She could feel the hot breath of its passage like the exhalations of a wild beast come to devour those that didn't belong, as it had devoured her pursuer only seconds before. Her nerves were screaming and all she wanted to do was run away, but she knew if she left the niche she would be splattered from here to Pennsylvania Station. It took all of her willpower to stand still and not move. Her ears were filled with the howl of the train's brakes as the conductor realized that there had been something more than just the usual rats in the tunnel and he tried to bring the train to a stop, but he was far too late.

It swept past her and Annja sucked a great gasp of air into her lungs, not even aware until that moment that she had been holding her breath.

That was too close.

AS ANNJA WAS RUNNING FROM her pursuers in the tunnels beneath Midtown Manhattan, a Gulfstream aircraft under private ownership arrived at Kennedy International Airport. Aboard were Henshaw, Roux and a half dozen of Henshaw's operatives he'd decided to bring over to help supplement the team that was already in place.

They passed through customs without difficulty and then split into two groups. Henshaw accompanied Roux to the car he had waiting outside, while his men headed for the safe house in Brooklyn overlooking Annja's loft apartment. Henshaw would meet up with them later, once he was satisfied that Roux had been safely ensconced in his usual hotel.

For a man like Roux, nothing but the Waldorf-Astoria would do. He'd been staying there under a variety of names for more than one hundred years and saw no reason to change now. Exquisite accommodations, superb service and a devotion to the privacy of their guests were the attributes Roux looked for in a hotel and the Waldorf did not disappoint.

Reaching the car, Henshaw dismissed the driver and took over that chore himself, not trusting anyone else to do it when he was personally available. He waited until Roux was buckled in and then eased out into traffic, ready for the hour-long drive through the Queens–Midtown Tunnel and across Manhattan to where the hotel stood on Park Avenue and Fiftieth.

Along the way, Roux asked for an update on the intelligence that Henshaw had been gathering on the Dragon.

"What little information we've been able to obtain seems to indicate that the Dragon became operational again about three years ago. He has done odd jobs here and there during that time—nothing too flashy and certainly nothing along the lines of his previous activity.

It is almost as if he was injured for a long while and is now testing his skills, learning again just what he is capable of."

"But it is him for certain?" Roux asked.

Henshaw nodded. "I believe so, sir. The hallmarks are there. The risky, maybe even reckless, nature of the contracts he takes on. The precision in which they are carried out. The telltale symbol—the paper dragon—left behind at each scene."

"Damn!" Roux said, and Henshaw mentally agreed. If the Dragon was after Annja, and it was looking more and more as if that were the case, then they were going to have to step up their security in order to keep her safe.

Annja was a fiercely independent person; he didn't want to think about how angry she'd be when she found out that she was being followed, even if it was in her best interest.

Henshaw had spoken to his people on the ground right after deplaning and now he shared what he had learned with Roux.

"She went where?" the older man exclaimed, after hearing what Henshaw had to say.

"To see a hypnotherapist," his butler repeated.

"Whatever for?"

"I don't know. Shall I have one of the men break into the therapist's office to obtain the records of her visit?"

Roux shook his head. "No, that's not necessary. At least, not yet. Annja will probably tell us herself."

"Very good," Henshaw said, and put down the cell phone he'd just picked up. He wasn't sure Roux was correct, but he'd learned a long time ago that it wasn't his place to argue with his employer.

Just as he disconnnected, though, it rang. He answered it, listened for several minutes, thanked the caller and then hung up again.

"There's been a new development," he said grimly. "A team was waiting outside the television studios where Ms. Creed is employed. She was chased into the underground and there was apparently a bit of a scuffle."

"Was she injured?" Roux asked. Henshaw was the master of the understatement. A "scuffle" in his view was other people's idea of a major combat engagement.

Henshaw shook his head. "No, sir. Our people involved themselves in the confrontation as soon as they were able to and in the resulting confusion, she slipped away from both groups."

"So she still doesn't know that we are watching her?"

Henshaw shrugged. "She clearly knows someone is watching, sir, but whether or not she has figured out that it is us is another question entirely. If I had to guess, I'd say no, though it won't take her long to figure it out if we have to interfere again."

He waited a moment while Roux digested the new information and then asked, "Shall I call off the surveillance?"

"Heavens, no! Clearly she needs it. Tell your people to stay close."

"Very good, sir."

They passed the rest of the ride in silence. Arriving at the Waldorf, Roux stepped out of the car and walked into the hotel, heading directly for the main dining room, intent on a late supper. He knew Henshaw would deal with the various details while he ate—take care of checking him into the usual suite he reserved each time he stayed there, seeing that his bags were brought up and unpacked properly, even arranging for breakfast at the proper time in the morning. After all, it was what he paid Henshaw for and Roux was not stingy with his personal comfort.

Later, Roux was relaxing with an after-dinner brandy when he heard the door to the suite open. A moment later Henshaw entered the room.

His majordomo had changed out of his usual perfectly pressed suit into casual slacks and a windbreaker, both of which, as well as his athletic shoes, were a very deep blue in color. Roux nodded appreciatively. The color wouldn't look entirely out of place in a crowd and the deep shade would actually help him to better blend in with the shadows than a pure black outfit.

"Are you all set, sir?" Henshaw asked.

Roux nodded. "I take it you are off to see our girl?"

"Yes, sir."

"We need to find this Dragon character before he finds Annja, Henshaw. Her life may depend on it."

Henshaw nodded. "We're working on it."

Roux waved a hand in dismissal. "All right, I won't keep you."

"Good night, sir."

THERE WAS LITTLE TRAFFIC AT this time of night and Henshaw made good time crossing from Manhattan over to Brooklyn. He located the correct street, then parked in the garage below the apartment building where his team had set up shop two days earlier.

He rode the elevator to the fifth floor and knocked on the entrance to apartment nine. After a moment the door opened slightly and Henshaw found himself looking down the barrel of a 9 mm handgun. Its owner recognized him and let him through the door.

The surveillance team of eight individuals allowed them to box the target and handle the job properly. If one of them was in danger of being seen, then another member of the team could either step up or fall back, preventing them from blowing their cover because Annja had made some sudden move or change of direction.

They thought she might have seen them the day before, because she'd suddenly gone crazy, sprinting down side streets and dashing across traffic. But when she stopped right next to Olivia, and didn't realize that she was part of the surveillance team, they knew she must have caught wind of someone else. That was when they figured out they weren't the only team on the job.

They had relayed the information to Henshaw before he'd left France and he'd given them explicit instructions what to do should they discover who, besides themselves, was following her.

As it turned out, it was a good thing he had.

He went into the kitchen where several of the team were congregating around a fast-food dinner. Pulling up a chair next to Marco, his team leader, he said, "Give me an update, please."

Marco did. He took Henshaw through the entire evening's operation, from when they had picked up Annja that morning outside her loft, all the way to their involvement in the confrontation between Annja and the Dragon's hit team in the subway tunnels hours later.

"Where is she now?"

"She's back in her apartment. You can see her from in there," Marco said, nodding at the closed bedroom door on the other side of the living room.

"Who's got the watch?" Henshaw asked, getting up.

"Jessi and Dave."

"All right, good." Henshaw addressed everyone around the table, and not just Marco, when he said, "Good job, everyone. Get some rest while you can, as I think things are going to start heating up and we want to be ready."

With a chorus of "yes, sirs" at his back, Henshaw crossed the darkened living room, knocked once on the bedroom door and then slipped inside.

The lights in the room were off, to prevent what they were doing from being backlit and allowing someone outside to see in, but there was a little light coming in through the window, at least enough to see the shapes of Jessi and Dave over by the window.

"How's it going?" he asked.

Jessi's soft voice came floating out of the darkness and over to him. "That woman's obsessed. You'd think she'd be exhausted after what happened down in the subway, but she acts as if it was just a walk in the park. She started practicing those crazy martial-arts moves she does the minute she returned and she hasn't stopped since."

Henshaw joined the two of them on the other side of the room. Without saying anything, Dave handed him the binoculars he'd been using to keep their charge in sight.

Annja's building was across the street and one over from the one they occupied. They were on the fifth floor and she was on the fourth, giving them an excellent downward viewpoint into the loft she called home. She had the curtains open at the moment and through them Henshaw could see her working out in the large open space in the middle of the room. She was dressed in a white tank top and a pair of gray sweatpants, with her hair pulled back into a ponytail and her feet bare. In her hands she held her sword and even as he watched she threw herself into another sword kata with deadly concentration.

Henshaw remembered the way she'd handled it that night at Roux's and for the first time he realized just how good with it she had become. It was like an extension of her body and as she twisted, turned and flowed around the room in the midst of her practice; he sometimes had a hard time recognizing where the sword ended and she began.

Keep it up, Annja, he told her silently. You might just need it.

And she did keep it up.

Long into the night.

With only her silent, watchful guardians to keep her company.

20

Switzerland, 2003

Shizu entered the room with more than a bit of trepidation. It had been several years since Toshiro had pronounced her ready to take her place in the world and she had used the time as she'd been instructed, traveling and learning. She had grown up considerably in those years, her core toughened and her edge sharpened by what she had seen and done, just like a sword that is tested again and again until it is pronounced ready.

Less than a week earlier she had received a message through the special channels that had been set up just for that purpose, a series of dead drops and hidden Internet communications. The message had asked her to travel to Switzerland. Sensei had a new mission for her. The summons had filled her with excitement, had shaken off the lethargy she'd been feeling for the past few months, and she quickly made the necessary arrangements.

The address turned out to be a small, private chateau in the Alps, hidden at the end of a long road that she would have missed if she hadn't known what to look for to find the turnoff from the main road. She arrived late at night and had been met at the door by a manservant who led her to her room, stating that Sensei would see her in the morning.

After breakfast she'd been asked to join Sensei in the study. She entered the room to find him seated behind his desk, reading through a report. He pointed at a chair in front of the desk and went on reading without looking up.

Obedient to his wishes, Shizu sat.

After a few minutes he put the report down and looked at her.

"You are well, Shizu?' Sensei asked, smiling in welcome.

Hearing his voice sent a thrill of delight through her body. It had been years since she had heard him speak to her aloud, but she heard his voice in her dreams each evening and knew she would never forget the sound of it.

"Yes, Sensei," she replied. She did not ask how he was doing in return, as a Westerner might, for he was the master and she was the servant. He would tell her if he wanted her to know.

"Do you know why I have asked you here today?"

"No, Sensei."

"I have a mission for you, Shizu."

She remained silent, patient, content to sit there with

him until he chose to tell her more or not. Either one would be okay with her, if that was what he decided to do.

It wasn't hero worship; it was far beyond that. The man had saved her from slavery. He had given her purpose. Trained her, schooled her. He had made her into who she was today. He'd done it all from a distance, through a menagerie of teachers, but that didn't matter. He was still the one who made it all happen, and long ago Shizu had pledged her heart and soul to him.

She would die for him.

In fact, she had no doubt that some day she would do just that. She couldn't think of a more fitting way to end her life.

Sensei stood behind the desk, looming over her in his height. "As you no doubt have guessed, I have been preparing you for a specific purpose. Like clay in the potter's hands, I have molded and shaped you to fit that purpose, to let you live the life that you were born to live.

"Now the time has come to set you on your way, to make you the light burning in the wilderness, the key for every lock, the whisper behind every door. To set you free so that you can become all that you are destined to become."

He paused, and she could feel his eyes on her, looking her over. "Are you ready, Shizu?

"Only if you say I am, Sensei."

"You are a weapon, Shizu, and it is time to point you at a target."

Shizu's heart raced and her blood sang. It was finally time to put all she had learned to the test.

"Come," he said. "Let me show you your purpose."

He led her across the room and into the next, which was set up like a command center—the walls were covered with charts and photographs and long stretches of dates and names; the tables were littered with boxes of files and computers running massive database searches.

Sensei stepped into the center of the room. Raising his hands, he gestured at the information gathered around him.

"A man died recently. His name is not important. In fact, I doubt we could find three people outside of those who have been in this room who could tell you what it actually was. He acquired a new identity long ago, one that he built into a legend, and it is that legend that I am interested in. Go on, take a look around."

It soon became apparent that the man, whatever his name, had been an international assassin of no little skill. His long list of targets included ambassadors, government ministers, diplomats, even bankers and prominent businessmen. They were from more than a dozen countries. He had been like a ghost, infiltrating heavily guarded locations to deliver death by his own hand rather than with a bullet or a bomb, and the more she read, the more respect and admiration Shizu felt for this man. The work he had done. The skill with which he had done it.

Sensei must have noted her reaction. He said, "He was known as the Dragon and he elevated killing to an art form. You, Shizu, are going to take his place and be his successor."

Shizu spun around, shock and surprise flooding her system.

"Successor?" she asked.

Sensei nodded. "The man was unimportant, but the legend he created, the symbol he represented, that is something too precious to be lost. For the past ten years, Shizu, I have been training you to revive the legend, to become the new Dragon."

He gestured at the information around him again. "Study what is here. Learn who he was. How he killed. What it was that let an ordinary man, a cheap killer, become the myth that the world feared. This chateau will be your home, your base of operations. The staff has been instructed to serve your every need and there is money in an account to cover any expenses you might have.

"And when at last you are ready, I have a very special target for you."

21

The news the next morning was full of stories about the shoot-out in the subway. Only one of the television stations mentioned the mysterious woman who, they claimed, was at the heart of it all, Annja was relieved. The last thing she needed was to be in the middle of a major news story, never mind have someone recognize her as the host of *Chasing History's Monsters*. If they did, she'd have paparazzi camped out up and down her street. The police would certainly want to hear her side of the story as well, to say the least. She was happy to see the majority of the news channels were calling it a gang-related event, which she knew would sink people's interest in it faster than the *Titanic*.

Besides, she had more important things to concentrate on. She knew that the sword the Dragon carried was the key to the whole situation. If she could understand the weapon, she could understand its bearer. So as soon as it was late enough the following morning, she made a series of phone calls and arranged to meet with Dr. Matthew Yee, curator of the Asian Hall at the American Museum of Natural History and the closest thing that New York City had to an expert on samurai culture.

He agreed to see her when she mentioned a Japanese sword with a dragon emblem etched into the blade. He had some free time late in the afternoon where he could fit her in, which meant that she had the whole morning to kill while she waited.

She decided to pay a visit to the New York Public Library, specifically the research section, and see if they had any information on the Dragon's past or present that she might not yet be aware of.

The New York Public Library actually consisted of eighty-nine separate libraries—four nonlending research libraries, four main lending libraries, a library for the blind and physically handicapped and seventy-seven neighborhood branch libraries in the three boroughs it served. But it was the building on Fifth Avenue between Fourtieth and Forty-second streets that most people thought of when the library came to mind. The two stone statues of the lions outside the main entrance, named Fortitude and Patience, seemed to guard the entrance from unwanted troublemakers and were the public face of the library the world over. As Annja walked past them on her way into the building, she gave the closest one a quick pat on the head.

"Good kitty," she said, and laughed aloud at her own joke.

The library held in excess of fifty million items, from books to periodicals to film and video. She hoped that somewhere, in all that data, she could find something new to help her understand just why the Dragon had taken an interest in her.

She started with the periodicals first. The assassinations had occurred in different countries, but the targets had all been prominent enough that the American media had reported on them, as well. Unfortunately, the reports were dry, devoid of all but the most basic of facts, and Annja gleaned little from them that she didn't already know. Her fluency in several languages allowed her to check out some of the foreign editions, too, but the end result was the same.

After an hour Annja decided to switch tactics. If she couldn't find anything specific about the Dragon, maybe she could track down the Dragon's sword.

Much of what she uncovered in the next hour was material she already knew, such as the fact that Japanese swords were classified by the length of the blade, with the shortest being a *tanto* and the longest being a *katana*, and that the majority of them came from five houses, or schools, of craftsmanship. She discovered a catalog of signatures for swordsmiths all the way back to the twelfth century, but none of the images matched the one she had drawn while in her trance. There were a few that were close, and she made a note to ask Dr. Yee about them later.

THE DRAGON HAD NOTED THE watchers of Annja's apartment the day before. They were good, just not good enough, and sometimes it was that little bit that made all the difference in who came out on top.

Like now.

Dressed as a plumber in a grease-stained coverall and driving a battered old van, the Dragon showed up outside Annja's apartment building about fifteen minutes after she had departed. The building had a security gate, but getting inside was just a matter of pressing several of the buttons on the directory and waiting for someone to hit the buzzer without bothering to ask who it was.

It didn't take more than two tries. It rarely did.

Once inside the building, the Dragon went directly to Annja's apartment on the fourth floor, knocked and pretended to be waiting for someone to answer the door. A long look around showed that the hall was empty, so out of the tool bag the Dragon was carrying came a crowbar. The locks themselves might be sturdy, but the wood around them was as old as the rest of the building. It didn't take long to pop the locks and gain entry.

The loft was an open floor plan, with a large window occupying one entire side. Thankfully the curtains had been left drawn and the Dragon didn't have to worry about the observers across the way taking note of what was happening.

At first, the Dragon just stood there in the center of the room, soaking up the atmosphere of the place, trying to get a feeling for the woman who lived there. There was a sense of a life lived in constant motion, of comings and goings without any real time in between.

It felt more like a way station than a home to the Dragon—a not-unfamiliar feeling.

After that the loft was searched quickly, efficiently and with the kind of care that would make it nearly impossible to prove that anyone had gone through the place. If cabinets were opened, they were closed again. If objects were moved, they were put back in the exact position as before.

The Dragon wasn't looking for anything in particular—just the opposite, in fact. The goal was to learn as much about the target as possible and the best place to do that was in the target's own home. That was where people felt safe, where they were free to let their hair down and be themselves, where all the secrets they kept hidden from the world were revealed. The types of clothing they wore, the magazines they read, the shows they recorded on their DVRs—all these things could reveal important character quirks that might help the Dragon complete the assignment.

There were some interesting facts on display in this apartment. The clothing in the closet and in the wardrobe indicated a woman who was comfortable in her appearance; she didn't need fancy clothing to make her feel more feminine or attractive. The books scattered throughout the place indicated a curious mind, one that was able to compartmentalize a whole host of topics at the same time, if the number of volumes that held bookmarks were any indication of her current reading habits. The food in the pantry—or rather, the lack thereof—

gave mute witness to that fact that this was a woman who rarely cooked for herself.

In one corner of the apartment the Dragon found a padded workout area and a wall covered with a collection of martial-arts weapons—a *sai,* a pair of *bokken,* a *bo* staff, assorted throwing knives of different lengths and weights, even two different sets of samurai swords.

The weapons came from a variety of countries and a mix of styles. Forget being proficient, if she even had a working knowledge of all of them she would be an opponent worth fighting.

The mix of ancient pottery, artifacts and mementos from dig sites across the world supported the Dragon's view of the woman as being a modern nomad. She was in so many other places that she did not have time to be at home.

Nearly half an hour had passed since the Dragon had entered the apartment and that was pushing it. The target might come back at any moment, so it was time to finish and get out of there.

The final bits of stage dressing didn't take long. The tool bag was a bit heavier upon exiting than it had been on entry, but that couldn't be helped.

The Dragon left the building, climbed back inside the van and drove off. The items that had been taken from the apartment would be tossed into various Dumpsters a few blocks away; they were just window dressing, after all.

ANNJA STEPPED AWAY FROM the stairs and noticed the damaged door right away. It hung slightly open and even from this distance she could see the gouges in the frame where a crowbar or tire iron had been used to force the locks.

"Crap!"

Annja considered returning to the street and calling the cops. After all, the thief might still be inside. But she'd faced down much worse than a punk involved in a little breaking and entering, so she decided to have a look around first. If she still needed the cops, then she'd make the call.

She approached her apartment and cautiously pushed the door open the rest of the way. She stood in the doorway, listening for sounds of someone moving about inside, but didn't hear anything.

Emboldened, she stepped inside the apartment, and closed the door behind her with her foot.

She called forth her sword and, with it in hand, she made a thorough search of the premises. When she was satisfied that she was alone, that the thief had long since fled, she sent the sword away and tried to make a list of what was missing.

It didn't take long. Her Blu-ray player, her Xbox console and a few other assorted electronics, stuff that could be pawned off easily without too much of a hassle. Her passport and other documentation were still in the desk drawer where she normally left them and none of the artifacts in her collection had been disturbed, which led her to believe that this was a simple smash and grab.

The fact that the thief had chosen her apartment rather than the one on the third floor was pure chance, it seemed.

Or was it? She wondered if there might be a connection between the events of the past few days and the break-in, but after giving it some thought she dismissed the idea as being just a bit too paranoid. Unless the Dragon had suddenly taken a liking to Guitar Hero 4, she couldn't see any reason for her stuff to be missing.

No, she decided, it had to be a simple B and E.

And the truth was that break-ins like this happened all the time in New York, and Annja had been around long enough to know that the cops wouldn't be able to do much about it. Maybe her stuff would turn up, maybe it wouldn't; they weren't going to go out of their way to track down a petty thief with all the other problems the city had.

A glance at the clock told her it was getting late. She didn't have much time before she had to get to her meeting with Dr. Yee. The police report could wait, she decided. It was only for insurance purposes, anyway. She had to get the door fixed.

It cost her extra to get the guy to come out immediately, but inside of an hour she had the doorframe fixed and new locks installed. By then it was time for her to leave for her appointment.

As ANNJA PULLED UP IN a cab in front of the museum's entrance on Central Park West, with its towering white columns and its bronze statue of President Theodore Roosevelt on horseback, Annja was hopeful that Dr. Yee's expertise could fill in the missing pieces that her research that morning had not. With his help, maybe she could identify the sword.

The museum was one of the largest in the country, with forty-two permanent exhibits and a handful of temporary ones at any given time. Its massive stone edifice stretched out over several city blocks, attracting tourists just for its architecture alone. Even in midweek it was busy, and Annja stood in the foyer for a moment, trying to decide the best course of action to take in order to find Dr. Yee. As it turned out, he found her, having been waiting in the area and overhearing her tell the guard that she had an appointment.

Dr. Yee turned out to be a good-looking guy in his mid-thirties, with a quick smile and an encyclopedic knowledge of Japanese culture from the early Heian period to the Meijii Restoration and the dismantling of the samurai class.

"It is a pleasure to meet you, Miss Creed," he said, shaking her hand and looking her over with an openly appraising eye. "I must say that you are not quite what I was expecting."

"Annja, please. And why is that?" she asked, curious.

"While all geeks might dream of meeting a beautiful woman with knowledge about a legendary sword, very few of us actually believe it will ever happen and even fewer get to fulfill that dream. And you can call me Matthew, by the way." He said it all rather lightly, with a just the right hint of self-deprecation, and Annja couldn't help but laugh.

Good looking and a sense of humor. An interesting combination.

"Come on. We can talk in my office."

He led her down the hall to a door marked Staff and removed a plastic key card from his pocket, which he swiped through a security reader next to the door. There was a click as the lock disengaged. He pulled the door open and held it for her, then resumed his position beside her as they walked through the maze of corridors on the other side. Annja had done a few odd jobs for the museum and had been there before, but she still couldn't help but peer inside each room as they passed, looking to see what treasures they were unearthing elsewhere in the world.

They finally reached their destination—a corner office overlooking the park—and Annja's estimation of the power Dr. Yee held within the museum hierarchy rose a few notches. Then she noticed the beautifully restored *yoroi,* or samurai battle armor, standing in one corner. The black leather and gleaming iron was set off by the glaring aspect of the battle mask, or *mempo,* that sat atop the figure. She stepped closer, intrigued.

Noting her admiration, Dr. Yee asked, "Like it?"

"It's gorgeous," she breathed, unable to take her eyes off it.

Yee stepped closer. "Isn't it, though? See the butterfly pattern?" he asked, pointing at the gold filigree that formed the shadow of a butterfly in the center of the chest piece.

Annja nodded.

"It's the symbol of one of the minor houses of the Taira clan, who favored it for its elegant symmetry and delicate design. Unfortunately, they were wiped out by the Minamoto clan at the battle of Dan-no-ura in 1185 and very few of their arms and armor remain intact. It took me fourteen months of around-the-clock work to restore this one to the shape it is in today, but it was worth every second."

She could hear the pride in his voice over a job well done and she knew that she had found a kindred spirit, at least when it came to an appreciation of history and the lessons they could teach.

"I've been meaning to add it to the Hall of Asian Peoples all week, but somehow, every time I go to do so, I find some excuse to keep it here a few days longer. Silly of me, I know, but I just love to look at it."

Annja could totally relate.

After a moment, Yee finally tore himself away from his admiration of the armor and said, "I'm sorry. Where are my manners? Please, have a seat," indicating a chair in front of his desk. As Annja sat, he walked around to the other side of his desk to the room's only other chair.

"Now, what can I do for you?"

Annja explained that in order to help support her time in the field, she occasionally took on privately funded work confirming the provenance of various items for museums, auction houses and the like.

"About a week ago I was asked to investigate a man's claims that the *katana* he had in his possession was of a unique nature, with serious historical value. He plans on auctioning it off in a few weeks and wanted to get a better understanding of the market value before doing so."

"This is the weapon you mentioned on the phone?"

"Yes. I've never seen anything like it and I'm concerned by that. My knowledge of weaponry is fairly extensive and I can recognize many of the primary swordsmiths from the period, but this is one I've never seen before."

Yee smiled. "Given the number of swordsmiths who have practiced the art through the years, it's not surprising that you didn't recognize one of the minor houses. There were literally hundreds of them, though they could all be traced back, eventually, to the big five."

Annja had studied martial arts, particularly sword arts, long enough to be able to recite them from memory and she did so now, to show Yee she really wasn't a complete novice. "Right, the Yamato, Yamashiro, Bizen, Soshu and Mino."

"Very good," Yee said, and Annja noted that he at least had the decency to blush at little at the professorial air he had assumed.

"The collector in question wouldn't turn over the sword even temporarily for an independent examination, nor would he allow any photographs to be taken for fear that they would leak on to the Internet, but I took the time to recreate the etching and the *mei* by hand and I have that for you to examine."

The *mei* was the set of kanji characters on the end of the blade just above the hilt, the signature of the artist who created it. She'd tried to identify it through the usual channels, but hadn't had any luck.

She took the page from her backpack that contained the drawing of the sword and passed it over to Dr. Yee. A little self-consciously he removed a pair of wire-framed glasses from his pocket, put them on and then took the drawing from her to have a look.

Annja watched as his expression grew more intent and he pulled the picture closer to his face for a better look.

His voice was tight when he asked, "This is the *mei* exactly as you saw it on the blade?"

As exact as you can be when the blade is trying to take your head off, was Annja's first thought, but she didn't say that. Instead, she replied, "The mark was worn and faded, so I'm not one hundred percent certain. Why?"

Dr. Yee looked up at her. "We're faced with two possibilities here. If the mark is complete as it is, then I have to admit that I am not familiar with the swordsmith who fashioned it, either. That would mean he would have been a very minor player and would disprove your client's claim that the weapon was of serious historical value."

Dr. Yee got up and came back around his desk to stand next to her, holding the drawing so she could see it. "However, if we assume that the *mei* is, in fact, incomplete due to the condition of the blade and we add one little mark here—" he drew a single short line extending outward from the edge of the rest "—well, then, I'd have to say that not only is this sword of rather important historical significance, but it just might be the archaeological find of the century with regard to Japanese history. Never mind, for all practical purposes, priceless."

Annja felt her heartrate quicken and it had nothing to do with the nearness of the good-looking doctor. "Okay, I'll play along. Let's say that I did miss that little mark. It is small, as you said, and it is in an area of the blade that is rather worn, so it's possible that's exactly what happened. What does that mean? Who created the sword?"

Yee straightened, a big smile on his face, as if he had just won the lottery not once, but twice.

"I'd bet my career that Sengo Muramasa fashioned that sword. And if he did, it isn't just any sword, but the last sword he ever produced, the famed Juuchi Yosamu, Ten Thousand Cold Nights."

As Yee pronounced the sword's name, a chill ran down Annja spine. Totally appropriate, she thought, for the weapon that had nearly decapitated her. She didn't know much about Muramasa. She'd heard the name, but she wasn't sure where or in what context. She said as much to Yee.

"I'm not surprised," he replied. "There was a definite campaign to eradicate his work from history and most of the references that survive today are so fanciful in nature that most think he is just a figure of myth and folklore. They couldn't be farther from the truth.

"Come on, let's go down to the hall so I can show you a few things and I'll tell you about Muramasa along the way."

Yee went on to explain that Muramasa had been one of the most accomplished swordsmiths in all of Japanese history, second only to Soshu Masamune himself. Both men lived and worked in the Kamakura period. "In fact, there is a legend that a contest was organized between the two to see who could produce the finer blade. The contest was designed so that each man would dip his sword into a small stream with the cutting edge facing the current. Muramasa went first, plunging his weapon into the flow of the river. Anything and everything that passed by the weapon, from the drifting leaves in the current to the fish that swam in the depths to the very air hissing by the blade, was cut in two."

They stopped for a moment while Yee negotiated locked set of doors with a pass card and a key ring, and the continued.

"Next it was Masamune's turn. He lowered his sword into the water and waited patiently. Everything that came toward the blade was redirected around it, unharmed and undamaged. From the leaves to the fish to the air itself—all of them passed around the blade without resistance.

"As you can imagine, Muramasa was certain that he had won the challenge—after all, his sword had cut everything, and wasn't that the purpose of a sword? He began to insult Masamune for his poor weapon. But a wandering monk had witnessed the whole affair and he offered his own conclusions. 'The first blade is, of course, a worthy blade, but it is a bloodthirsty, evil blade that does not discriminate between who it will cut and who it will spare. The other blade, on the other hand, was clearly the finer of the two, for it did not needlessly cut or destroy that which is innocent.'"

Annja smiled. "An interesting tale."

"Ah, but it gets better, it really does," Yee said. "The reason that you are most likely not familiar with Muramasa blades is that they gained a reputation for being evil swords that lusted after blood. Some even thought that such a blade should not be resheathed until it had drawn blood. Doing anything less was terribly bad luck."

"So what about the dragon etching?" Annja asked. "What does that tell us?"

"That is how I recognized the sword as possibly being the Juuchi Yosamu. You see, Muramasa's name has not enjoyed the fame it deserved because the shogun, Tokugawa Ieyasu, ordered his blades outlawed and destroyed whenever found. Regardless of whether or not the blades were actually evil, they did seem to have a negative effect on the Tokugawa House. Kiyoyasu, the grandfather of the first shogun, was cut in two in 1535 when his retainer attacked him with a Muramasa blade. Ieyasu's father, Matsudaira, was killed by another man wielding a Muramasa blade, and even Ieyasu cut himself severely on his own *wakizashi,* or short sword, which was also made by Muramasa. When his own son was beheaded with a Muramasa blade, the shogun had finally had enough. He banned their creation, possession and use throughout the empire."

By now they had entered the public areas of the museum and Yee had to speak louder in order to be heard as they cut across a busy exhibit hall.

"The response to the shogun's edict was mixed. Many went out and sold off their Muramasa blades hoping that no one else had yet heard the news that they were about to become worthless. Others defaced the blades, scraping off the *mei* so that no one could tell that it was a Muramasa blade. A few hoarded the weapons, believing they might bring them personal power and financial gain. Those who were found to be hiding Muramasa blades were often executed on the spot, including the magistrate of Nagasaki who, in 1634, was discovered to be hoarding more than twenty-four Muramasa blades."

At last they reached the Asian Hall, which, as fortune would have it, was actually closed until the morning for renovations of the existing displays. With his pass card, Yee let them inside and the noise level dropped considerably.

"So what makes the Juuchi Yosamu so special? Just the fact that it is a Muramasa blade?" Annja asked.

Yee shook his head. "Not just any blade, but *the* blade. The last weapon he ever produced.

"You see, legend has it that it was just before winter when Muramasa found out about the shogun's edit. He knew that the imperial troops would be coming soon to destroy his forge and seize any weapons he had produced. But the swordsmith lived in a small valley between three major mountain ranges. The shogun's men did not make it up the mountains in time before the winter snows came and so they were forced to wait another three months until the pass cleared enough for them to reach the swordsmith's home.

"Muramasa used those months wisely, creating his ultimate masterpiece, blending every bit of his anger, jealousy, hatred and desire for vengeance into the blade until the blade itself took on a darker hue than normal.

Some say it even gleamed with hunger whenever it drew close to its enemies."

Annja turned her eye inward until she could see Joan's sword, her sword, hanging there in the otherwhere, waiting for her to need it again. The blade glowed with a faint luminescence. Did the Dragon's blade do that? she wondered.

"Unlike other swordsmiths, Muramasa never etched designs into the blades of his *katana*. He felt that it was doing the weapon a disservice to deface it in such a manner. But he made an exception with his final masterpiece. That one, legend has it, had the image of a rampant dragon added to the blade just above the hilt, its claws stretching downward along the length of the sword as if reaching for the sword's target, a visual representation of all the darkness he had poured into its construction.

"I would suspect it probably looked very much like the dragon in the drawing you just showed me."

They were deep in the Hall of Asian Peoples and Yee steered them over to a large display focused on the samurai eras of ancient Japan.

Stopping in front of a particular case that held several different types of sword, he said, "Ah, here we are!"

He took a *katana* from its stand inside the case and withdrew the blade so that Annja could see it.

"Look here," he said, pointing at a line that ran down the middle of the blade from the narrow tip toward the hilt. "This is known as the *hamon*. It is the point where the sharper steel, which forms the blade's edge, meets the softer steel at its core, which gives the blade its exceptional flexibility. During the sword-making process, the smith would paint over this line with a very thin mixture of clay and ash and then heat it all over again, to help bond the two sections together. What was unique about a sword fashioned by Muramasa was the identical *hamon* that could be found on either side of the blade. It was one of his trademarks."

He flipped the sword over to show her that the line tracing down the opposite side of the blade was identical to the former. Annja gasped when she realized that the blade in his hand was a Muramasa.

"May I?" Annja asked.

"Certainly," Yee said. "But be careful because the blade is very sharp."

Annja had stopped listening, however. She had taken the sword, leaving the scabbard in Yee's hands, and had stepped into the center of the room where there was more open space than by the displays. She wanted to get a feel for this blade, get a sense of what she was facing in the presence of its more famous cousin. She slid into the first of several moves of an advanced sword kata, testing the weapon. It was lighter than her own sword, and more maneuverable, but did not have the kind of reach that she liked. She realized quickly, in fact, that she preferred the heavier blade of her broadsword. Still, there was no doubting the craftsmanship inherent in the *katana;* it was perfectly balanced and cut the air with precision.

She stopped what she was doing and turned, only to find Dr. Yee staring at her with an open mouth.

"That was so incredibly sexy," he breathed, as if afraid to break the spell, then blushed scarlet when he realized that he had said it aloud.

Annja laughed. "Look out, Uma Thurman, here I come," she said, knowing Yee would get the *Kill Bill* reference.

She brought the sword closer to her face so that she could get a look at the *mei* near the hilt. Yee had been right; it was identical to the one on the sword used by the Dragon, if you added in the missing crosspiece on the H-like character.

She walked over to her companion, accepted the scabbard from his hands and moved to slide the sword back inside. As she did, she felt a sharp pain in her finger and looked down to find she had nicked herself on the edge of the blade. A drop of blood welled up as she stuck her finger in her mouth.

"The curse of Muramasa strikes again," Yee said, with a little something in his voice that said he was more than familiar with the bloodthirsty nature of that particular weapon.

Talking around the finger in her mouth, Annja got back to her cover story. "So, how do I tell if my client's sword is really the Juuchi Yosamu?"

"The first thing I would do is check the *hamon*. If they are identical, front and back, you will have your first bit of proof. Then see if the owner will let you examine the *mei* under magnification or after it has been polished and cleaned. That might help bring out the missing crossbar to confirm it.

"I have to say this, however. If it is the Yosamu, your client is going to be hard-pressed to sell it for what it is worth. That weapon would be considered by many to be a cultural treasure of the Japanese and I, for one, would want to see it returned to its rightful government. It should not be in the hands of a private individual."

Annja was in total agreement with him. Relieving the Dragon of the sword was her highest priority.

"I couldn't agree with you more, Dr. Yee," she said.

22

That night, Annja dreamed of the Dragon.

She was being hunted through the woods by the scaled beast from which the assassin had derived his nickname and it would only be a matter of moments before the creature found her.

Annja ran frantically through the thick underbrush while behind her the beast closed in. She could hear its breathing, could smell its sulphurous stench, and knew that it was gaining ground faster, that she wouldn't be able to outrun it.

She ran on until the trail she was following opened up into a canyon in the midst of the woods, a canyon with only one way out.

She was trapped!

A shriek filled the sky around her and sent her heart hammering into overdrive. Slowly Annja turned to face the beast...

She woke up.

It was just a dream, she told herself as her heart beat frantically and she fought to catch her breath.

She was about to roll over and take a sip of water from the glass on her bed stand when she realized that she wasn't alone.

There was someone in the room with her!

She lay still on the bed, doing what she could to keep her breathing steady, and looked around through eyes that were barely open.

There was a shadowy form off to her right, slowly crossing the room and moving closer to her bed.

Wait, Annja said to herself.

The intruder didn't make a sound, crossing the floor like a ghost in the night. He stood at the very foot of the bed, looking down at her. Annja could feel the other's gaze, could see eyes gleaming in the morning half-light. Whoever it was, he was dressed to disguise his appearance, in dark clothing and a hooded mask.

Just as the Dragon and his men had worn back in Paris.

Wait...

As Annja lay there, doing all she could to make it seem as if she were still asleep, the intruder slowly brought a hand out from behind his back, revealing the long gleaming blade in it. Slowly the weapon was raised over the intruder's head, ready for the strike.

Now!

As the intruder's sword came whistling down toward where she lay in the bed, Annja threw herself to the side, summoning her own sword as she went.

The intruder's blade slashed through the mattress of her bed, but Annja wasn't there any more. She was on her knees beside the bed and was already in motion, her sword swinging toward the other in a well-executed counterattack.

The intruder reacted with lightning-sharp reflexes, dancing backward out of reach of her weapon.

The move, however, gave Annja the space she needed to get to her feet and brace herself for the next attack.

No sooner had she gotten into a defensive stance than the intruder rushed forward. They exchanged several blows, their swords ringing in the early-morning quiet.

Annja lunged, hoping to slip her sword past the other's guard, but the intruder was too quick for her, jumping on top of the bed and then trying to use the extra foot or so in height he had gained by doing so to his advantage. A vicious overhead stroke nearly took Annja's arm off at the shoulder; she saved herself only by throwing her body backward out of the way and then was forced to scramble to defend against a blistering rain of blows.

She knew the apartment's layout instinctively, something the intruder did not, and so she gained a moment's respite when she managed to put the length of her sofa between them.

That's when the intruder spoke.

"Give it to me and I'll let you live."

The voice was thick and gruff, but obviously disguised as well, and didn't tell her anything about her opponent.

She didn't know what the intruder wanted. Nor was

she naive enough to believe the offer. If she were to lower her guard for even a moment she'd be run through without hesitation. And then he would be free to do whatever he had come here to do.

Fat chance, buddy.

They circled the room, keeping the furniture between them for the moment, each of them preparing for another onslaught. As they did so, the light from the rising sun shot through the window and illuminated the sword held in the intruder's hand. Annja's gaze was immediately drawn to the etching on the blade, just above the hilt.

The etching of a dragon, rampant.

Her eyes widened in shocked recognition and her gaze shifted from the intruder's sword to his face. He wore a mask, but familiar eyes stared back at her from out of its depths.

She was facing the Dragon for a second time!

The Dragon must have seen the recognition in her eyes, for he suddenly rushed forward, intensifying his efforts to catch her in an error and slip a thrust past her guard.

But she was ready for him this time, and it was actually Annja who drew first blood. She feinted to the left, drawing his thrust, and then spun about, her sword slashing out and drawing a furrow down the length of his thigh.

The scent of fresh blood hit the air.

The Dragon faltered, perhaps surprised at having been so marked, and Annja used that moment to put a little more space between them. She was ready and waiting for the next onslaught when he did a surprising thing.

The Dragon abruptly turned and rushed across the loft, headed for the front door.

By the time Annja had managed to recover from her surprise, the other had made it halfway across the apartment.

Oh, no, you don't, Annja thought. You're not getting away that easily.

Annja rushed after the intruder. As she did, she switched the position of the sword in her hands, until she was holding the blade like a spear.

When the intruder was forced to slow down for a second to negotiate the door, which had been closed again behind him, Annja wound up and let fly.

The sword whistled through the air across the remaining space of the apartment.

The intruder managed to get the door partially open and was trying to slip through it just as the sword slammed point first into its surface.

It had been a good throw, and if the door hadn't come open right at that second, the sword might have buried itself in the intruder's back. As it was it managed to grab a piece of his sleeve, pinning his arm against the door.

As Annja charged forward, the intruder looked back in her direction, and for the first time she got a good look at the intruder's face.

Even covered by a hood and mask that left only the eyes free, Annja recognized the face she was staring at. She'd been staring at her drawing of that face for days. She'd been seeing it in her dreams. She had absolutely no doubt that she was gazing at the face of the Dragon.

After all she'd been through trying to find him, she couldn't let him get away!

The Dragon pulled on his sleeve, trying to free himself, but the sword had driven itself deep into the wood and there was no way he was going to be able to pull himself free.

Annja was closing in fast, thinking she just might reach the door before anything else could happen, when the Dragon raised his sword and brought it down sharply on edge of his sleeve where it was nailed to the door.

As Annja reached for him, he used his now-rescued limb to fling the door open, directly into her path. When she skidded to a stop to keep from colliding with the door, the Dragon slipped through into the hallway beyond.

Rather than spending precious seconds to yank the sword free, Annja simply willed it back into the other-where, freeing it from the door.

She followed the intruder into the hallway.

She turned left outside her apartment, assuming her uninvited guest would head for the ground floor, and as a result she lost a few precious seconds before she realized that he had gone the other way, toward the stair-case leading to the roof instead.

Annja skidded to a halt and turned around, heading back in the other direction. She could hear footsteps on the stairs, just above her head. By the time she reached the steps, a crash echoed from above. Annja knew that sound; the door to the roof had just been thrown open.

She took the steps two at a time and as she reached the landing above she summoned her sword again.

The door to the rooftop was directly in front of her. She grabbed the handle, said a quick prayer to lady luck, and, yanking the door open, threw herself forward in a somersault onto the rooftop.

The Dragon was standing on the small structure that covered the stairwell door to the roof and would have cut Annja's head from her shoulders had she gone through the door upright.

Rolling to her feet, Annja realized that she was standing on the rooftop in her pajamas with nothing on her feet while waving a large sword around in the air.

If any of her neighbors caught sight of her…

The Dragon wasn't waiting around, however. As dawn's red light burst over the horizon, he was silhouetted there for the briefest of moments and then he jumped off and raced across the rooftop, intent on making the leap to the next building.

Annja gave chase.

The rough surface of the rooftop cut into her feet, but she was so close to catching the Dragon and getting some answers that she wasn't about to stop. She released her sword, knowing she could call it again. She needed the extra speed she could gain by sending it away.

The edge of the roof loomed ahead of the Dragon.

"WHAT THE HELL?"

Dave bolted upright in his chair, frantically rubbing the sleep from his eyes. He had the watch, but apparently he'd dozed off a little because one moment he was watching the darkened windows of Annja Creed's apartment and the next thing he knew there was a sword battle going on inside.

"Hey, guys! We've got a situation in here!"

A moment later the door to the bedroom that served as their observation post burst open and Marco rushed inside, Jessi right on his heels.

"What have we got?" Marco asked.

Dave simply pointed.

The two of them, Annja and whoever the guy in the black mask was, were racing around the bedroom, and not in a good way. It was still pretty dark, the sun just starting to peek over the horizon, but because of their position they had a pretty good view inside the apartment and could see them hacking and slashing away at each other.

Suddenly the intruder made a break for the door and they all watched in near awe as Annja reversed the sword she was using and hurled it, spearlike across the room to pin her opponent in place.

"Son of a… Did you see that?" Dave gasped.

Marco was already headed out the door, rallying the troops as he went. "Code Red!" he yelled. "Code Red."

They'd worked out a system for all their problems when they had first come together as a team. Code Red was the highest warning level they had, reserved for when a principal was in deep trouble.

Marco stuck his head back in the door to the room where Dave was. "Keep watch," he said sternly. "Don't turn this into a fiasco."

Dave waved him away. "Yeah, yeah, get going!"

As Marco rallied the troops, Dave kept watch. Like

Annja had done only moments before, he thought the intruder would go down instead of up.

"They're on the roof!" Dave yelled when he realized what was happening. Marco and the others charged out the door. Dave couldn't run, not with a lame leg from a previous operation, so he always got left behind. But this time he didn't mind, because out of all of them, he was the one with the front-row seat.

He sat back and watched the battle unfold on the rooftop.

Despite the danger to their principal, one thing kept running through his mind.

Damn, does she look good in pajamas!

As THE DRAGON SPED toward the edge of the roof, Annja realized his intent. The next building was close enough to reach with a decent leap and it looked as if that was exactly what he intended to try.

If she could catch him when he came down…

Annja reached deep and found a bit more speed, ignoring the added pain she felt as her feet cut deeper into the gravel covering the rooftop.

Worry about your feet later, she told herself.

When the Dragon jumped, Annja was only a step behind.

She slammed into him in midleap and rode his body down onto the adjacent rooftop. The impact knocked her clear, but she was up again in a heartbeat, already moving in with hands and feet at the ready.

The Dragon stood and Annja waded in, throwing a

jab, uppercut, jab combination, but the Dragon blocked all three. He lashed out with a side kick, designed to cave in a rib or two, but Annja skipped away and his foot hit only empty air.

They circled each other, hands weaving back and forth, both a distraction and a means to stay loose, ready to respond no matter what the strike.

This time it was the Dragon who attacked first, coming in hard and fast with a wave of punches followed by a high kick to the head. Annja blocked the punches and then dropped to the ground, swinging her legs around in a scything motion, trying to cut the Dragon's feet out from under him. Anticipating the move, the Dragon leaped over backward in a somersault that put him a few feet away from her.

Again they closed, trading blow after blow. Annja blocked most of what came at her, though a few strikes did manage to get through. She took one to the ribs and then caught a glancing blow off the side of the head that momentarily stunned her.

She shook it off, but the damage was done. That blow had given the Dragon a few precious seconds to break away and start the run for the next rooftop.

Doggedly, Annja went in pursuit.

MARCO AND THE REST of the surveillance team spilled out onto the street, headed for Annja's building. They kept looking upward, waiting for one of the combatants to make a wrong move and end up splattered on the sidewalk after a four-story fall.

Back in the observation room, Dave continued to give them the play-by-play over the radio.

THE DRAGON REACHED THE edge of the roof and jumped. He did it without hesitation, without a second thought, and so Annja followed suit.

Unfortunately, the blow to the head had slowed her down a bit, and the cuts on her feet dropped her speed even more. When she reached the edge of the roof she planted one foot on the small ledge that ran around the top and launched herself into space, only realizing that she didn't have enough speed when she was halfway across the gap.

She wasn't going to make it.

As she watched, the Dragon touched down on the other side and kept going, widening the distance between them without looking back.

The edge of the roof was coming up fast and Annja could tell she was going to be an inch, maybe two, short. She stretched as far as she could, reaching out with her fingers, praying all the while.

One hand caught the edge of the roof, barely grabbing on with just the tips of her fingers.

Her body slammed into the side of the building, the force of the impact almost jarring her loose, but Annja held on with all her strength, crimping her fingers the way she'd once been shown in rock-climbing class. By some miracle she managed to remain hanging on to the edge of the building, though by only the thinnest of margins.

Having originally been worried that the Dragon was

going to get away, now all Annja could do was hope that he didn't come back. If he wanted to kill her, now would be the perfect time. All it would take would be a little tap on the fingers and she'd plunge to the concrete below.

"LOOK!" JESSI SHOUTED AND as one the group turned to follow her pointed finger. Above their heads, between the buildings, they could see someone hanging off the edge of the roof.

Marco radioed Dave. "Can you tell who it is?" he asked.

"No. They're out of my sight now, behind the next building over."

Terrified that Creed was going to die on his watch and he'd have to explain how it had all gone wrong to Henshaw, Marco rushed for the entrance to the building, praying he'd be in time.

SLOWLY, EVER SO SLOWLY, Annja reached up with her other hand, being careful not to twist and pull herself off the roof. Gradually, inch by inch, she managed to get her other hand over the edge of the rooftop.

She rested there a minute, then began to pull herself upward, as if doing a chin-up, intending to get herself high enough to throw an elbow over the edge and secure some leverage to pull the rest of her body back to safety.

Unfortunately, the roof had other ideas.

The low wall that lined the outer edge of the roof had seen more than its share of harsh winters, acid rain and time's steady but corroding hand. The section Annja was clinging to chose that moment to voice its displeasure at the conditions it was forced to endure by crumbling beneath her weight.

One minute she was pulling herself upward, the next she was twisting in the wind again, barely hanging on with one hand, while chunks of masonry plummeted to shatter on the street far below.

She wanted to kick her legs and flail about with her arms, but she fought the instinctual motion that her body cried out for and willed herself to hold still. Any extraneous motion at this point could pull her right off the roof.

To make matters worse, her left hand was starting to slip, as well. She could feel her fingers slowly sliding backward, one millimeter at a time.

She guessed she had less than a minute before her hand would slide totally free.

After that, it was all over.

MARCO DASHED UP THE STAIRS three at a time, muttering under his breath all the while.

"Hold on," he was saying. "Hold on, hold on."

He kept a sharp eye out for whoever it had been that Annja had been chasing, but he didn't meet anyone on the stairs, and by the time he burst onto the rooftop his attention was solely on rescuing the woman whose life he was supposed to be protecting.

He couldn't see her from where he stood and he didn't have time to search every side.

He keyed the radio.

"Which way?" he asked, nearly frantic with worry.

Dave was immediately on the line with an answer. "Left. In the middle."

Marco rushed over to the edge.

ANNJA TRIED TO SWING her right arm up and over the edge, but the motion only served to make her other hand slip faster. She wrapped her thumb over the tops of her fingers, bearing down, but it was too late—she'd slid too far and couldn't find any traction to keep from slipping farther.

"I am not going to die like this!" she said through gritted teeth, and was about to call her sword, thinking she could jam it into the masonry or something as a last-ditch effort, when she heard footsteps charging in her direction.

The Dragon.

Apparently letting her fall to her death wasn't good enough; he had to help her along the way.

Well, two could play at the game.

As her fingers began to slip faster, Annja brought forth her sword. If she was going to die, she would do what she could to take the Dragon with her.

MARCO RUSHED OVER TO the edge. As he drew closer he saw her hand, and watched in dismay as her fingers slid backward.

"No!" he shouted, and dove forward, arms outstretched.

The fingers of his left hand touched something soft, something alive, and he seized it with all the desperation he could muster.

He felt her fingers wrap around his wrist in return, locking them into a mountain climber's grasp.

Then her weight asserted itself and he felt himself being dragged forward.

His head popped over the edge the roof and he found himself staring into those amber eyes he'd first noted in that photograph back in Paris.

The sword that was suddenly thrust upward at his face was a shock.

He closed his eyes and instinctively jerked his head back, while simultaneously trying to brace himself against the pressure that was pulling him forward.

"Hold on, lady!" he shouted, trying to preserve his cover without even thinking about it, so ingrained was the instinct to keep from revealing who he was or what he was truly doing there.

He got his knees braced against the wall and planted his feet, stopping their forward slide. Now all he had to do was pull her up.

ANNJA HAD NO IDEA WHO the guy was or where he had come from, but she was suddenly glad she hadn't skewered him when he'd poked his head over the edge. Jabbing her sword into his chest might have ended his rescue attempt a bit prematurely.

As it was she was starting to doubt that he had the strength to pull her up, but she'd let him worry about that because she could barely feel her arm.

The minute she'd realized he wasn't the Dragon she'd released her sword back into the otherwhere, and now she used her right hand to reach up and grab on to his wrist from the opposite side, trapping his arm between both of her hands.

Well, if you're going to fall, at least you won't be going alone, she thought grimly.

Her Good Samaritan was stronger than he looked and with a few heaves backward he managed to pull her up and over the ledge and back onto the rooftop.

Then he collapsed onto the ground and tried to catch his breath.

Annja didn't blame him; her heart was racing a bit wildly at that moment, as well.

"Are you all right?" he gasped out eventually.

"Yeah. Thanks to you," she said.

He shrugged it off, apparently not the prideful type.

But something wasn't feeling quite right to Annja and she wanted to know more. "How did you know I was in trouble?" she asked, and despite nearly falling off the roof she watched him closely.

He waved his hand vaguely in the direction of the stairwell. "I was on the stairs, headed for my apartment, when I saw you through the window. I knew there was no way you were going to make that jump," he sucked in another lungful of air. "So I ran up the stairs."

"And here you are."

He nodded, and then turned to look at her for the first time since he'd pulled her to safety. "Yep. Here I am."

Good enough, she thought. So far he hadn't said anything about the sword, so maybe she should get out of there while the going was still good.

She climbed shakily to her feet, thanked him again for saving her life and quickly left the roof, and his protests, behind.

It was only when she was halfway down the stairs that it occurred to her to wonder what he was doing up and about at that hour of the day.

Just be thankful he was, she thought, and left it at that.

MARCO MADE SEVERAL HALFHEARTED protests to keep Annja from leaving, but he was relieved when she did. If she had started asking any more questions he would have been hard-pressed to answer them. This way, he at least had a shot at keeping the surveillance team from being compromised.

He waited a good half hour before making his own way back down to street level. Annja Creed was nowhere in sight, so he kept his head down and headed for the preplanned rendezvous point.

Marco wanted to have a long talk with Dave. If he found out he'd been sleeping on watch again…

EXHAUSTED FROM THE FIGHT and from the release of all that adrenaline, Annja returned to her loft just long enough to pack a change of clothes, grab a first-aid kit and throw on a pair of shoes. The Dragon had been in her apartment once, possibly more than that, so it wasn't safe for her to stay there anymore. She knew a decent hotel a few blocks away and she decided to hole up there for the time being until she could figure out just what to do.

She checked in, took a shower and then, using the supplies in the medical kit, tended to her torn and bloody feet.

Remind me never to do that again, she told herself, wincing as she applied hydrogen peroxide to the cuts and then wrapped them in soft gauze to help them heal.

When she was finished, she collapsed onto the bed and fell into a dreamless sleep.

She awoke later that morning to the insistent buzzing of her cell phone.

"Hello?"

"Annja! Thank God I found you. You've got to come down to the studio and fix this!"

She sighed; Doug in a frenzy was really not what she needed right now. "Fix what, Doug?"

"The episode! We've got to trim another six minutes and thirty seconds from the footage. Maybe we could…"

Annja let him drone on for a moment, then cut in when she could. "I'll be down within the hour, Doug. Don't do anything until I get there." She hung up before he could protest further.

Spending a few hours in the editing room with Doug wasn't her idea of a fun time, but she needed to take her mind off the Dragon and her close call from earlier that morning.

Fighting with her producer might be just the thing.

23

Most of Annja's day was taken up with correcting the issues that had come up after Doug had begun to do the final edits on the episode. She spent the afternoon working with him and by the time she was done night had fallen and the streets were full of commuters trying to get home from work. People pushed past on both sides, but she barely noticed, her focus completely inward.

The past few days had been a blur of action and reaction. She was being stalked by an international assassin for reasons unknown, though she was pretty sure it had to do with the sword she carried. She'd been attacked twice in the past forty-eight hours, more than likely by men in the assassin's employ. The assassin himself had broken into her hotel room, sent someone to interrupt her lunch and was, more likely than not, out there, somewhere, right now, watching.

She'd seen a hypnotist, allowed herself to be put in a trance and been able to draw a perfect replication of the emblem on the assassin's own sword, a sword that was most likely cursed and just as mystical as her own. She'd even watched a man die only inches away from her, and she couldn't imagine that death by subway was an easy way to go. Last but not least, the assassin himself broke into her loft and tried to kill her while she slept.

Frankly it was a lot to take in.

Annja walked down the street, lost in thought. She had lots of questions but few answers. What did the Dragon want? How had he found out about her? What did he know about the sword she carried? How did her sword compare to his?

What made it all the more frustrating was that she felt as though the answers were all right there in front of her and she just wasn't seeing them clearly enough to put everything together into a coherent whole. Like having all the pieces of a puzzle but, without a picture to work from, she didn't know if the blue pieces represented the ocean, the sky or some other colored object.

As a scientist, she was used to looking at things through a logical progression that more often than not was based on a cause-and-effect relationship between two items. In order to sort through the mess she found herself in, she decided to apply the same elemental logic and see where that got her.

So what did she know?

She knew there had once been an international hit man known as the Dragon, who apparently had survived the explosion everyone else thought had killed him, and he was following her around New York City.

Garin had claimed that the Dragon carried a sword that was the mystical opposite of her own, the dark to her light. The information she'd managed to haul out of her subconscious while under hypnosis had provided her with the image she'd seen etched onto the Dragon's sword, and her visit to Dr. Yee had revealed that the sword itself might be the fabled Juuchi Yosamu, Ten Thousand Cold Nights, the final *katana* produced by the master swordsmith, Sengo Muramasa. The sword was said to have been instilled with all the bloodthirsty madness that had characterized Muramasa's final days. All of which confirmed what Garin had been suggesting.

The Dragon had passed up the opportunity to kill her on two different occasions; first, during the assault at Roux's estate, and later while she lay sleeping in her hotel room in Paris. Since then his agents had not only followed her about New York, but had tried to kidnap her, as well.

Clearly he wanted something from her.

And there was only one thing, she knew, that was possibly valuable enough for him to go through all the trouble. One thing that he wouldn't be able to get his hands on simply by killing her outright.

Her sword.

It came when she called. It existed to do her bidding and her bidding alone. While she wasn't positive, she suspected that killing her would leave the sword lost in the otherwhere until it chose another bearer, and who knew when that might be?

It was the only thing that made sense.

The Dragon wanted Joan's sword.

With that realization the Dragon's demands from the night before finally made sense. "Give it to me!" he'd said. At the time she'd had no idea what he was referring to. She had, in fact, assumed that he'd been mistaken in thinking that she had some rare or unusual artifact in her possession.

You were right, in a way, she told herself. Except the artifact in question was none other than her sword.

Annja had no intention of giving it to him.

She found herself at the Eighty-first Street entrance to Central Park and decided that a walk through the park would be a nice way to end the evening. The thought of going back to her apartment, the one the Dragon himself had been in on more than one occasion, just wasn't all that appealing at the moment. If she had to, she could always catch a cab back to Brooklyn when she got to the other side, on Fifth Avenue.

There were quite a few people still in the park, despite the fact that evening had come and the sun had already set, and Annja enjoyed the sensation of getting lost among them, anonymous even if only for a few stolen minutes.

She had been wandering the grounds for about fifteen minutes when she saw him.

He was hanging back, not making it too obvious, but

there was no doubt that he was keeping her in sight, lingering in her wake.

He was wearing a dark windbreaker and slacks, with a hat pulled low over his face so that she wasn't able, especially from this distance, to get a good look at his features.

It was at least the second time in as many days that she had been followed and she was starting to resent the attention. They hadn't been shy about chasing her through the subway system and she had the same feeling now; the tourists around her would not be a deterrent to her capture, if that was indeed what he wanted.

For a moment she was tempted to confront him directly, to shout, "Hey, you!" and start striding determinedly toward him, just to see what he would do. Only the idea that he might just pull a gun and simply shoot her, prevented her from such a brash course of action.

Instead of a direct confrontation, she opted for a more covert approach.

ROUX WAS BORED.

He'd only been in the hotel for a little over twenty-four hours, but laying low and staying out of sight was not something he was interested in doing. For a man who had lived as long as he had, he had surprisingly little patience.

He knew Henshaw had things under control with regard to the Dragon's sudden interest in Annja. That wasn't the problem. The problem lay in the fact that if he had to sit there and stare at those same four walls for another minute he was going to go nuts. Why did

Henshaw have him hiding out anyway? Annja was the one in danger, not him!

"Enough of this!" he said to himself, and got up to dress for dinner. Roux had old-fashioned tastes and one of the things that he appreciated about the Waldorf was that you were expected to be properly dressed for dinner. None of this casual-dress nonsense that seemed to have become the norm, and thank the heavens for that, he thought.

Attired in a crisp blue suit and matching tie, Roux headed for the main dining room.

Two hours later he was relaxing after his meal over a glass of brandy when he spotted the most exquisite young woman sitting alone several tables away. She was Asian, looked to be in her twenties, and was dressed in a figure-hugging black dress that highlighted her every curve. She had that classic porcelain-doll look—pale skin, full red lips, her long hair as dark as oil at midnight.

Her beauty wasn't what had attracted his attention, however, but rather the fact that she had been casting surreptitious glances in his direction throughout his meal.

It appeared he'd found something that would make a worthwhile diversion for the evening.

Roux's success with young women was matched only by his skill at the poker table. The trick, he knew, was to make them think it was all their idea.

He caught and held her glance for a long moment, then signaled for his bill. When the waiter brought it, he signed it to his room and, taking his drink with him, he moved across the restaurant to the bar on the other side of the room.

He intentionally chose a seat several chairs away from anyone else and waited, knowing the conclusion was already a foregone one.

"Is anyone sitting here?" a feminine voice asked.

Roux turned to find the young beauty from the restaurant indicating the chair beside him, a smile on her face and a spark in her eyes.

"Please," he replied, smiling back. "Be my guest."

She slid deftly onto the seat, managing to look extraordinarily graceful and at the same time giving him a flash of tanned and supple thigh through the slit in the side of her dress as she did so.

Roux couldn't help but smile.

It was going to be an interesting evening, after all.

The bartender wandered over. Roux's new companion glanced at his glass and said, "I'll have one of what he's having."

Roux raised an eyebrow but didn't say anything.

She turned to face him. "Aren't you even going to ask me my name?" she asked with a smile.

"No. If you want me to know it I'm sure that you'll tell me eventually."

"And if I don't?" There was amusement in her voice.

"Then our lovemaking will be all the more passionate for the mystery."

She laughed aloud at that one. "That's rather forward of you. What gives you the idea that I intend to sleep with you?"

"Because a woman like you can't resist a challenge." Roux grinned and extended his hand. "But if it will set you at ease, my name is Roux."

Her grip was strong. "Hello, Roux."

Now it was Roux's turn to laugh when she didn't give her name in return. "I take it that puts the ball firmly in my court?"

The bartender returned with her drink and she took a healthy swallow of the one-hundred-and-thirty-year-old brandy as if she had it every day.

"Do you think you are up to it?" she asked.

"We'll never know unless we give it a try, now, will we?"

Her eyes smoldered. "What did you have in mind?"

Roux shrugged. "How about we retire to my suite and see what we can do with a full bottle of this fine brandy?"

"An excellent suggestion." Her smile turned mischievous. "Maybe, if you're good, I'll tell you my name when we're finished."

"Whatever the lady desires," Roux replied.

He signed the check, asked for a bottle to be delivered to his suite and then extended an arm to the gorgeous young creature by his side.

They didn't say much in the elevator, though more than a few sidelong glances passed between them. They made some small talk about nothing of consequence on the way to his suite and arrived to find room service already waiting outside with their order.

Roux opened the door, let his guest inside and then dealt with the room-service waiter. He left the cart in the entrance hallway where it wouldn't be in their way and, drinks in hand, Roux returned to living room, only to find it empty. The bedroom door was open and a pair of high heels lay discarded in the entrance. Just beyond, her cast-off dress lay in a pool of silk.

Her voice floated out of the darkened bedroom. "Bring me that drink, Roux. I'm thirsty."

Never one to deny a beautiful woman, he did as he was told, an I-told-you-so grin on his face.

The lights were off in the bedroom, but there was enough illumination coming through the thin curtains covering the windows to reveal his guest, now naked, languishing across his sheets. The light cast dappled shadows across her sensuous form and as she rolled to face him the tattoo of the dragon that covered much of her taut young flesh seemed to ripple and writhe, as if the creature was rising to life from the surface of her skin.

"Come to bed, Roux."

As uncharacteristic as it was of him, Roux again did as he was told.

24

Annja kept walking, but began to steer herself toward one of the side paths, away from the crowds. She knew the layout of the park pretty well and was counting on the fact that her mysterious follower more than likely did not. It would give her the chance to spring the trap that she was getting ready to set.

The direction she chose led the two of them along a paved footpath through a thick copse of trees. A few hundred yards into the trees was an old discarded construction pipe, the kind that was large enough to drive a truck through. At night it would be a haven for drunks and junkies, a place to avoid the police patrols that routinely went through the park, but at this hour it would more than likely be empty.

It was there that Annja intended to spring her ambush.

The trail took a quick little dogleg before it reached that particular point in the walkway, and as soon as she knew she was out of sight, Annja broke into a jog. Reaching the construction pipe, she slipped inside, her back to the wall.

It took a few minutes but soon she heard the hurried pace of her pursuer. Annja waited until he stepped past the mouth of the pipe and then she struck.

Stepping out of the shadows, she grabbed him by the shirtfront and hauled him back into the pipe, using her momentum to slam him against the nearby wall hard enough to make his teeth rattle. Half a second later she had the tip of her sword against his throat.

"You've got ten seconds to start talking," she said, applying a little pressure to the blade for emphasis.

"No need for violence, Ms. Creed," a familiar voice said in response.

Lowering her sword, Annja stepped back, surprise and annoyance vying for dominance on her face. "Henshaw! What are you doing here?"

In his typically unruffled kind of way, Roux's man replied, "Following you."

He glanced down at the sword in her hand. "And not very well apparently."

Annja released the sword. She wasn't in any danger. Not from Henshaw.

"Following me? Why would you do that?"

Henshaw didn't say anything.

It didn't take her long to figure out what his silence meant. Henshaw would be acting on orders and those orders came from one person only. "Roux," she said.

But why?

Henshaw didn't know. Or if he did, he wasn't saying. When she asked, he simply shrugged his shoulders.

"Was it your people in the subway the other night?"

Again the shrug.

"Fine," she said, and she let the heat show in her voice. If Henshaw wouldn't tell her, she'd just have to ask Roux himself. "Give me your phone and I'll speak to Roux myself."

He handed it over without objection and perhaps the slightest trace of relief.

She hit the redial button, figuring that Henshaw would have been in constant contact with Roux as he followed her through the city streets. She waited for her mentor to answer.

The phone rang several times.

She began to get an uneasy feeling as it went on and on. If Roux had said he would wait for Henshaw's call, then that was what he would do.

She hung up and handed the cell phone back to Henshaw. "No answer," she told him. "Are you sure he's waiting for your call?"

Henshaw looked concerned. He immediately pressed Redial and waited through a set of rings. The longer it went on without an answer the more concerned Annja became.

Something wasn't right, an inner voice told her.

The longer she watched Henshaw waiting for Roux to answer the phone, the more certain of it she became.

Something had happened to Roux.

"Come on," she said, and headed for the exit to the park. Once on Fifth Avenue she flagged down a passing cab, waited for it to come to a stop and then climbed inside with Henshaw at her heels.

"Waldorf-Astoria," Henshaw said as the cab pulled away from the curb and headed into traffic. "Please hurry."

Annja's anxiety ratcheted up a notch. She'd never seen Henshaw in a hurry, not even when under fire. Apparently his inner alarms were going off, too.

The cabbie got them through the city streets in record time. Henshaw shoved a handful of bills through the slot and the two of them were out the door and rushing into the hotel before the doorman could even get out his usual "Good evening."

The elevator seemed to take forever and Annja was grateful that no one else tried to get on board with them. Henshaw was practically vibrating with tension and she didn't think listening to the prattle of civilians, for lack of a better word, was going to do him any favors.

When they hit the eighth floor, Henshaw drew a gun from his jacket and led the way down the hall, toward the suite at the other end where Roux was staying for the duration of his visit to New York.

They were still a half dozen rooms away when they saw that the door to the suite was partially open.

Annja called her sword to her, getting a firm grip on the hilt with two hands, ready to deal with whatever might be waiting for them inside.

Henshaw glanced back, saw that she was ready for a confrontation if it came to that and crept down the corridor to the room itself. Reaching out with his free hand, he silently pushed the door the rest of the way open.

There was a short corridor between the front door and the living area and this naturally limited what they could see from outside in the hall, but even from there they could tell that a struggle had taken place inside the room. Cushions had been pulled off the coach and a chair had been knocked to the ground.

Cautiously they stepped forward.

The living room looked as though it had been the scene of a fight. In addition to the furniture that had been knocked over, the glass top of the coffee table had a starred crack in the center, as if someone had driven the heel of their foot into it, and the television had been knocked out of the entertainment cabinet to lay shattered in a heap on the floor.

Seeing the damage, they quickly checked the rest of the suite, doing it as a team so that they could provide cover for each other if they found someone or something unexpected.

In the end, they didn't find anything more.

The suite was empty.

Roux was gone.

"Maybe he wasn't here," Annja suggested, trying to see the bright side. "Maybe he's down in the bar or in the dining room right now."

She could tell by his face that Henshaw didn't think it was very likely, but he pulled his cell phone out of his pocket and called down to the front desk where he asked to speak to the manager. They spoke for a few minutes and then Henshaw thanked the man and hung up.

He did not look happy with what he had learned.

"Roux left the restaurant in the company of a young Asian woman around nine. The manager says he'd never seen her before, so that reduces the possibility she was one of the professionals that they're used to seeing who use the hotel as a meeting place. They tend to be known quantities in a place like this. Then he checked with room service and they confirmed that they delivered a bottle of brandy to an older gentleman and a younger woman here in this room about an hour ago."

Annja's mind went immediately to her encounter at the café with the mysterious Shizu. Was that who Roux had been seen with? If so, how had she found him? Had the Dragon had them all under surveillance without their knowing it? Could they be under observation even now?

She was just about to say something along those lines to Henshaw when she was startled into silence by the ringing of a telephone.

The two of them immediately checked their individual cells, but neither one was receiving a call, which left the hotel phone somewhere beneath all the debris. Luckily the caller just let the phone ring until, at last, Annja was able to locate it.

"Hello?"

"Ms. Creed. What a surprise to find you there."

The voice seemed to be older, deeper, but Annja recognized it nonetheless.

Shizu.

"You're not surprised and you know it. Where's Roux?"

At the mention of his employer's name, Henshaw walked into the bedroom next door and Annja soon heard him searching around in the debris, looking for another extension to listen in on.

"The old goat is fine. For now," Shizu said.

Annja heard a gentle click and knew Henshaw had found the other phone.

"Whether or not he remains that way depends on you, however."

Annja frowned. "What do you want?"

"I thought that would have been obvious by now. I want the sword."

The bold statement left her at a momentary loss for words.

Shizu laughed. "My, my, my. Has the proverbial cat got your tongue?"

At last Annja found her voice. "I don't know what you're talking about. What sword?"

Shizu said something to someone else in Japanese and in the background there came a sudden wail of pain. When silence returned she said to Annja, "I can do this all night, if you'd like, but I don't think your friend Roux is up to it. Are you sure you want to play it this way?"

Annja bit down on her lip, fighting for control. "I told you, I don't know what you are talking about," she said again, trying to stall for time as she fought to figure out just what to do.

This time Roux let out a long mewling cry of such pain and terror that it didn't even sound human. Annja felt her stomach churn at the thought of what they had to do to a man, particularly one as tough as Roux, to get him to make a sound like that, never mind keep it going for several very long minutes. In the other room, she thought she could hear Henshaw retching.

Yeah, you and me both, buddy.

To Shizu, she said sharply, "All right. Lay off. I know what sword you mean."

"Of course you do. Seems you're not so tough, after all, Ms. Creed."

We'll see about that, she thought.

"Bring the sword with you to the Brooklyn Botanic Garden tomorrow at sunset. Come alone. Walk to the viewing pavilion inside the Japanese Hill-and-Pond Garden. I will meet you there with the old man and we'll do an exchange, your sword for your friend's life. Understood?"

"Yes, I understand. I'll be there," Annja said.

"Good," Shizu said, her voice dripping with satisfaction. "And one other thing. Be sure to leave that British bastard, Henshaw, behind. You don't need him trying to be a hero and messing up what should be a simple exchange."

With that parting shot, Shizu hung up the phone.

25

Henshaw came out of the bedroom, his face set in a mask of fury. "I can have that garden flooded with men inside of twenty-four hours. We'll grab her and…"

Annja wasn't listening. A sudden suspicion had swept over her, one that would change everything if it was correct. She dug through her backpack for the drawing pad that she'd been carrying around with her since her session with Dr. Laurent. When she found it, she pulled it out and flipped to the first image, the one of the swordsman's face.

She stared at it intently, trying to see beyond the mask and hood. She studied the bridge of the nose, the shape of the eyes, the overall sense of what the picture was telling her, trying to answer a single question.

Could the Dragon be a woman instead of a man?

"What is it?" Henshaw asked, noting the intensity of her study and the way she'd stopped listening to him.

"I'm not sure yet…." She trailed off, not ready to explain. Her thoughts went back to that day in the café, to the young woman she'd met. Shizu. Could she have been far more than she appeared to be? Annja had been convinced she was an agent of the Dragon, sent to harass her, throw her off balance, just like those who had been following her and the men who'd been sent to try to kidnap her on the streets later that night.

But what if she was something more than just a foot soldier?

What if *she* was the Dragon?

It would certainly explain a few things.

Annja summoned up a memory of Shizu's face and tried to mentally impose it over the image of the swordsman she'd drawn on the pad.

As best as she could tell, the two were a match.

Annja explained her theory to Henshaw, showing him the drawing and explaining how she'd arrived at her conclusion.

He was shaking his head before she was finished. "That can't be right, Annja. The Dragon has been operating since the late seventies. Every single scrap of information about him points to the fact that he is a man."

She moved to interrupt him and he held up a hand. "Hell, even if that was all a front, even if she cleverly used misinformation to throw everyone off track for decades, you've still got a problem with the time frame. The girl you saw couldn't have been more than thirty, yet the Dragon has been claiming credit for political assassinations for more than three decades."

But Annja had already considered that. "She's his successor," she said, and the act of verbalizing it made the theory crystalize into fact in her mind. She was right; she knew it.

"I'm sorry, she's what?"

"His successor." Annja began to pace back and forth. It helped her think things through sometimes, just like walking did. "Most everyone, and by that I mean the various law-enforcement agencies, believes that the Dragon, the real Dragon, died in that explosion in Madrid, right?"

Henshaw nodded.

"Okay, so let's assume that is true. The Dragon *did* die. And I'll bet that your intelligence information would support that theory, too, wouldn't it? For years there was no further activity associated with the Dragon after the failure in Madrid."

Again, the nod. "Word that the Dragon had resurfaced didn't start up again until about three years ago," Henshaw said.

Annja stopped pacing and turned to face him. "You see, that's the key. Someone else has taken up the mantle of the Dragon, has suborned his identity and has been using it as their own for the past several years."

"But why? What would be the point?"

Annja shrugged. "Fame. Fortune. A sense of adventure. Who knows?"

"And the rumors about the sword?"

Annja didn't have an answer for that and it was the one part of her theory that was bothering her. Had it been the sword that had influenced Shizu to pick up the tattered image of the Dragon and wrap it about herself? Had the sword somehow guided her actions, given her the skills she needed to step into the role, to fool the law-enforcement community for so long?

If so, then it was all the more important for Annja to stop her and destroy the sword.

Perhaps even more important than rescuing Roux.

"I'm not sure," she replied. "But I think I know the reason."

She explained about the conversation she'd had with Garin and his theory that the Dragon and her weapon were a polar opposite to Annja and the sword she carried.

For the second time that day Annja was treated to a view behind the mask that Henshaw usually wore. She could see the wonder of it all on his face.

"Two swords, created for cross-purposes, one representing the light and one representing the dark," he said, his thoughts distant and his gaze focused on something far away.

He shook his head as if to clear it and asked, "So what do we do now?"

"We get Roux back, whole and in one piece," she said, letting her anger at how one of her friends had been treated in order to influence her show through. "And then we deal with the Dragon once and for all."

It didn't take them long to come up with a plan. Using Annja's laptop they discovered that the park opened up at eight every morning and closed again at six. Sunset would happen just a few minutes before closing, so they should have the park to themselves at that point and they intended to use that to their advantage.

Henshaw would go in shortly after the park opened the next morning. He'd find a suitable position where he wouldn't be stumbled upon by park visitors, but one that at the same time would allow him to keep the pavilion itself under observation.

They had little doubt that Shizu would have the park under surveillance, but they hoped she wouldn't have it in place that early. Just to be safe Henshaw agreed to wear a disguise when he made the entrance attempt.

By arriving so far in advance of their scheduled meeting time, Annja hoped to be able to spot Shizu's people getting into position. Once Henshaw knew where they were, he could relay that information via directional radio to Annja. It would be a lot easier for her to take them out once she knew where they were.

Henshaw would be armed with a high-powered rifle and he would keep Annja in view at all times. When the Dragon appeared, hopefully with Roux in tow, it would be Henshaw's job to deal with anyone who posed a threat to Roux's continued well-being. Annja, on the other hand, would focus her energy and attention on the Dragon. If things got too dangerous, she'd call in a little extra help from Henshaw.

In order to pull it off, they were going to need a communication system that would be difficult to intercept. Henshaw knew where to get one. Just in case the phone in Roux's suite had been bugged, Henshaw went down to the lobby and used a pay phone to make arrangements.

While he was gone, Annja tried to clean up things a little; she put the cushions back on the couch, put the chairs in their places and swept up the loose glass from the smashed coffee table and television set.

When Henshaw returned half an hour later, he had a well-built dark-haired man who looked a bit like Antonio Banderas with him.

Seeing him, another piece of the puzzle fell into place in Annja's mind.

"Well, if it isn't my rooftop savior," she said. She shouldn't have been surprised, but she was. Score one for Henshaw, she thought.

The newcomer at least had the grace to look sheepish about the deception. "Sorry I couldn't say anything to you then. Operational parameters and all that."

If there had been even a trace of smugness in his response she would have made him regret it, but since he sounded entirely sincere, Annja let it go.

"Thank you," she said.

"You're welcome."

Henshaw made the formal introductions. "Annja, meet Marco. Marco, Annja. Now let's get on with this."

Marco explained that he was there to show Annja how to wire herself up with a microphone and receiver for the next night. "Have you ever used anything like this before?" he asked.

She shook her head. "I know how to use a walkie-talkie. Does that count?"

Marco laughed. "Technology has come a long way since then, but at least the principle is the same."

He walked over to the desk and took several small black cases the size of jewelry boxes from the pockets of his light coat.

He opened one of them and removed two flesh-colored pieces of plastic from inside. To Annja they looked like earbud headphones minus the wires.

Marco handed one to Annja and one to Henshaw.

"This is your receiver," he said. "It sits inside your ear just like a hearing aid does, except it is so small it is practically invisible to anyone standing nearby. They would need to actively look inside your ear to spot it. Go on and try it—we need to make sure we get the fit right."

Henshaw had obviously used one before. He popped it, tugged on his earlobe for a moment and announced that it was fine.

Annja, on the other hand, had to twist and turn hers for a moment before she got a good fit.

Marco picked up one of the other boxes, opened it and showed them both the wafer-thin piece of flesh-colored plastic it contained. "This is a microphone disk. Peel away the protective covering to expose the adhesive and then just press it firmly against your skin. Somewhere near your neck or upper chest is usually the best place. It's extremely sensitive, but I wouldn't count on it picking up your words if you stick it on your calf, for instance."

Marco picked up the mini-walkie-talkie from the pile of gear on the table in front of him. "Go ahead and put on a mike, then we'll give them a test."

He waited to be certain they both followed the instructions he'd given and then walked into the bedroom, closing the door behind him.

A moment later Annja could hear Marco's voice in her ear. "Testing, one, two, three. Can you hear me, Annja?"

"Yes, I can hear you."

"All right, hang on a minute while I check Henshaw's gear."

He repeated the sequence with her partner and then returned to the living room. He collected their equipment, put the each set of earpieces and corresponding mikes into a single case and handed a case to each of them.

"They have a battery life of twenty-four hours, so don't put them on until you're ready to go—" he hesitated for a moment "—wherever it is you're going."

Annja eyed the box in her hand thoughtfully. "What about interception or interference?"

Marco shrugged. "The radios use a pretty rare frequency and the signals are encrypted automatically, so you won't pick up anyone else's traffic, nor will they pick up yours. The transmitter might be small but it's powerful. You should be able to remain in contact with each other up to two miles away. It will even penetrate solid rock up to five hundred feet thick, so the walls of a building or even an entire house shouldn't be any kind of problem for you. That's the best I can do on short notice."

Annja nearly laughed. If that was what he could do on short notice, she wasn't sure she wanted to know what he'd be capable of when given more time.

Probably reroute the NSA's supersecret satellites just to get his voice mail, she thought.

With the communications issues resolved, Henshaw saw Marco out the door. He was gone for a few minutes, and when he came back Annja was waiting for him with an annoyed look on her face.

"Let me guess. He's an old friend who just happened to be hanging around down the street when you called. Out with it, Henshaw."

He mumbled something about not knowing what she was talking about.

But after all that had happened, there was no way she was going to settle for a feeble excuse.

"I said, spill it!"

Henshaw hesitated for another moment or two, then sighed. "No sense in keeping things a secret now, is there?" he asked.

Annja chose to take that as a rhetorical question and simply waited for him to continue.

"We've had you under surveillance ever since the day you left the estate," he said.

"Why?"

"Roux was worried. He knew about the Dragon— knew what he was capable of, how far he would go to get something he wanted. At the same time he'd heard rumors about an artifact the Dragon was supposed to possess."

"You mean Muramasa's sword?"

"Yes, right, the sword." Henshaw tried but failed to hide his surprise that she knew about the weapon.

Of course she knew about the weapon. Did they think she was an idiot?

"And then what?" she prompted, feeling her anger rise. "Did he think he was going to just dangle me out there as bait? Wait and see what happened?"

Henshaw's face went still. "I wasn't privy to all his plans, Ms. Creed."

So they were back to Ms. Creed now, were they? "I have half a mind to just leave him there, Henshaw. He was playing games with my life!"

Wisely her companion remained silent.

After several minutes, Annja said, "Okay, we both know that I can't leave him in her hands any more than you can, no matter how angry I am. So let's figure out the rest of this plan and call it a night."

They talked for another hour, getting everything straight so that when the time came they both knew what they were supposed to be doing and when. It was a reasonable plan, straightforward, without too many things that could trip them up. Of course, she thought, there was always the unexpected, but that couldn't be helped.

Afterward they made arrangements with the manager to have a cab waiting for them in the hotel's underground garage so they could slip away from the hotel without being seen.

Assuming that Annja's loft was being watched, they staged an argument just outside, with Annja yelling at Henshaw through the cab's window, telling him she didn't want anything to do with him and that she would handle things on her own, all in an attempt to convince the watchers they knew were out there that Annja was following the Dragon's instructions to the letter.

Sleep was a long time in coming for Annja that night.

26

Several months earlier

Shizu eyed the lodge in front of her through the curtain of falling snow. Inside that building was the man she had come to kill. All she had to do in order to complete her contract was to enter the house, kill its occupant and get out again without being caught.

Not a problem, she thought with a grin.

She circled the property, noting the position of the security cameras and how often they moved in their preset arcs, and laughed silently. Whoever was in charge of security was an idiot; the cameras moved in defined, repeatable patterns. All she had to do was wait for the right moment.

When it came, she raced across the lawn directly toward the house in front of her. She was dressed in white, from her head to her feet, blending perfectly with the snow all around her. Even if someone had chosen that moment to look out through the windows, they wouldn't have been able to pick out her form in the midst of the swirling snow.

She reached the side of the building without incident and flattened herself against it. The cameras only faced outward, so she was beyond their reach, but she wasn't certain yet if there were armed guards wandering the property and she didn't want to make herself a visible target.

There was a door several yards farther along. From the plans she had stolen from the contractor who'd built the place she knew that it led into a utility room.

It was as good a choice as any to provide her entrance.

She removed an electric lock pick from the pocket of her coat. It resembled a pistol but instead of a barrel it had a long thick tongue sticking out of the front end. She shoved the tongue into the lock and then pulled the trigger. There was a brief rattle as the pick vibrated inside the lock, causing the pins to fall into place, and then the door was opening before her. She shoved the pick back inside her jacket and stepped forward.

Slipping inside, she shut the door quietly behind her and listened, making certain that the rattle of the pick, quiet as it was, had not attracted undue attention.

She left her coat and shoes behind, not wanting the heavy fabric or wet soles to give her away. On stocking feet she moved deeper into the house.

The utility room door opened to a short corridor, which, in turn, led into the kitchen. That was where she found the first guard. He was standing at the island making a sandwich, a loaf of bread and a jar of mayonnaise open on the counter in front of him. He never heard her as she crept up behind him, covered his mouth with one hand and, with the other, drove a knife deep into his brain through the base of his skull.

She held him as he died and then lowered him quietly to the floor.

Wiping the blade of her knife on his shirt, she moved on.

The next guard was standing in a pool of light at the foot of the stairs leading to the second floor, his arms crossed in front of him.

Her sword barely made a sound as she drew it from the scabbard she wore on her back.

Breathing deeply to fill her lungs with oxygen, the Dragon burst out of the hallway, a shadow moving through the dimly lit room. By the time the guard's mind managed to receive the message from his eyes that he was under attack, it was too late. He died with his hands still reaching for the weapon on his hip, the Dragon's sword thrust through his heart.

Pulling her sword free from his chest, she was already moving past the body and up the stairs as it crumpled to the carpet behind her with a thump.

She could see the floor plan in her mind, knew that the bedroom she wanted was the third door on the left, and she was already passing through it into the room itself when she heard the first shouts of alarm from downstairs.

Someone had found the body in the kitchen.

But that didn't matter; she was where she needed to be. She could see the man's sleeping form on the bed in front of her and she moved forward confidently.

One more thrust would be all it took.

Three steps from the bed the lights suddenly flared to life around her and Shizu found herself looking down the barrel of the pistol held in the hand of the man on the bed.

The one she had been sent here to kill.

Staring at him, Shizu nearly died of shock.

The man on the bed was Sensei.

"Hello, Shizu," he said gently.

She could say nothing; it was as if she had lost the capability of speech.

Sensei did not lower the pistol. "You did exceptionally well. While I know your skills are extraordinary, I did not think you could penetrate my security so easily. My hat is off to you and your teachers."

Shizu still said nothing.

The pistol did not waver. "I am sorry I had to test you this way, but it was necessary. I needed to be certain that you had developed the skills for what comes next and this was the only way to do that."

He paused, watching her closely for a moment. "Do you understand that this was just a test? You are not to complete the mission as instructed, now that you know it is a test."

Shizu slowly nodded.

"Let me hear you say it," Sensei told her.

"This mission is aborted. You are not the target,"

she said softly, the tension of the previous moments still in her voice.

He nodded in reply. "Very good, Shizu."

Then and only then did he lower the pistol and place it on the bed beside him. Rising, he said, "Well done, Shizu. Well done indeed."

Finding her voice at last, Shizu spoke up. The fact that she did so was a testament to how unnerved she was by what had just happened. "But I could have killed you!" she gasped, appalled at the very idea.

Sensei smiled, but there was little humor in his eyes. "You could have tried. I'll give you that."

He reached out and pressed a button on the intercom beside the bed. A moment later the door behind Shizu opened, revealing a muscular man in a dark suit.

Addressing the newcomer, Sensei said, "Show her to her room and see to it that she has anything she needs."

The man nodded.

Turning back to Shizu, he said, "Get some rest. I'm sure your exertions tired you out. We will talk in more detail in the morning."

Mystified, but obedient as always, Shizu did what she was told.

By THE TIME SHE AWOKE the next morning, the damage to the estate had been repaired. She walked through the central room and saw no sign that she had killed a man there the night before. Even the bloodstains were gone from the thick carpet.

Hungry, she wandered into the kitchen. There she

found breakfast prepared—a buffet-style table laid out with fruit, eggs, meat—on the same island the guard had been using to make a sandwich the night before. A place setting had been laid out and next to her plate was a small card.

"Join me in the dojo when you are finished," it read, and included a few additional instructions. It was unsigned, but Shizu had no problem recognizing the handwriting. She hadn't seen it in some time, but that didn't matter. One does not forget the signature of the man you consider to be your personal savior.

The dojo was in a separate wing of the house and it didn't take her long to find it. She moved directly to the changing room as she'd been instructed. There she found a large tub filled with water and a pure-white kimono made from the finest silk hanging on a rack nearby. A full-length mirror stood next to the tub beside a small table holding a silver pitcher, a folded towel, a natural sponge and another card. "Cleanse yourself and meet me on the floor when you are ready," it read.

If Sensei wills, so be it, she thought.

She stripped out of her clothing and carefully placed it off to the side so it wouldn't get wet. She caught a glimpse of herself in the mirror as she did so, her tattoo rippling across her muscles as she moved. She was not a vain woman, however, and the idea of standing in front of a mirror admiring herself was so out of her frame of reference that the thought didn't even occur. Picking up the pitcher, she poured the contents—water hot enough to still be steaming—all over her head and body. She endured it stoically, not flinching once at the pain. She put the pitcher down, picked up the sponge and scrubbed herself clean.

She turned to the tub. A stool stood nearby and she used it to get up over the edge of the waist-high tub, then dropped down into the water.

As she had expected, it was icy cold. She dunked beneath the surface three times, then climbed back out again, drying off with the towel before putting on the kimono.

It fit as if it had been tailored for her and Shizu had no doubt that was, indeed, the case. She spent a few minutes clearing her head and preparing for what was to come before stepping through the door into the dojo proper.

In the middle of the room, Sensei waited, kneeling on a mat in front of a traditional Japanese tea set. He wore a black silk kimono the same color as his hair, which was loose around his face. It made him look younger, less harsh.

Behind him, on a wooden rack, was a sword in a wooden scabbard.

Shizu's curiosity burned at the sight of the weapon, but she knew better than to ask about the sword. It wasn't the way these things were done. She would remain quiet until Sensei mentioned it or until she was given permission to speak freely.

She crossed the floor on bare feet and settled down lotus style next to the tea set. As she reached out to begin the tea service, Sensei shook his head, indicating that she should leave the service alone.

When she sat back, he shocked her by preparing the tea himself, something he had never done in front of her before. First, he added hot water to the delicate porcelain cups and then added some green tea leaves. Next, he whisked the mixture together to produce a foamy green tea. Turning the cup to face her, Sensei bowed low and offered her the first taste. She took it, then offered it back to him, as was traditional, but he declined, indicating she should drink. Once she had, he repeated the process, taking a sip for himself before putting the cup down on the table.

They passed another moment in silence, and then Sensei spoke.

"You have done well, Shizu. I am proud of your accomplishments."

It was high praise for her and she sat a little taller before him, honored to have him think so highly of her.

"Now at last, we come to the reason for all you have done over the past several years. I have a specific mission for you, a mission I am now convinced you can carry out successfully."

Shizu bowed her head. "Whatever you wish, Sensei."

He was smiling when she looked up again. "You have always been faithful, Shizu, and I admire you for that. Such dedication is a rare and powerful thing. Because you have been so devoted, so unflinching in all that you have done for me, today I want to return that dedication. I have a gift for you, a gift fitting for one known as the Dragon."

Sensei stood and turned to the sword rack behind him. He bowed low, then picked up the scabbard in both hands and returned to his former position, the sword resting across his knees.

"Like you, this sword was crafted for a purpose. The artisan who fashioned it poured everything he had into its creation. He gave it a destiny and then turned it loose in the world to carry out its ends. So it is fitting that on this day, when you, too, are turned loose to carry out your mission, you should receive a gift of equal value."

To Shizu's shock and surprise, Sensei bowed once, short and sharp, and then handed her the sword.

She cradled it lovingly in her hands, not trusting herself to speak. Holding the scabbard in one hand and grasping the hilt in the other, she drew the sword out slightly, revealing about four or five inches of the blade.

The *katana* was old; she could tell just by looking at it. The blade was too sharp, the etching too exquisite, for it to have been made in the modern era. Toshiro had taught her to recognize the old blades, those actually fashioned during the samurai period itself, and she had no doubt that this one originated from that time frame.

Just beneath the hilt, a dragon had been etched lovingly into the blade's surface. It was lunging forward, its front claws reaching toward the pointed end of the blade, smoke pouring from its mouth and between its whiskers.

"It hungers, Shizu. Hungers for death and destruction and misery, hungers for everything its creator wished upon his enemies."

That last was said quietly, almost reverently, and she wondered for a moment if there were hidden meanings behind the words.

"It is the sword carried by your predecessor, the original Dragon. Now it is yours."

Shizu stared at the blade in her hands and vowed to do the gift justice. She would be better than the original Dragon; she would make the legend live as it never had before.

Sensei gently took the weapon from her, sliding the blade back into the scabbard and returning the sword to the rack behind him.

"It is there for you when you need it," he told her.

He moved to stand before her again, his gaze capturing her own.

"I have one more gift for you," he said.

Stepping in close, he bent his head and kissed her passionately on the lips.

For a moment she froze in shock and then the hunger and passion she had been hiding inside for years exploded. She clung to him, losing herself in his touch and his taste and his very closeness. Her love for him knew no bounds and she had prayed for years that this day would come, but had never actually believed that it would.

His hands found the ties of her kimono and deftly released them, sliding the garment off her shoulders to let it pool on the floor at her feet. His lips traced their way down her neck and Shizu nearly screamed in delight.

Sensei took her on the floor of the dojo and every move of his body upon hers cemented her allegiance to him. When he was finished he left her alone. He had won her over, heart, mind and soul. She would do whatever he asked, whenever he asked, without hesitation or doubt.

WHEN HE SUMMONED HER to his study a few hours later, he gave no indication that anything out of the ordinary had happened between them.

Recognizing what she thought was his need for discretion, Shizu did not refer to it, either.

It would be their secret.

Sensei handed her a file folder. Inside was a color photo of a stunningly beautiful woman with chestnut hair and amber-green eyes. A name had been printed across the bottom of the photograph.

"That woman carries a certain sword that I wish to possess. I want you to get that sword for me," Sensei said.

Shizu nodded. "She'll be dead before the week is out," she replied, displaying a sense of newfound confidence that was as surprising to her as it was to her master.

"No!" he said sharply, and then calmed himself. To Shizu it seemed as if he was embarrassed at having shown even that little emotion.

"No," he repeated, this time in a calmer tone. "She is not to come to any harm, nor can the sword be taken from her by force. It must be given of her own free will. Anything less and my plans will be ruined. Do you understand?"

Shizu hid the confusion she was feeling and simply nodded. She had been trained to kill, to eliminate her enemies as ruthlessly and as quickly as possible. The woman had something Sensei wanted and she was not allowed to use the one skill she could most easily bring to bear on the problem? Was this another test?

Sensei saw her confusion. "The sword is an item of

considerable power, but that power is only available if its current bearer still lives and if the sword has been given freely, rather than taken under duress. She must remain alive," he explained.

"Hai!" Shizu said, bowing to show her complete agreement.

Sensei pointed at some materials in a file folder. "Everything you need is in here—habits, locations, even her travel schedule for the next several weeks. An account has been opened for your use—the access codes are in the folder, as well. Once you have the sword, reach me through the usual channels."

He moved out from behind the desk and Shizu understood that her audience was over. It was time for her to leave.

"I will await word that you have succeeded," he said, "as I have no doubt that you will do so. Good hunting."

Later, in her own room, Shizu stared at the photograph, studying the woman. Her gaze drifted to the name at the bottom of the image.

"What secrets are you hiding, Annja Creed?" the Dragon asked. "And why is preserving your life so important to Sensei?"

She did not know the answers, but she was certain she would find out.

Maybe then she could quench the fire of jealousy that was suddenly burning in her heart.

27

Now

Annja slept badly that night, her dreams plagued by faceless samurai soldiers and a massive feathered dragon that breathed fire in great scorching arcs. Roux appeared more than once, as well—a gagged and bound captive who endured torture after torture at the hands of a beautiful porcelain doll with long dark hair.

By the time she awoke for the fifth time, heart pounding, Annja decided that it wasn't worth trying to sleep any more. She got up to greet the sun.

She ran through a series of katas to get her blood flowing and her head clear, then settled down in front of the windows for some meditation and deep breathing. The sun kissed the rooftops nearby, then rose high enough to shine its light directly into her loft, illuminating her as she sat lotus style on the floor.

Satisfied she was ready for what was to come later that day, Annja got up, showered and ate a hearty breakfast, knowing she was going to need the energy reserves later.

All the while, her thoughts were on her sword. The plan called for her to give it up to the Dragon and do what she could to hold it here in this world as she and Henshaw tried to free Roux. Then she would call the sword back to her, ultimately returning it to the otherwhere.

It wasn't half-bad as plans go.

There was only one thing wrong with it.

They had no idea what would happen when she voluntarily gave up the sword. Would it still be bonded to her at that point? Would the link between them be shattered? Would she ever be able to command the sword again?

She didn't know.

And not knowing scared her.

HENSHAW ARRIVED AT THE park just after it opened. He carried a backpack over one shoulder and had several cameras slung around his neck, emulating the look of just another picture-obsessed photographer come to document the beauty of the garden in bloom. A tour bus with New Jersey license plates was unloading passengers as he approached the entrance to the park so he merged with the crowd and struck up a conversation with one of the tour's patrons as they waited to buy their entrance tickets.

If the park was under surveillance as Annja suspected, then they would be looking for a solitary individual and might not pay too much attention to the group as it entered the park.

He stayed with his newfound friend until they had moved through the entrance pavilion and into the park itself, then wandered away on his own.

When he was certain that no one was taking an undue interest in him, Henshaw took out the little map he'd been given when he'd bought his ticket and quickly located the Japanese Hill-and-Pond Garden.

He'd entered off Flatbush Avenue, which was on the opposite end of the park from where he needed to be. It seemed a prudent move; the two entrances off Washington were certainly closer, but were also more likely to be watched for just that reason. In order to get to the Japanese garden, he was going to have to stick to the outer walkway, past the Steinhardt Conservatory, the Lily Pool Terrace and the Magnolia Plaza Visitor Center before he was even close. From there he could cut through the Celebrity Path or the Fragrance Garden to reach his destination.

Henshaw took his time, using his cameras on a regular basis, doing what he could to remain in character and not appear out of place. Several passersby smiled and said hello. He nodded or waved hello in return, but kept his mouth shut at all times. He didn't want people to remember the man with all the cameras and the British accent, just in case something went wrong later.

At last he reached the southern edge of the lake. The viewing pavilion was directly in front of him; this was the location of the meet.

He had to find a suitable watching place.

He consulted his map and tried to match it up with

his surroundings. He could see that on the other side of the narrow lake the land began to rise toward a wooded ridgeline. A second path wound along about halfway up the hillside and he decided to follow that to see what he might find.

Another ten minutes of walking found him looking directly back across the lake at the viewing pavilion from that second, higher walkway. This is the place, he thought.

He left the path and climbed through the trees, emerging on a narrow ridge above the edge of the Japanese garden. From there he could look across the lake to the viewing pavilion, as well as both walkways, the one on this side of the lake and the other that led up to and away from the pavilion itself.

He found a small copse of trees that provided him with a clear line of sight to the pavilion, as well as some shade. Setting his pack on the ground, he walked fifty paces in every direction, looking back at his selected spot from a variety of locations. He was pleased to find that he couldn't see the backpack no matter how hard he tried; the position was a good one and would provide the cover he needed to carry out his part of the plan. Later, when the sun was setting, the whole area would be layered with shadows and he'd be almost invisible.

Returning to his chosen location, he removed a pair of binoculars from his pack, found a comfortable sitting position with his back to a tree and settled in to start his watch.

BY MIDMORNING ANNJA WAS going stir-crazy. When something needed to be done she was the type who just went out and did it, so waiting around was driving her nuts. She paced the floor of her loft like a caged lioness, back and forth, until she just couldn't take it anymore.

She had to get out of there.

She threw on her sweats and went for a jog, sticking to the main streets and avoiding any of the alleys or short cuts she might have used. She wanted to be certain she was around people in case the Dragon's goons tried to make another move ahead of the meet.

When she returned to her apartment she showered for the second time that morning and then dropped in front of the television in her bathrobe for some mindless entertainment. Halfway through whatever show it was that she was watching—it was that interesting—she decided to call Garin.

If there was one thing Garin was good at, it was self-preservation. Since both he and Roux were tied to Joan's sword in some indefinable way, she knew he would want to be kept abreast of what was happening. He'd also want to know what had happened to Roux; just because their last encounter had ended badly didn't mean that they wanted nothing further to do with each other. If that was the case, they would have stopped talking to each other hundreds of years ago.

Annja dialed the cell number she had for Garin and listened to it ring several times before the call was finally routed to a general voice-mail system. There wasn't even a message; it just beeped to indicate that it was recording.

She left a message, explaining that Roux was in trouble and that she needed Garin's help. After that, there wasn't anything more she could do.

THE HOURS PASSED SLOWLY.

The park had a fair number of visitors and Henshaw watched them all in turn, looking for that one telltale sign that something was out of place, the one little detail that would give them away for who they really were, but he didn't see anything that made him suspicious.

He found himself admiring the tranquility of the place—the calmness of the lake waters, the gentle cascade of the landscape. Even the soft breeze that wafted over the garden seemed to have been designed to enhance its very features.

Several times he saw solitary figures showing interest in the lake and the viewing pavilion. One even took the time to pace off the inside of the structure, but when the bride and groom showed up fifteen minutes later for the picture-taking ceremony, Henshaw knew the photographer was just that, a photographer, and not a threat.

Around noon two men in a small boat paddled out across the surface of the lake to where an odd-looking wooden gatelike structure floated. Henshaw had noted it when he'd first caught sight of the lake and the brochure he'd been given with his entrance ticket had told him that it was known as a torii. It had been painted such a brilliant shade of red that the eye couldn't help but be drawn to it amid the deep emerald green of the surrounding trees.

The men in the boat seemed to be checking something at the base of the torii. Probably a pair of maintenance men, he thought, and after growing tired of watching them eventually dismissed them as unimportant. He barely noticed when they left a few minutes later.

He made sure to shift positions occasionally so that his limbs didn't go to sleep, and when he needed to relieve himself he did so with a bottle he had brought along for just that purpose.

Not once during the long afternoon did anyone glance in his direction, never mind leave the path and climb up toward the ridge where he might have been in danger of being seen. Nor did he see anything suspicious. If the Dragon or her people were out there, they were doing one hell of a job of staying hidden.

Eventually the sun began to set and the time for Annja's arrival drew near. Confident that the shadows now hid him sufficiently well that he wouldn't be seen even if he stood, Henshaw reached for his backpack. He removed what he needed and then assembled it carefully. When he was finished he took the spotting scope out of the pocket of his shirt where he had been carrying it all day and clamped it on to the barrel of the now-reassembled rifle.

He was ready.

"Hang in there, sir," he whispered to the wind. "We're coming."

28

When the time had come, Annja dressed in a pair of jeans, a long-sleeved jersey and her usual low-cut hiking boots. She put the receiver in her ear and attached the microphone to the space between her breasts, just below her collarbone. Then she caught a cab over to the garden.

Founded in 1910 on the site for a former ash dump, the Brooklyn Botanic Garden occupied fifty-two acres between Washington and Flatbush avenues near the Prospect Heights section of Brooklyn. It held more than ten thousand varieties of plants and welcomed more than seven hundred thousand visitors per year.

At least, that's what the sign near the ticket booth read. In all the years Annja had lived in Brooklyn, she'd never been to the gardens.

I have to get out more, she told herself sternly.

She paid for her ticket and passed through the gates, examining the little map they handed out in the process.

She found the section of the park containing the Japanese Hill-and-Pond Garden and headed in that direction. Wandering down the path a short way from the entrance she found an isolated spot and, pretending she needed to retie her shoe, she squatted and tried to reach Henshaw.

She knew the microphones were sensitive, that they could pretty much pick up anything, even a whisper, so Annja kept her voice low and her head turned away so no one could see her seemingly talking to herself.

"Henshaw, you out there?"

There was a long moment of silence and then, "Right here, Ms. Creed."

Annja breathed a sigh of relief. She hadn't realized until just that moment how much she was depending on the radio system to keep her in touch with Henshaw. Or how much his presence helped calm her nerves. She'd already faced off against the Dragon and lost; the idea of doing so a second time was in the forefront of her mind. But this time, her life and Roux's depended on her success.

It was a heavy burden to bear.

"All right, I'm inside the park. I'll make my way around to the pavilion and we'll see what's what," Annja said.

It took her fifteen minutes to reach the Japanese garden. This particular one was the first Japanese garden built within an American public garden, and its creator, Takeo Shiota, had done the city proud. It blended the ancient hill-and-pond style with the more modern stroll-garden style and managed to carry it off wonderfully. Annja thought the beauty of the place was amazing.

Evergreen trees and bushes dominated the landscape, and here and there bright splashes of color from flowering plants were used with restraint. Annja could see a wooden bridge extending out to a small hump of an island that reminded her of a turtle's back, but it was the building standing right at the water's edge that drew her like iron to a magnet.

The viewing pavilion was a large, wooden pagoda-like structure made in typical Japanese fashion. The wood had been stained a deep brown and stood out against the trees without being conspicuous or seeming to be out of place. A vermilion-colored torii, or floating gateway, could be seen in the middle of the lake. Annja knew that the torii indicated the presence of a shrine somewhere nearby, but when she looked around for it she couldn't see it.

She walked over to the pavilion and entered. It appeared to be empty, just one large room without furniture but which offered several places from which one could look out upon the lake.

"Still with me?" she whispered.

"I'm here. Looks like you're about to get company. Someone is approaching from the opposite entrance."

Annja waited a moment, then turned to face that direction just in time to see Shizu enter the Pavilion

HENSHAW BROUGHT THE RIFLE to his shoulder and centered the sights on the Dragon as she approached Annja.

A twig snapped behind him.

Henshaw whirled around, thinking he'd find a stray hiker or a runaway dog. Instead, he saw a figure standing in the shadows not half a dozen yards away. The gun in his hand was a dead giveaway that he didn't have Henshaw's best interests at heart. Henshaw couldn't believe what he was seeing; he'd been so careful all day long, so intent on making certain he wasn't seen, that his mind just couldn't accept that someone else had gotten the drop on him. He made an effort to get his gun up and around in the right direction, but the other man fired before he made it.

Henshaw was close enough to see both muzzle flashes as the pistol in the man's hand went off. What a sledgehammer slammed into his chest, followed immediately by another one, and as he went over backward, the darkness already closing in, Henshaw had a moment to wonder about the lack of the sound of the gunshots.

Then the darkness closed in and he knew no more.

ANNJA WATCHED AS THE Dragon seemed to step right out of the shadows as she entered the building. Shizu glanced around, saw Annja and began walking toward her.

"Here she comes, be ready," Annja whispered into her microphone.

But she didn't get the reply she expected. Instead, from her receiver, came a harsh grunt, then nothing else.

"Henshaw?" she asked, doing what she could to keep the look of concern off her face. She was supposed to be alone and didn't want to jeopardize the meeting.

There was no reply.

By that time the Dragon was too close for Annja to take a chance with another message. She'd just have to hope that he'd heard.

It wasn't an auspicious beginning.

The Dragon stopped about ten feet away from Annja and the two women looked each other over. Gone was the slightly over-the-top fan from the other day. Annja could see that in her place was a stone-cold killer with dead-flat eyes. She was dressed in loosely fitting dark clothing that Annja knew had been chosen not just to allow for ease of movement but also to hide her amid the shadows that were settling all around them now. The hilt of a sword rose up over the edge of one shoulder.

"Where's Roux?" Annja asked, leaning to the side to look past the Dragon, as if he might be waiting back there in the darkness from which she had emerged.

Shizu laughed. "He's here. You'll be reunited with him in a moment. Where's the sword?"

Knowing that only one of them was going to make it out of this encounter alive, Annja didn't care about the Dragon seeing the truth and so she reached into the otherwhere and drew forth the sword.

One moment her hand was empty and the next it was filled with the hilt of an ancient broadsword, the tip of the blade pointed directly at the Dragon's throat.

Shizu's face showed surprise, though it was masked very quickly.

Annja had seen it, though, and she wondered about it. Did the Dragon's sword operate differently? Is that why she wore it openly on her back rather than letting it rest in the otherwhere? Or was it all just a trick to throw her off the track, to lull her into making a mistake?

The Dragon made a strange flicking motion with her hand and suddenly there was a pistol in it. She pointed it at Annja.

"Put the sword down on the ground."

Annja stood resolute. "No, not until I know where Roux is."

"I told you, he's nearby. You'll see him soon enough." The pistol rose slightly, until the barrel was level with her face. "It would be a shame to mess up those pretty features," Shizu said.

Annja clicked her tongue twice, one of the pre-arranged signals she and Henshaw had come up with for when they were in the thick of things. This particular one meant that he was to put a warning shot right across her bow, to show the Dragon that she wasn't the only one with arms and support.

Nothing happened.

She did it again.

Click, click.

Still nothing.

Apparently she was on her own.

Annja suddenly felt very inadequate for the situation she faced.

The Dragon chambered a round into the barrel of the pistol. "I said, put the sword down."

Not seeing any other alternative, Annja did as she was told.

As she prepared for the sword to leave her hand she

had a momentary flash of panic. She didn't know what it was that made the sword bond to her in the first place, nor did she know what it took for it to remain in this world. She had always assumed that it would stay in her possession until she died, but here she was voluntarily relinquishing it to another. Would the sword pass on to its new owner as a result? Would it abandon her in the mistaken belief that she was abandoning it?

Easy, Annja, she told herself. The sword will understand. Have faith.

At this point, that was all she had left—faith.

She put the sword on the ground and willed it to remain and not vanish into the otherwhere.

"Now, move over there," the Dragon said, pointing with the barrel of the gun to where a screen in the side of the pavilion had been pulled back, revealing a small balcony overlooking the lake.

Slowly Annja did as she was told. She never took her gaze off the Dragon. If this was going to be it, she wanted to meet death with her eyes open and spit into the face of her adversary. While she watched her enemy, she also continued concentrating on keeping the sword in the here and now; having it disappear into the otherwhere would probably earn her a bullet in the head.

The Dragon kept her distance as she circled toward where the sword rested on the ground. By the time Annja reached the balcony, the Dragon was standing over the sword. She bent over, slid it into a cloth sheath that she'd produced from somewhere on her person and slung the entire package over her back, next to her own weapon.

"We had a deal," Annja said. "The sword for Roux."

For a moment Annja thought the Dragon was just going to run off, but then she realized the woman was enjoying this. Whatever was about to happen, it would probably not be pleasant for Roux or Annja.

"Look to your left," Shizu said. "Do you see the line tied to the railing?"

Annja looked that way and then quickly back again. "Yes, I see it." It was a narrow piece of fishing line, nearly invisible in the fading sunlight, tied off at the railing and disappearing out into the pond.

"Untie it and pull on it," the Dragon said.

Annja eyed her warily but made no move toward the line.

The gun swiveled in her direction again. "I said, pull on it."

Annja didn't see that she had a choice, so she stepped closer and began to work at the knot. While she did so, she tried reaching out to Henshaw again.

"Are you out there?" she whispered.

She heard nothing but static.

When the line was finally untied, she gave it a good yank. Behind her, out on the water, something splashed.

"Reel it in," Shizu ordered.

Again, Annja did as she was told, but this time a cold sense of foreboding was stealing across her body. Something had gone very wrong; it seemed likely that both Henshaw and Roux were already dead, which left her alone to escape the Dragon's clutches.

It only took a few seconds to reel in the line and when

she did she discovered that it was attached to a long hollow reed that resembled nothing so much as a wet piece of narrow bamboo. As she stared at it, something began to churn and splash at the base of the floating Torii marker in the middle of the lake.

"I promised I'd deliver Roux alive and unharmed," the Dragon said, with a vicious smile. "I always keep my promises. It's just too bad that you're the one who just took his air hose out of his mouth. Old guy like that, he probably won't last two minutes."

As Annja made the connection between the long narrow reed in her hand and the churning commotion in the middle of the pond, her mind screamed at her to act before it was too late.

She backed up, took three running steps and dove over the railing into the lake, all thought of the Dragon forgotten. She struck the water in a shallow dive and let her momentum carry her along as far as it could before she surfaced and swam toward the floating torii with hard strokes of her arms and legs. The cold water sucked the heat from her limbs and her wet clothing threatened to drag her down, but she knew she had only minutes to save Roux from drowning so she fought her way forward.

Behind her, unnoticed by all but the gun-toting watcher on the ridge above, the Dragon walked briskly out of the pavilion.

As she drew closer to the floating signpost, Annja ducked below the surface. The torii wasn't actually floating, she discovered, but was held in place by a long shaft that was sunk several feet into the muck-covered bottom of the pond.

Roux was tied to that shaft.

He was flailing, trying desperately to get himself free. Air bubbles streamed away from him as he fought to hold his breath and his eyes were wide with the sense of impending death. Annja couldn't even be sure if he saw her, nor did she have time to find out.

She surfaced, grabbed another lungful of air and then shot back down to help Roux.

Up close she discovered she'd been wrong; Roux wasn't tied to the shaft.

He was chained.

A shiny steel chain was attached to the pole and then wrapped around his body several times, securing him in place. It was all held together by a thick, brass lock.

There was no way she could pick that lock in the time she had, nor could she smash it open with anything at hand. She was going to have to focus her efforts on the chain and hope for the best. But when she tried to pull the long loops away from Roux's body enough for him to slip free, she found they were wrapped too tightly to budge even an inch.

Roux continued to thrash frantically beside her and one of his feet lashed out, connecting with her thigh, sending a wave of numbness shooting down its length, but she ignored the injury and swam in close against the shaft. She held on to the chain with her left, opened her hand and summoned her sword.

She felt the solid weight of it against her palm. She

jammed the blade down between the first loop of the chain and the pole itself and then pulled against it with all her strength.

For a moment she thought it wouldn't work, that she wouldn't be able to get enough torque, but she was surprised when the link snapped quickly.

Annja wanted to shout for joy, despite being several feet underwater, but she knew she wasn't out of the woods yet. She still had several more lengths to go before it would be loose enough to free Roux.

She shot for the surface, filled her lungs with another gulp of cool spring air, and then dove back down. Annja could see that Roux had stopped struggling; he was just hanging there in the chains, his mouth open and filled with water.

Annja had run out of time.

She wasn't ready yet to give up the fight, however.

She repeated what she had done before, sliding the sword between the pole and the links of chain. Planting her feet against the pole, she hauled down on the sword with all of her might.

As if in answer to her prayer, several links of chain parted and Roux's body began to slip downward toward the bottom of the pond.

Annja dropped her sword and grabbed for him before he could drift out of reach. Hugging him to her, she kicked for the surface.

Below her, the sword flickered and was gone.

29

With her arms wrapped around his chest from behind
and his head resting in the crook between her shoulder
and neck, Annja struggled to get Roux to shore. The
minute she stopped kicking with her feet, their combined
weight would start to drag them down and she'd have to
heave him upward with her arms to keep his head from
going under again. It was tough, tiring work. Eventually
her feet found the bottom and she stood, relieving her
back of some of the burden. She dragged him up and
onto the shore and laid him flat on the ground.

He was a mess. His face had been severely beaten
and the right side was so swollen that his eye was barely
visible. The fingers on one hand were broken and it felt
as though his shoulder was dislocated, as well, though
whether that happened before he went into the water or
when struggling against the chains that bound him,
Annja didn't know.

It had taken so long to get him across the pond and out of the water that she feared for the worst. Would CPR even work after this long? If she did get his heart beating again, would his brain be damaged by the lack of oxygen it had sustained? What was the longest someone could go without oxygen, anyway?

She didn't know and, as usual, it was the lack of knowledge that scared her the most. Things did not look good. Still, she would give it her best. She wasn't one to quit before she even began.

She rolled him on his side to let some of the water drain out of his lungs and then set to work. It had been a while since she'd had any formal CPR training, so she quickly found herself repeating the steps aloud to be sure she didn't miss anything.

"Tilt the head, pinch the nose and breathe."

His lips were cold and hard beneath her own. She could taste the brackishness of the pond water.

"Check for air."

She put her ear in front of his nose, hoping for an exhale. Nothing.

"Hands on the chest. Pump one, two, three, four," Annja continued the count to fifteen.

Nothing.

"Come on, old man."

She went back to breathing again.

Tears streamed down her face as she worked, afraid that for once she hadn't been good enough, hadn't been quick enough.

"Pump one, two, three…"

Roux couldn't die like this. Not drowned while chained to a pole in a public park. Not sacrificed so that someone else could be the new bearer of Joan's sword. Not because she had failed him when he needed her most.

"Breathe."

She was crying so hard that she couldn't even see. Not that she needed to. Her whole world had devolved down to three simple activities.

Breathe.

Pump.

Check for air.

"Don't die on me, Roux. Not yet."

In a way she was surprised at the depths of her grief. Roux could be an infuriating, stubborn, old-fashioned pain in the butt, but he was also her friend and her mentor and until now she really hadn't understood what he meant to her.

She pumped harder.

"Breathe, damn you!" she said.

As if in response, Roux suddenly convulsed, coughing up what looked to her to be half the water in the pond behind them.

She quickly rolled him on his side and pounded his back, helping him evacuate the water from his lungs. He gasped for breath several times and then settled into a more normal rhythm.

After a moment, he opened his eyes and blinked up at her.

As always, he was direct and to the point.

"Did you kill her?" he croaked.

"Not yet," she said, and the cold gleam of justice danced in her eyes. It wasn't a question of *if,* but simply a question of *when.* She would not let this go unpunished.

Roux went through another fit of coughing, then said, "I heard them talking. Before they…"

He waved his hands vaguely at the water and Annja understood. Before they tried to drown me, he was saying. Continuing, he said, "The shrine is the rendezvous."

"The one behind us here in the woods?"

He nodded, then turned his head and spent a few minutes spitting up more pond water.

When he had cleared his throat and realized she was still there, watching him, he asked, "Well, what are you waiting for?"

Annja nearly laughed. Save him from drowning, drag him out of a lake, pound on his chest until he starts breathing again and he wants to be critical of her choice in priorities?

"You sure you'll be all right?" she asked.

"Fine," he said, and then retched up more pond water.

She reached for him but he waved her off. In between coughs, he said, "Go. She has to be stopped."

He was right.

Annja went.

The sun had set while she had been in the water with Roux and it was fully dark. The old-fashioned street lamps that lined the walkways had come on with the growing dark and now lit the path with a soft light. Yet despite their ambience, the calm, tranquil feeling she'd experienced earlier was gone, replaced by a sense of imbalance, a disruption in the flow, as if the landscape around her was reacting to the events playing out upon its surface.

She followed the path a short distance until she came to a fork in the road. A little sign stood nearby, with an arrow pointing down each arm of the fork. The first was directed to the right and the word *Shrine* had been etched into its surface. The second pointed farther along in the direction she'd been traveling and read, *Esplanade.*

Annja chose the right-hand fork.

It didn't take her long to spot the small structure set back in its own nook amid the white pines. It was made from wood and had a green tiled roof that made it seem as if the structure itself had simply grown out of the ground rather than having been built by human hands.

Leaving the pathway, Annja crept through the trees until she had a clear view of the front of the shrine. Four steps led up to the entrance. Beside the steps was a pair of stone foxes, symbols of Inari, god of the harvest. The Dragon was nowhere to be seen.

Annja moved forward.

When she reached the side of the shrine, she stopped and listened. She could hear the Dragon's voice from inside the structure, though she couldn't make out what was being said.

It didn't really matter though, she'd found what she was looking for.

Annja walked to the front of the building, calmly climbed the steps and entered through the front door.

The interior of the shrine was lit by an entire wall of candles. By their light Annja could see the Dragon speaking to two men dressed in the uniforms of the park maintenance crew.

As one, they turned to look at her.

"You can't have the sword," Annja said, looking directly at Shizu.

The Dragon laughed. "Do you think you can take it from me?"

Annja smiled, and by the way the two men stepped back upon seeing it, she knew she had conveyed her intent clearly enough. "Oh, I think so," she said.

Reaching into the otherwhere, she summoned her weapon.

The Dragon's eyes fell on the sword and then on the wrapped bundle she had set aside several minutes before. Annja could almost see her playing it back in her mind, wondering how Annja could have managed to regain possession of the sword when it had been in the Dragon's custody since she'd left the pavilion.

Chew on that one a bit, Annja thought, and now it was her turn to laugh.

Fury seized Shizu in its iron grip. "Kill her!" she screamed, even as she drew her own sword with a lightning quick maneuver.

The men were already in motion, rushing toward Annja with their own weapons drawn.

She didn't wait for them to reach her, but moved to intercept instead. She was done running; it was time to stand and fight.

She would avenge what they had done to Roux and most likely Henshaw, as well.

She met the first of the Dragon's henchmen in the center of the room. She knew right away he was no match for her; he held his blade poorly and relied on his brute strength to get him through. He came forward with clumsy, overhand attacks that Annja had no problem avoiding. Annja gave back a little ground, forcing him to move closer to keep her in range, and when he followed she made her move.

Annja deflected the swing of his sword and continued to turn, spinning around to bring her left elbow smashing upward toward his face. When she hammered him on the temple, he stumbled backward, dropping his sword in the process. Annja moved in on him, kicking his sword away as she did so. When he turned to run, she slashed her blade across the backs of his knees, cutting his hamstrings and effectively taking him out of the fight.

A knife whistled by her head, taking her attention away from the downed man at her feet. The other man was standing where he'd been originally, but rather than facing her with sword in hand, he was pulling knife after knife from slots on his belt and hurling them at her.

She used her sword to knock them out of the air as she advanced. Just like swatting a fly, she thought. When she reached him, he drew his own sword and put up an inspired defense, but the end result was the same.

Annja shortly found herself standing over his dying form, the blade of her sword slick with the man's blood.

Annja looked around. Where did the Dragon go?

The notion occurred to her just as the Dragon came running out of the shadows, sword in hand, and almost managed to cut her head off at the shoulders. Only the fact that Annja stumbled over something on the floor kept her from losing her head.

They moved around the interior of the shrine, trading blow after blow. Eventually the battle began to wear on Annja. Where Shizu was fresh, Annja was not. She'd fought to save Roux's life, and the events in the pond and the effort to deliver CPR afterward had sapped her strength. Her timing was off; her attacks were a split second too slow and getting slower all the while.

Sensing this, the Dragon pressed her attack, driving Annja back. Step after step, blow after blow, Annja could do nothing but retreat. Her sword was heavier than her opponent's, bulkier, and if this went on for much longer her ability to fight back would be severely hampered by fatigue. At that point, it would be all but over. The Dragon would be able to deliver the coup de grâce whenever she felt like it.

As Annja's strength ebbed, her doubts began to creep in.

She couldn't do it, a voice in the back of her head whispered. Who did she think she was, anyway? Joan had been a hero, a true warrior. But her? She was nothing more than a glorified trench digger looking for broken bits of pottery and other garbage. She didn't deserve to carry Joan's sword.

Her mind flashed to the first fight between them, the one at Roux's estate. The Dragon had bested her then and was sure to do so now. What did she have that the Dragon did not?

The answer was at the heart of all she did.

Annja did have faith in her own destiny, in her right to bear the sword.

And that faith was enough to silence the voice of doubt in her head.

The Dragon chose that moment to smile at her, just as she had during their first encounter, as if to say, *See? You can't face me and expect to win.*

That little grin, that slight quirk of the mouth, was enough to turn the tide of the battle.

Annja felt a newfound strength pour through her limbs as adrenaline flooded her system, and she used it to her advantage, her blade like a dervish whirling in the dim light.

This time it was the Dragon who was forced back. This time it was the Dragon who came out of the exchange bleeding as the tip of Annja's sword slashed her skin when she failed to move fast enough.

This time it looked as if it would be the Dragon who lost the battle, and apparently the Dragon thought so, too. She maneuvered her way around the building until she stood in front of the stairs leading back down to ground level.

After delivering a powerful blow, she turned and ran down the stairs.

Annja gave chase.

30

By the time Annja managed to get outside, the Dragon had disappeared into the trees. Annja caught the barest glimpse of her just before she was lost from sight and without hesitation Annja raced to catch up.

There was no path, no easy route, and Annja was forced to push her way through. Branches tore at her, brambles cut her flesh, and when she came out on the other side she was certain she was bleeding from a dozen new wounds. She could imagine she looked quite the sight, covered with cuts and blood and gore-stained clothing.

Annja emerged on a grassy hill above a walkway and once she reached it she realized that it was the continuation of the left-hand path she'd encountered earlier. Since the path was well lit and would provide both her and the Dragon the fastest and most direct escape route, Annja chose to follow it.

Eventually she emerged from the trees and found

herself standing near what could only be the Cherry Esplanade.

It was a wide-open area on which seventy-six individual cherry trees had been planted in four identical rows, leaving a wide carpet of green grass in the center. Large spotlights had been set up all around the edges of the esplanade, illuminating it even though the park was closed.

The cherry blossoms were in full bloom, their bright pink and purple petals transforming the space into a riot of color. They rustled, like the whisper of a thousand voices, in the cool evening breeze.

In their midst, death awaited her.

The Dragon stood in the center of the grass. In her hand she held the Muramasa blade—the Ten Thousand Cold Nights—that Garin claimed was the dark counterpart to Annja's own sword. Maybe it was her imagination, but to Annja the steel seemed to gleam with eagerness for the blood that was about to be spilled. The sword and the Dragon expected her to fall.

Annja had no intention of letting that happen.

With a thought her sword materialized in her hand and she stalked forward onto the field, coming to a halt several yards away from her enemy. She could see Shizu almost vibrating with fury. Good, she thought, maybe she'll make a mistake.

Annja kept her own anger bottled up and locked away behind a wall in her mind. The woman in front of her had almost killed Roux, and had probably taken care of Henshaw, too. She had more than likely broken into her home, chased her through the streets and had endangered her life. But Annja knew she couldn't think about that now. There was no place in a sword fight for anger—just attack and counterattack, thrust and parry, until only one was left standing on the battlefield.

The Dragon looked at her through narrowed eyes. "Surrender the sword and I shall let you live," she said.

Annja shook her head but did not say anything in return. She knew the Dragon's words were meant as a distraction and when she sensed her opponent shift her weight from her rear foot to her front, Annja knew what they were supposed to conceal.

Without another word the Dragon launched herself at Annja, in a spinning whirlwind of an attack, her sword coming around and down toward Annja's unprotected flesh.

But Annja was no longer standing there, she had moved several feet to the right. She'd seen the shift in weight, had known what it signified, and had reacted by twisting to her right, away from the deadly blade.

The Dragon was on her in an instant, trying to overwhelm her with the sheer ferocity of her attack, using the same tactics she had utilized that night in Paris when they had first crossed blades. Slash and parry, cut and jab. Back and forth they went, neither of them gaining any significant advantage, their blades ringing in the night air.

They broke apart, gaining a momentary respite.

Annja tried circling to her left, watching Shizu closely, searching for some opening in her guard that she might exploit, when the opportunity presented itself.

The Dragon was doing the same, however, and apparently saw one before Annja.

Shizu exploded in movement, her weapon swinging toward Annja's midsection in a vicious strike, and the assassin was faster than Annja had expected her to be.

Annja dropped the point of her sword and met Shizu's blade with the edge of her own, channeling the energy of her attacker's strike away from her and toward the ground instead. She twisted and brought her own weapon around in an arc that was aimed at the Dragon's midsection.

But Shizu was gone before the blow landed, dancing out of range on nimble feet.

Back and forth they went, blow after blow, twisting and turning, moving across the grass while cherry blossoms drifted through the air around them, each of them striving to gain the upper hand and deliver the winning blow.

It was Shizu who drew first blood, cutting in beneath Annja's guard and slashing the tip of her sword across Annja's shoulder. Blood flowed, staining her jersey, and Shizu grinned in triumph.

"The beginning of the end," she mocked.

Annja ignored her and the wound, as well. She could tell it wasn't too deep and she wasn't in any real danger from it at the moment, though eventually the blood loss would take its toll, she was sure.

She'd just have to redouble her efforts and put an end to this before that happened.

Shizu came at her again and they traded another

series of blows, the sound of their swords colliding ringing out across the field. This time, when the Dragon stepped in close, Annja took advantage of the situation and lashed out with her leg, striking the Dragon straight in the chest and causing her to stumble backward.

Annja kept up her forward momentum, driving the Dragon back across the field with a combination of sword fighting and martial-arts moves, throwing out strikes and kicks between sword blows.

Finally the Dragon began to tire and came in with a new overhand blow, trying to end it all.

Seeing it coming out of the corner of her eye, Annja shifted her hold on her weapon and struck out at the hilt of her enemy's.

Their swords slammed together and the Muramasa blade rang like a crystal bell in the second before it flew out of Shizu's grasp, tumbling through the air.

Annja hadn't expected the maneuver to work. The Dragon was shocked. She turned her head to watch the blade go flying from her.

Afraid that Shizu would simply call her weapon back again, just as Annja regularly did with her own sword, she didn't hesitate but drove home a short, sharp thrust.

Looking the other way, the Dragon never even saw it coming.

The broadsword entered Shizu's body between the third and fourth ribs and exited out the back just to the right of her spine.

Annja released her sword and stepped back.

The Dragon tottered for a moment and then sank

slowly to her knees, her bloody hands searching for and finding the hilt of Annja's weapon but without the strength to pull it free.

"How did you take the sword from me?"

Her eyes glazed over and she crumpled to the ground.

The Dragon was dead.

And with her death Annja's sword, which just a moment before had been shoved horizontally through the Dragon's body, vanished back into the otherwhere, ready for the next time Annja would need it.

Annja knew she should have felt satisfaction at the end result, but all she could think about was that final question.

She didn't understand. She knew instinctively that the Dragon had not been talking about her own weapon, but about how Annja's sword had vanished right out of the Dragon's very hands. And that didn't make any sense.

How could the Dragon not know about the sword's ability to vanish and reappear at will? Surely the weapon the Dragon carried had been able to do the same?

Annja looked across the field, expecting the Dragon's weapon to have vanished the minute its wielder died, only to find it right where it had fallen, jammed point first into the earth about ten feet away.

For a long moment, Annja couldn't look away.

The sword was still there.

Her thoughts churning at the implications, Annja climbed to her feet and cautiously approached it.

The sword was as she remembered it, right down to the etching of the dragon on the surface of the blade just below the hilt. Even now the etching seemed to be snarling in defiance.

Reaching out, afraid of what might happen should she touch it but needing to know nonetheless, she wrapped her hand around the hilt.

Nothing happened.

Where she expected to feel something from the blade, some sense of its bloody history and evil reputation, she felt nothing.

It was just a sword.

An inert piece of metal.

While it might have historical value, there was nothing otherwise special about the weapon.

Garin and Roux had been wrong.

Priceless historical artifact it might be, but that was all. The only mystical sword Annja knew of was the one she carried.

epilogue

From the shadows beyond the rows of cherry trees at the edge of the esplanade, Garin Braden watched the woman he had selected and trained specifically for this day, for this very battle, fall beneath the point of Annja's sword.

This was not the way things were supposed to end.

No longer content to leave the sword, and hence his future, in the hands of anyone other than himself, Garin had carefully planned and orchestrated events for years to arrive at this point in time. Originally created to eliminate Roux, the training of his beautiful assassin had been redirected when Annja had reunited the pieces of Joan's shattered sword, irrevocably changing the status quo. Garin had adapted, however, and modified his goals. His intent to steal the sword for himself and eliminate both his former mentor and his mentor's new protégé had seemed flawless, but apparently he'd done something that he kept telling himself, and even the Dragon, not to do.

He'd underestimated Annja Creed.

Both she and Roux still lived, while the blood of Garin's carefully groomed champion pooled upon the ground at Annja's feet beneath the beauty of the cherry blossoms.

How poetic, he thought in disgust.

To add insult to injury, he'd even let that bastard Henshaw live. His two shots had been true, but when he'd checked the body he'd discovered that Henshaw had been wearing a protective vest; he was unconscious rather than dead. All Garin had to do to eliminate a future threat was put one more bullet through the man's skull, but the previous shot had ruined his silencer and he hadn't wanted to alert Annja that her partner was in trouble.

He'd let the man live and might someday regret it.

No matter, he thought.

There will be another time, another opportunity.

He was sure of it.

Just as he was sure that he and Annja Creed would one day face each other over that sword.

And on that day, Garin Braden intended to come out on top.